HOWARD

THE PROUD
AND THE FREE

HOWARD FAST is well known for a literary career that spans
more than sixty years. He is the author of over seventy novels,
including *Spartacus, April Morning, Moses, Citizen Tom Paine,*
The Immigrants, and *Freedom Road,* which has been published
in eighty-two languages. Among his most recent projects are the
novels *Redemption* and *An Independent Woman,* and the screen-
play for *The Crossing,* a television movie for the A&E Television
Network.

After the loss of his wife Bette, he is now living happily in
Connecticut with his new wife, Mercedes O'Connor.

THE HOWARD FAST COLLECTION
Published by ibooks, inc.:

HISTORICAL FICTION
Bunker Hill: The Prequel to The Crossing
The Crossing
Moses
The Proud and the Free

THE IMMIGRANTS SAGA
The Immigrants
Second Generation

MASAO MASUTO MYSTERIES
Masuto Investigates
Masuto: The Hollywood Murders

THE PROUD
AND THE FREE

HOWARD FAST

ibooks
new york
www.ibooks.net

DISTRIBUTED THROUGH SIMON AND SCHUSTER, INC.

To the memory
of the brave men of the Pennsylvania Brigades,
and of their still unrealized dream

THE PROUD AND THE FREE

AN INTRODUCTION

We might feel that this generation knows all there is to know about the American Revolution. Unfortunately, this is not the case. We teach history poorly, here in America, and no part of it more poorly than the circumstances that led up to the American Revolution, and the Revolution itself.

Ask any graduate of an American secondary school to talk about the Foreign Brigade of Pennsylvania—either they will look at you blankly, or babble something about the French Foreign Legion.

Actually, the Foreign Brigade of the Pennsylvania line was the backbone of General Washington's army, the very best troops he had; and without them, the Revolution would have gone differently.

The Proud and the Free is their story, a very true story of the Foreign Brigade and the great mutiny of 1781.

The brigade was called "foreign" because it was composed, not of New Englanders or Southerners, but of Pennsylvania Germans, of Irish immigrants new to America, of European sailors who had jumped ship, of Polish volunteers, Spaniards and, interestingly, of a handful of Jews from Pennsylvania and Rhode Island.

The First World War quelled any desire by Americans to deal with the German contribution to our history, and until Carl VanDoren tracked down the facts and figures, the story remained untold.

I tell the story here as a novel, but the facts are true.

They were the only American troops who could stand up to the British Regulars, and again and again, for five years, they proved their courage and steadfastness.

Here is their story.

Howard Fast
January 2002

PART ONE

Wherein I describe how it came about that I am telling
this tale, which no other has told.

IT IS AN UNCERTAIN thing when an old man sits down to write a tale of his youth, in the long ago; for even if he remembers well, his memory will be cold with time; and no matter how well he remembers, he is making a drama in which the players are dead and the scenes have been shifted. . . .

I remember not so long ago that we were in New York and saw a production of *King Lear*, where Hammond Drice played the old man so well that I was moved to return the next day to tell him how much I understood, and how much I was touched by him. I would perhaps have gone back-stage that same evening, but I was awed at the thought of the grand and glamorous personality of the ac-tor—since we have no theater in York in Pennsylvania, where I still live—and I put it off until the next day. But the next day, my wife urged me to it and I went; for even if I was not at ease with large city things, I was twice representative in the State House, and never playing a stick of politics to get there, and once in Congress too, and the law I practiced was law in which I tried to find justice at least as much as I tried to find a living.

... But you see that already I am off and drifting, the way an old man drifts when he sets out to put down a simple sequence of events, and I mention this simply because the show had finished the next day. The flats were taken down and piled around the big, bare stage, and the costumes had that awful, deflated and lifeless look which comes to old-fashioned dress cast off and aside. Thereby, I lost all desire to meet any of those who had looked so gallant and fine under the bright lights of the evening before; and I went away as I had come, only a little sadder.

I said that was not so long ago, but it was six years, the way time passes, and in those years my wife and many other good friends passed away; so that more and more I get to feel that I, Jamie Stuart, have overstayed my leave. For that reason, with what strength I have for concentrating on so exhaustive a task, I would write down the one tale I have always meant to tell: the tale of the foreign brigades of Pennsylvania in the faraway days of my youth. I would write it down as nearly as I can in a truthful way; for I know of no one else but myself who remembers what took place in those old and trying times, and the story is one which should not be forgotten.

Well may you ask, Who is Jamie Stuart, that we should listen to him? And why should we be bored with the ramblings of these ancients, who will not consider that the world moves on?

It moves on, that I know; but a little from the old along with what is new, and there is the taste. Like those good Pennsylvania housewives who could never tolerate food

wasted. In the corner of the stove they kept a pot of soup—
and very good and peppery soup it was—and each day's
leavings went into the next day's pot. So there was ever
fresh soup for eating, but always a taste of the old as well.

And of myself, when my wife died and left me an old
and lonely man of seventy-seven—I am past eighty now—
I had little desire to live any more. It was less grief than a
sort of absolute hopelessness. Day in and day out, I sat and
counted the passing of time. Life is like a moment, and you
can sit in the gathering cold and eat your heart out, if you
are so minded; and that way I was sitting one night, filled
with a sort of senile pity for myself, when there was a quick
and angry hammering at the door. I went there and asked
who it was.

Does Lawyer Stuart live here?

He lives here. He does live here. And this is Lawyer
Stuart; and who the devil are you at this hour of the night?

Well, open the door and see, by God! We're on quick
business, so would you yammer with us all night long?

I opened the door, because there was nothing much that
I had to be afraid of, and if they wanted to rob an old man
like myself, or break my head, why that was as good a way
as any to put an end to the fright of sitting alone and
waiting for death. Six of them there were altogether, two
white and four black men, and the two white men carried
guns. They were young, hard, quick-talking men who laid
it right out in front of me that they were a part of the
underground line for taking black men out of slavery in
the South, and this was four of a group they were running
through to the border of British Canada. Their regular contact was Pastor McGilcuddy and the manse of the Presbyterian church was their regular station; but a band of

armed men from below the Virginia Line had broken a link of contact at some point and now were waiting for these at the manse; and what would I have? Would I have a bloody slaughter here in the peaceful village of York—for, as they said, they were determined not to give up their cargo without laying down their own lives first and making a real price of it—or would I grant them shelter for the night, a stable for their horses, and a chance to bind the links of their chain together again?

Come inside, I said, and don't stand outside there yelling, as if this were the first pot of tea you ever tipped over.

And all the while I was trying to straighten out in my mind the fact that the gentle and soft-spoken Pastor Lyton McGilcuddy was one of the Devil's brew of Abolitionists, and here were two more of them right in my own hallway, the first I had ever seen or spoken to in the flesh—that is, not counting the Pastor.

Who told you to come to me? I asked them, looking them up and down now and seeing that they were not much different from other men—dirty in boots and overalls and cotton shirts, with three days of beard on their cheeks, but otherwise plain-looking lads, and the black men behind them were tired and dirty and frightened too, but no menace in them; they brought back to me memories I had not dabbled with this long, long while—memories of other lads who had had a wild venture in freedom; and this you will see if you read through the tale I set down here.

... The Pastor, they answered; the Pastor, he said: When it comes to a pinch, go to the old man, Jamie Stuart.

Well, you have come to me, I said, so leave the black men here and go out and stable your horses. . . .

*   *   *

It was that way that I fell in with them, and became one of the underground chain, a way station on it, a stopping place for men who fled through the nights for their freedom; and it is that way too that I, Jamie Stuart, an old man in the twilight of his life, have become a part of the little, hated—well-hated, well-loved—group of men and women who call themselves Abolitionists.

There is a tale—but for others to tell. I have a little bit of it, but I am an old, old man, and when I see the young ones come in and out of my home—when I see the black men, whom I see only for the moment, coming and going and bold for liberty—I am filled with a different kind of sadness than I had before. I want to know the end of this, and I realize that such knowledge is for others, not for me. Little use I am to them, crouched by the fire in the cold days, trying to warm the ache from my bones; but my house is theirs and all else that I have. In another way, I am joined to them, and it is of this other way that I would tell.

It has often seemed to me that while man cannot look into the future, he can make a good deal out of the past; and in my own past, there is an adventure not wholly without meaning. How many lies have been told about those times! But how many lies have been told about the young men who call themselves Abolitionists today! So it may be that if I look back, it will not only be the rambling memories of an old man, but a clue to that which lies ahead. Or so I tell myself.

In any case, there is no other left alive today—of whom I know—who can tell the tale of the great revolt of the foreign brigades.

*　　*　　*

They are all dead, my comrades, scattered like leaves to the four winds, and their time is dead with them. They were not men eager for growing old, for the winter of their lives came with the springtime; and the fruit I have tasted was not for them, but a more bitter fruit indeed. What a strength they had, that wasted away and went sighing off; and sometimes it seems that their cold bodies were filled with honey, such a swarm of activity and wealth arose from them!

They were soldiers, you know: the men of the Pennsylvania Line of the Continental Army, a rock for those strange and troubled times. I was one of them. Eleven regiments of us there were, hard soldiers of hard times; and I myself, Jamie Stuart, was master sergeant in the 11th Regiment. Originally, I was part of the 1st Regiment, and then I was only seventeen years old; but later on, when the 11th and last regiment was formed, they took me and Danny Connell, and made us sergeants in it; and there I was when the great rising took place.

Often enough, as time went past, as the war slipped into the faraway and everyone tried to forget and wanted to forget, I brooded over the circumstances of our revolt, so that I might extract some meaning from it. But the meaning apparently became more and more difficult to grasp. I found a way of life; I worked and studied and became a lawyer. Here, I said to myself, you have done this, Jamie Stuart, and therefore you are an outstanding man and unlike that devilish rabble that fought in the brigades—for where are they? Scattered like chaff, they are. But you, Jamie Stuart, you have reaped a real harvest and you have married your own sweet Molly Bracken and made a home and watched your children grow and blossom, and buried some children too, and tasted a little of this honor and that honor—and therefore what is right is right.

Could you also say that what is wasted is wasted, and that the dreams and the pains of the men I once knew were wasted? For when I was left alone in my old, old age, my life was bereft of meaning as well as companionship, and it was not until those two young men came to my door, and with them the four black men in flight, that I had a glimmering of a story unbroken and continuous.

That is why I have determined to set down my part in it, and the adventures which befell me in the year 1781, so that you may see some of the meaning of the eleven foreign brigades which stood for the country of Pennsylvania in the old times, before there was such a union as we have today.

I must tell something of myself first and of my beginnings, so that I may establish a part of the logic I believe in; for I believe that neither in the lives of men nor in the lives of nations is there a lack of reason. This is a matter I once discussed with a very wise man, a physician in Philadelphia, Benjamin Rush by name, and it was he who first said to me that given sufficient facts and a truthful method to apply them, almost anything is knowable. And this I intend to do, putting down a narrative of our adventure as well as I can recall it.

Of myself, I must say to begin that I was born here in this same place where I will, in all probability, end my life—in the village of York in Pennsylvania. I was born in the year 1759, out of a mother and father who had been bound over as servants from Glasgow in the old country. I am not ashamed to state this, for my mother and father were good and honest people, for all that they were held in chattel slavery for a matter of twelve years. Nor am I ashamed to say that I was born out of parents who were slaves. It is the habit of thinking today that only black men are slaves or fit for slavery, such a proud and arrogant fetish have we made of our own freedom. But we know little enough today of the purchase price of this freedom, and, in my childhood, many of white skin were slaves, as well as those whose skin was black.

My mother was a MacAndrews of the Highlands, the daughter of a poor crofter; my father was a weaver by trade and a free man until he took sick with a condition that made it impossible for him to use his fingers for some months—nor did he ever regain the full dexterity of them. Because of this, to avoid death by starvation for my mother and himself, they both of them sold themselves into bond slavery in America for a sabbatical, or seven years. But when costs and sick charges and birth charges were added, it came to twelve years that they labored for their freedom on a Virginia plantation, and in that time, a boy and a girl were born to them, both of whom died. When they gained their freedom, they came to York, where my father thought he would set up a loom and go back to his trade of weaving, and there I was born; but my mother's labor over me gave her a lesion which killed her in two years. For the next eight years, my father raised me as best he could, which meant that without a mother's care I ran like an animal in the woods and the streets. Then he died of smallpox, and, ten years old, I was an orphan in the world.

So I was an orphan, without father or mother, and all

the wealth I got from them you could press into a thimble. Nor had I letters or anything of that kind, for this was before Pastor Bracken took a fancy to me and taught me to read and write.

My father was in the church, so the Presbyterian elders had me before them and they said: Well, Jamie, here you are, alone in the world by God's mercy, without kith of kin to lend you a hand, and what do you think of your future?

I'll be a robber, I answered, which seemed to me to be the only practical way of keeping body and soul together, and already I had had some indication that unless a little thievery was mixed in with an honest man, he did less than well in the world.

The elders, however, were unimpressed. They pointed out to me that this was hardly the attitude for me to take, if I hoped to be adopted into some good, God-fearing home, and they also pointed out that the likelihood of such was not too great, considering how my father had let me grow up. I stood in front of them, my toes coming out of my shoes, my knees coming out of my pants, my elbows coming out of my sleeves—a ragged, bony, unprepossessing little boy, I suppose; and to this day I remember well my bitterness and resentment against them, those pious, hard-jawed, sharp-nosed trustees of the Almighty who were sitting in judgment upon a lad of ten summers. A Scottish pout, they were thinking of me, no doubt, a wild one, an animal like all the young of the miserable Highland beggars and gillies who thought that gold was turned up at every step in the new country. My speech in those times was thick and broad and their own was sharp and narrow. So they looked at me as at some insect, and my own heart was full of repayment in kind.

Do what you will with me, I said to myself, but never will I rest with what my mother and father had, going to their graves in such sorrow! Do it and be damned!

I went home and lay down alone in the little shack my father had rented, with his loom and his bench and the two or three sticks of furniture he had in the world, none of it mine but all of it in pawn for back rent. And the next day I was called to Stephan Dobkin, the church head; and with him was Fritz Tumbrill, the cobbler, a monstrously large and fat man, pig-eyed, with a rolling collar of his own flesh in which his head sat like a pudding in gravy.

Here is good Master Tumbrill, and he has agreed to take you in and keep you for apprenticeship and teach you the trade, said Stephan Dobkin. Such is the charity of Jesus Christ, our own Master, he said, and God help you if you should ever prove ungrateful.

My father's trade was weaving! I cried. I'll be a weaver and no damned shoemaker!

So I learned my first lesson in the weight of Fritz Tumbrill's hand and the nature of his ethics. From the floor where he sent me with his blow, I listened to his instructions on language to be used in his presence and in his household.

Thus I went to serve him and to learn cobbling, and a full sabbatical I served before I threw his leather apron in his face and walked out to join the 1st Regiment of Pennsylvania, then being raised to march north and help the farmers in the siege of Boston town. I mention this because in the narrative I propose to tell, concerning what befell myself and my comrades in the winter of 1781, you may be moved to ask, now and again, How does one account for these men? What made them and what moves them, and why do they endure what they endure?

Also, you may ask, What of this one who writes the narrative? What of Jamie Stuart? He is native born in the American land. What kind of bitter cud does he chew over and over again, retching the acid into his teeth?

But it is not my intention to make such a compilation. If I at twenty-two was no lad, then I was little enough of a lad at ten. Childhood is for those who can afford it, and my own purse was light from the beginning. In the years I sat crouched over the bench in the workshop of Fritz Tumbrill, particularly before that day when Molly Bracken walked into the shop, like sunshine coming into a dark well, in those years I thought often of my father's lean and tired face.

A word about that face before I go into the tale I must tell; for I think that before you are finished you will have some curiosity about my own look, and if you see my father, you will see me too.

I remember him best at the loom. The light was poor in the shack where he worked, so when the weather was good, he took half a dozen shingles out of the roof, and through the opening a broad shaft of light fell upon the loom and upon his face as well. I would play on the floor facing him. Sometimes I would glance up and meet his eyes, and his whole face would smile, for I was all he had in the world. But at other times, he would be unaware that I was watching him, and I would note the incredible sadness of his face. Ah, what a sorrow was there! What grief for the thin crust of bread he handed to his child! A Scotsman is dour, they say, but the quality is not born into a man but comes rather from the soil he scratches.

My father's face was a long one, as mine is too. A narrow one. His brows arched, and on either side his forehead there was a slight indentation of the bone—as there is on mine. The nose was long and well-shaped, the curve of the head high, the hair a tarnished sand-color, and the eyes gray-green. The chin was large yet gentle, long and narrow, and the neck was lean, as the man was, a tall, lean, long-muscled man; and taking away a quarter of a century it is a fit description for myself, Jamie Stuart, when I signed my name to the enlistment papers and became a soldier in the army of the Revolution for the commonwealth of Pennsylvania. An ugly lad I was, to a way of thinking, but I had qualities that I little knew of, myself, until I was rubbed like a sword on a grindstone, and then because of those qualities men gave me a post not without honor for a lad of twenty-two, as you will see.

So I have told you a little of my life in each direction, a little of what was in the old days, when one day was not so different from the other while I learned the best way to ease my back so that Fritz Tumbrill's blows fell as lightly as possible, while I learned how to bevel the leather for the sole and how to sew it for the upper, how to cut, shape, trim and awl, how to drink and coddle and roll—and some of what came after, when I grew old and away from the memories of my youth.

But Fritz Tumbrill never made an animal of me, or I would have become like him. Instead, I hardened and I became something else, and through Molly Bracken—of whom you will hear more—I learned to read and write. So I was able to read in a newspaper of the incident that happened in Massachusetts in April of 1775, and I was able to read as well that they were raising a regiment of Pennsylvania men and all others who would enlist for pay, bounty and glory, to strike down the tyrant. I knew what to do and I did it, because the answers to my questions were written on my back and on my memory too.

That is enough of Jamie Stuart to justify this narration which I will set down. He was like the other men, of whom I will also tell, and he loved them deeply and came to know them.

May they sleep well, do I say, myself. They reached up for the stars and they made a crude key to unlock the gates of heaven. This, other men will do, and the key will become a better one; so I will not weep for them or have you weep, but only give them their due.

PART TWO

Being an account of the death of Tommy Mahoney,
and the Congress we held and the pledge we made on
the eve of the New Year of 1781.

THE FACTS WHICH I am about to set down in a narrative to do honor to my dead comrades—for no other honor has been done to them—had a beginning somewhere; but the more I ponder the interconnection of things, the more I come to understand that the beginning is not traceable—which is all for the best: for then a spark of hope burns in my heart, and I ponder the possibility that the end is as little traceable as the beginning. And if that is the case, then I for one believe that there was a meaning and a purpose and a final chapter still to be written out in life to what we did.

But however that may be, there must be a starting point, and for that I have chosen the death of little Tommy Mahoney, the Protestant drummer boy from Dublin town, who died on the eve of the new year of 1781, in the encampment outside of Morristown, New Jersey. I will also tell you that I choose the death of this poor, damned little lad because our first Congress of the Line followed; but there were other places for the beginning. Even before the war, there was a beginning to what we did, and even before any man there was born, and even maybe so long ago as when Christ led men not so different from ourselves, and no more poorly clothed and fed.

It is something we know and which doctors cannot explain, that a man will not go on living if he has lost the desire to do so; and it was plain to everyone after we had marched from Totowa to Morristown that little Tommy Mahoney was not long for this earth. It was not the cold winds that blew so cruelly from the northern forests; it was not the fact that we lived on a little parched corn with never a taste of meat; it was not our nakedness, our lousiness, our sickness—for all of these things we were used to, and these things we had lived through before and had a ripe belly of, when we lay at Valley Forge. It was because we had stopped hoping, and because we were bereft and betrayed; and the little lad knew better than some of us who were old enough to be his father what the situation was. His beardless face became gray and the sparkle went out of his eyes. When he beat on his drum, it was a new rhythm, a sad and hopeless rhythm.

I beat because my heart is breaking, his drum said.

There was a time when such a drumbeat with such a sad and frightened rhythm would have angered us, and then some of us would have said, Twelve on his backside, that drummer lad needs. And others of us would have said, Stop your chopping dirty sticks, if that is all the kind of a tune you can beat out. And there would have been many a clip alongside the head and chin for little Tommy Mahoney as a reward for the devilish and persistent means he took of beating that drum.

But we were changed too, along with the lad, and nobody clipped Tommy Mahoney and nobody shouted at him; for inside of us we knew that the tune he played was the truth and nothing but the truth. We had all of us, all of the men of the ten infantry regiments and one artillery regiment of the Pennsylvania Line who were marched from Totowa to Morristown to go into winter encampment, become gentle. We were soft-spoken; we were quiet; we were sad. And as we set to work to repair the little log huts that stood in various stages of decay from the encampment of the year before, it seemed to many of us that there was never a time but when we were what we were now, such homeless, lonely, lost men as the world had not seen before. The heart had left us; we did not fight; we did not beat our women; we did not sing—and one time when big Angus MacGrath strode forth to play on his pipes, the music that came forth in spite of himself was such cursed and lonely music that he laid his pipes away and vowed never to play upon them again, so long as he lived.

For that reason, we did not clip Tommy Mahoney when he beat his crying rhythms. The lad is not for this world, we said. He is making a requiem for himself, and who will deny him that privilege?

He was undersized, the way most of us in the Line were, coming as we had from foreign soil, or out of bondage and poverty. When Massachusetts or Connecticut had first marched alongside us, they made many a joke of it, shouting things like, Ho for the dirty little runts! Ho for the little men! Are you going to war now, little men? But the Yankees sang another song when the grape opened up, hissing like a great kettle boiled over, and when the muskets balls whistled from the British volleys. Then they ran away but we stood and died, even as we stood and died on every field, New York, White Plains, Trenton, Monmouth, Stony Point—how many there were, and we in our line stood with our Irish and Scotch and Germans and Poles and French and Portuguese, our black men and our Jews and our Romans—we stood and they stopped calling us little men!

Yet Tommy Mahoney was smaller than most. His arms and legs were like sticks; he had a pinched face, pocked and tired and sad, but for all that a little boy's face. He had sandy hair, close-cropped, that stood straight up from his head, and he had a dainty alto voice that was the sweetest thing men ever heard. How he loved to sing once! But he sang no more now. We urged him and urged him, thinking that music would be like medicine, but only when Christmas time approached did he lift up his head and sing, *On the first day of Christmas, my truelove sent to me, a partridge in a pear tree. On the second day of Christmas, my truelove sent to me, two turtle doves and a partridge in a pear tree....*

And then he sang on and on and we joined in the round, and made a real ringing roundelay out of it; and that was the only real roundelay we sang in all that Christmas time. The women kissed him and petted him; and Handsome Jack Maloney, of whom you will hear much more, beat time with the tears streaming down his face and said:

Sing more and more, my lad, with old tunes of the old country, so you will make my rotten old heart crack with the joy of it all.

I can sing no more, the drummer boy answered, for I remember the beauty of Dublin city, before me uncle sold me to go overseas into bondage.

But ye're not in bondage now, me lad, the girls pleaded.

I can sing no more, he said, for me heart is breaking, and I want to lay me down and die.

They went on with their persuasion until big Angus MacGrath roared, Now let the lad be, for will ye make music out of a broken lute, like the officers make war out of our own lifeblood?

He withered, did little Tommy Mahoney, like the apple that is picked too soon and then goes uneaten, and when the last day of the year 1780 came, he laid himself down and he died.

We were hutted up then with our own bitterness, and because you should know to understand what followed, I will tell you what our huts were like. This one of mine will serve, for I was sergeant over the drummer boy, and apart from myself, fifteen men were hutted there in my house. Also, in this same house, the first Congress of the Line was held, and also in this same house there came into being the Committee of Sergeants.

The hut was twenty feet long and sixteen deep, fronting on the parade—which made it somewhat bigger than most of the others. It was made of logs, and chinked with clay, and had a dirt floor and a bark roof, no windows and a clay and log hearth. We bedded in threes, one atop the other, and there was a sawbuck table and two benches down the middle, at which we ate when there was anything for eating. The bunks were split logs with straw bolsters, only it was years since we had sewn the last of the bolsters into shirts and the last of our blankets into coats, so that now we slept on the straw and under it too. Such were our hutments.

In this hut of mine, Tommy Mahoney breathed out his

last; and we laid the little lad out on the table, and Katy Waggoner and Olive Lutz came in to wash him and make him ready for the ground. We took off all his clothes and washed his poor skinny body clean, and then we washed the few rags he wore, dried them by the fire, and dressed him over again. Katy Waggoner went to the quartermaster general to beg a winding sheet, but for her pains all she got was a curse and a slap in the face—which was no way to treat her, for all that she was a loose and slatternly woman. But even if she had gotten a winding sheet of the purest linen, I do not think that what followed would have been noticeably altered. I start this narrative from the death of Tommy Mahoney, only because I must have a starting point somewhere and not because I believe it was the death of the drummer boy, from sadness, starvation and bleeding lungs, that caused what followed. Nor do I believe that the beating of the two Kelly brothers, John and Dobie, made any decisive difference. The two of them were Romans who had come to us as replacements, signing in for what they and theirs had suffered in the old country from the British and from their own tyrants; and not knowing that the boy was a Protestant lad, and not knowing that in such a village as Morristown there could be no Roman priest, they now set off, without leave, to fetch one.

They were men out of the 2nd Pennsylvania, in which there were many Polish and Irish, and particularly eleven Jews, which gave the officers a singular reason for hatred. It is such a long time back that I may have a name twisted here and there, but I think it was Captain Sudburry and four or five of his fellows who stopped the Kelly brothers, demanding of them:

Now where are you going, my lads?

We're off to Morristown to fetch a father for a little lad who died unshriven, John Kelly replied.

The hell you are! And where are your papers for leave? the officers said ungraciously.

We have no papers, John Kelly answered, courteously enough as we heard of it, but his brother spoke up and asked, Now would ye want papers to enter into the gates of heaven, or hell also? Here is a little lad from the old country, from Dublin town, from which me blessed mother came, and he wasted away into his death all unshriven, and we only seek a holy father to give him a little unction.

Whether they knew what either Kelly brother spoke of, I know not; but they fell into a fury and cursed them out.

Now to hell with ye, for ye talk like a damned Englishman, said one of the Kelly brothers.

That was all that was needed. The officers, of whom there were at least four or five, drew their swords and set about to belabor the two boys with the flats and backs. One of the officers was armed with an espontoon, a weapon like a pike and much in favor by officers in those critical days, and this he drove into the stomach of Dobie Kelly, while the other was bruised and cut all over the face and head. Then both of them were taken under guard, and when we heard about it, early on the eve of New Year, Dobie Kelly was already dead.

You can imagine how it was. We were sitting in a wake around the body of the little drummer lad, and the word came to us, brought by Stanislaus Prukish, sergeant in the 2nd. Already, there were grouped around the boy, in the flickering firelight, small delegations of one or two sergeants or corporals who had come from each of the ten infantry regiments and from the artillery company too, for the lad had been much considered for his singing and the good spirits he once owned. Prukish told us what he knew of the incident of the Kelly brothers.

There it is, he said, in his thick Polish accent, which I cannot reproduce. We are not fast enough dying, so they have begun the killing. We are the enemy instead of the Lobsters.

If there was a drop of rum in this cursed encampment, I would be howling drunk this evening, said Sean O'Toole of the 4th Regiment. I would spin my head like a top and go out into the white snow and howl like the devil at the stars. But there is no rum, and here we are sitting at the wake of two good lads, with never a little bit of a drop to wet our throats.

Be damned with it! I have not been paid these eleven months, not even in the lousy Yankee paper; I have not been clothed; I have not been fed. The cold is in me bones.

Silence fell, and in the next half-hour it was only interrupted when someone said to throw another handful of faggots on the fire. I don't know what would have been that evening had we been drunk, the way soldiers have a right to be on the eve of the New Year; but apart from the officers' quarters in the fine and genteel houses, there was not a dram of spirits in the camp. Sober we were, sober and moody and angry. Nor were we cold, for one by one, men entered to pay their respects, and women too, until more than fifty of us were packed into the one cabin, on the floor, on the bunks, sprawled, squatting, standing; and those who came stayed. Sergeant Billy Bowzar of the 10th came in, and with him Jim Holt, the black man who was corporal in the 2nd. The two Jews, brothers in the 2nd,

Aaron and Moses Gonzales, entered, and with them was Danny Connell of my own 11th. Connell had been a minstrel in the old country, and when I saw him first, in 1776, he was as fair a lad to look upon as you would find in all the tidewater countries, twenty-three years old then with black hair and black eyes and a swagger and a dash, and as ready for a fight as a cock with spurs. But now, in his rags, he looked fifty if he looked a day; his hair was gray, as was his big, bushy beard, and his eyes were deep-sunk into his head, and he was as dirty as we all were, and as smelly and as lousy. He had his lass, Mathilda, with him, a mountain girl from the buckskin folk over westward; she was faithful to him and stayed with him from year to year, so thin a breath of wind could blow her away, yet with her spirit in her. To look at her made my heart yearn for my own sweet Molly Bracken in York village, but I would not want her here to share my own misery and dirt.

Connell had been to look at the Kellys, and he said as he entered:

It was a wanton thing they did to the boy, and if I had ever raised my voice, they would have done as much to me. For it is in me head that they are stricken mad and that this is the end of everything.

If it's the end of everything, said Freddy Goulay, a black man and corporal in the 6th Regiment, it's an end they made. The only gift they got is to lead us to slaughter. They are whipping men, like overseers, and each of them would be a king. They fill their cup with hate, they do. The people hate them and the land hate them, and we hate them too. Now they don't come near us, they don't touch us, they afraid.

Each had something to say of that sort, but it was surprising with what little anger they said it, and how slowly and regretfully. Our tone was gentler than our appearance, for crammed into the hut, sitting almost one on top of the other, with the little lad's mortal remains stretched out on the table square in the center of us, we looked like something that man had never made of himself before. It was a long, long time, yes many, many months since we had been given money or clothes or a blanket to shelter us from the cold. Put a man in rags, feed him on cornmeal until his teeth are all loose in the sockets, and he will not look after his body as if it were a thing to be precious about; we had stopped shaving because we had stopped caring, and our hair was long and wild and knotted. When we had fought, we were taken into battle like cattle into a slaughter pen, and when the battles were lost, as almost every one was, we were left to hold the field while the Yankees fled.

. . . So I went into the fine house of Thomas Hardwick, continued Danny Connell, still telling of his journeys to know why and how the Kelly boy had died . . . and the officers of the 9th Pennsylvania Regiment—may it be glorious in battle, this heart and soul of the Revolution—they sat at dinner. And on the eve of this New Year, when there is no eating or drinking or dancing or singing, would you like me to spin you a tale of the officers at dinner?

You should be sitting with respect at a wake, with respect and sober sorrow, said Olive Lutz.

And have I no respect in me voice? And is my heart not breaking with sober sorrow—me, Danny Connell, who sang such songs of gladness when he was a lad? If ye don't recognize that, you dirty bitch, it's because you got the soul of a slattern!

To hell with that, I told him. If it's the Roman way to

have foul talk over the dead, you swallow your tongue, Danny Connell. For this is a Protestant lad laid out on the table.

Then would ye have a theological discussion? asked Connell, combing his beard with his fingers and looking at the ceiling. Here we are Jew and Protestant and Roman and heathen too, but I do not find discrimination among our officers. They hold with equality, me dear Jamie Stuart . . .

I was on a top bunk, perched with my head against the roof beams; I was bent over—a taller man than the foreigners—chin on knees, and staring with smarting, watering eyes.

. . . Me dear Jamie Stuart, ye are not the only lad in the regiment can read and write, and I got in me head here four hundred songs. Tell me I'm lying, ye scut.

When our anger rises, we fight each other, said the Jew Aaron Gonzales, so sadly that the tears ran down my cheeks; and Connell cried too, and said more gently:

I got in me head many things, and I don't know how to use them, like ye take me who was a minstrel and set me to coopering. Me father was struck down by the tyrant's hand when he led the march of the starving folk on Dublin town, and I was just a lad when he lay there, with a bullet in his chest and dying in me arms. Danny, he said to me, ye must not take it amiss that a bullet strikes down yer father and lose yer taste for freedom. We are a downtrodden folk, Danny, me lad, and we got no taste for the finer things; but we got a taste for music and a taste for freedom, and these are from the olden times. So he died out his life there, and for the sake of me poor mother, for ten pounds in her hand and passage for me, I bind out to Pennsylvania for two years. But I got this in me head: *We hold these truths to be self-evident—that all men are created equal; that they are endowed by their Creator with certain unalienable rights; that among these are life, liberty, and the pursuit of happiness.* In me head is all this, when I come into the Hardwick House tonight to see if I can find a smell of justice for the Kelly boy. I am a free man. I am no peasant sod, but a free man in the army of the Revolution, in which I enlisted of me own free will out of hatred for the Union Jack and for the rich tyrant who murders the poor. So I come into the Hardwick House, pushing aside Frank Meyers, the stinking orderly who is lapdog there, and there are the gentlemen of the 9th, fifteen of them sitting at this long table, with white linen and candles as bright as the sun, and all of them in their finest buff and blue, and all of them shaven clean, and all of them wigged, and all of them with lace at the cuff and lace at the throat, and all of them with wine in the glass and wine in the bottle, and I am standing there when in there comes a roast of mutton with the very smell enough to break me poor heart. But not even to smell it am I permitted, for I am rushed out of there like I am the plague, which maybe I am from the look of me, and as for Kelly, they said to me that the dirty dog got what he deserved. . . . So there it is, Jamie Stuart, who is not like myself, a dirty foreigner, but native born out of Pennsylvania. Where have we been and where are we going? . . .

They looked at me, all of them fanciful people—some good, some bad, some bright and some dull—but all of them fanciful folk or they would not have been there, and I looked back at the thick of their upturned faces, half seen in the dim firelight, with passion and anger wiped out through the mood of Danny Connell's tale, and only a question left. But the question was not new. With high hope and high heart, we answered the call to come to Boston in 1776 where the Yankees had hemmed the British tyrant into the tidewater town; and each and every one of us came with that curious, unspoken, unformed dream that is in the heart of every man with a foot on his neck. They were farmers around Boston town, but we were a different crew, and I came with a dream that no more would an apprentice work for grits and beatings; the sailors came with the dream that free men would sail ships with no lashes on their backs; and the Scottish buckskin men came with a dream of land, so that they would no longer hire out as hunters and pack animals, and so that some day they would wear woven Christian cloth instead of animal skin. The Jews came with a dream of standing up as men free, and so did the black men; and in the bellies of the Irish estevars and ropewalkers was a hunger ache a thousand years old and a hate almost as ancient. And the Poles and the Germans came with their heads bowed, but they would hold them upright now, and all of it because the British were hemmed in Boston town. We did not reason it out. Here was talk of freedom and we knew what side we were on, and we had nothing to lose. But then the years went by, and the question began to burn in us; still we were the poor led by the rich, the disinherited led by those who did inherit, and here were curses and whiplashes and blows from those who spoke the pretty words of freedom. Here was worse hunger, and we knew hunger; here was worse cold, and we knew cold.

The others went home; they came and they went, did the Yankees, which is something that is forgotten now, but the Pennsylvania Line stayed: the foreigns stayed. They had no place to go, and now the foreigns looked at me out of the shadows and out of bloodshot eyes, and I looked at Handsome Jack Maloney, who sat as I did on an uppermost bunk, his small, sharp face the only clean-shaven one among us, his little black eyes observing me narrowly, his mouth twitching a little, as it did in the excitement of an engagement—he who had been a master sergeant in a British regiment, and had deserted and had come to us and our hell with the cold logic of a man who chooses between two sides. That he was, cold and logical and hard as rock.

The first to do, Jamie, he said, is to lay poor Tommy out in the cold, for the lad is beginning to stink, and then we will talk it over until we get it out of our systems.

I am tired of talk, growled big Angus MacGrath.

It helps.

If we talk in a straight line then it may help, said the Jew Gonzales. If we talk in a circle, we come back to each other where is no solution. We must lift up our heads.

And our eyes, I agreed.

Jim Holt picked up the drummer lad in his arms, and the women wept.

When you return, said Jack Maloney, bring with you men from the 1st and the 3rd and from the artillery company. Tell them there's a Congress sitting in the hut of Jamie Stuart, and they should not send any damned navvies, but good men in respectful standing.

That was how our Congress came about.

We let the fire die to embers, for—the way that hut was packed with humankind, their smell and their breath and their warmth—we wanted no other heat; and on the table we lit a tallow lamp. The year turned. We had no watch among us, having long ago bartered away the last for food and drink, but the sound of the New Year came up, fretful and uneven, with a huzza here and there through the encampment, and then with the tolling of the bells from the village church. The door was opened to let us have a breath of air, and as the swirling snow eddied in, we saw a man or two run across the moonlit parade, in a grotesque imitation of what a New Year's Eve should be.

The tallow wick lashed and flickered, and in a voice as sober as a parson's on Sunday morn, Jack Maloney spoke and said:

By the rights invested in me by the race of mankind—to which I have tried to do some good, for all the whoring and drinking I have done—and by a part of that holy right which made me, a deserter from the tyrant George III, master sergeant in the army of this republic of Pennsylvania, in the name of the Line and the 6th Regiment, where every lad is a comrade of mine and calls me by name, I do call into being and session this Congress of the Pennsylvania Line. . . .

No one laughed. Our being there and our listening to those pompous words of Handsome Jack's had already committed us, and our necks were inside of fifty nooses and our hearts were beating faster.

Representing *who?* someone asked.

The Line.

Not enough.

The people of Pennsylvania.

We lie in Jersey now.

Is there a Jersey lad here? asked Jack Maloney.

There arose the Dutchman Andrew Yost, who said, That I am, and my father before me.

Then what in hell are you doing in a Pennsylvania regiment? asked Sean O'Toole.

Pulled in by my neck, by God, with a promise of twenty-dollar bounty I never got, a promise of a suit of clothes, I never see, a promise of a pint of rum a week I never even smell, and a promise of twelve-dollar-a-month pay I never get paid, not even once, you hear, not even once, God damn it to hell!

And are ye fit to speak for yer land and folk?

Maybe yes, maybe no, the Dutchman answered slowly. What we do will make me able to speak later.

That's good enough, nodded Jack Maloney, and if it's yer pleasure, I will put this Congress in your hands to elect a board and a president. But I would solemnly advise ye first to choose a protector, and let him beat up a corporal's guard of honest lads, so that we'll have no gentry walking in on us.

This was done. Angus MacGrath was made protector of the Congress, and he left to find a dozen true lads who would patrol the hut, watching for any dirty informer with his nose in the eaves or any of the officer gentry with a nose in the door. Then we set about discussing form and shape for the Congress, everyone trying to talk at once, until Danny Connell roared us down, and Chester Rosenbank, the pinch-nosed German schoolteacher from Philadelphia, advised:

You must have a chairman *pro tempore.*

And what in hell is that?

It is Latin and means "for the time being," and how else will you have each one talk in turn instead of together?

Then let it be Jamie Stuart in whose hut we are, said Maloney, and if ye talk, make it cutty and sharp.

So I was chairman, and then for an hour, instead of turning our thoughts to what we intended to do, we debated the point of what we were and whom we represented and what our form should be. Maloney and Rosenbank and the Gonzales brothers, and the black man Goulay, and three buckskin men from the 1st Regiment and a handful of others all held that we represented the people, and that therefore we were a Congress of the people; but the rest of us opposed this, pointing out that aside from the officer gentry, there were none the people hated more than the foreigners of the Line, as witness the way they let us starve and die in the midst of their plenty.

After we were set on to rob their trees and pilfer their stock, said Goulay.

Be that as it may, we do not represent them, and it will be our burden in the future to see if we represent them or if their own guns are turned against us.

Then who do we represent?

The soldiers of the Line, said Danny Connell, and then only if they follow us.

When we ourselves don't know where we be going, but sit here quacking away?

Then let us get to where we are going and the hell with the shape of it, whether we are a Congress or a Committee or a Board, Jack Maloney said. And if ye want a president to sit over it, Jamie Stuart is as good for me as any other.

No, no, I said. Give it to some other.

Dwight Carpenter is Pennsylvania man, said Prukish slowly. So is Jamie. So is Button Lash.

Carpenter I remember well—a long, bony man, with a

great hatchet chin and a somber way of speech. He had been a powder maker before the war, and he went as pow-derman for the first cannons we rolled from Philadelphia. Now he was a layer and a sergeant, but always to follow and never to lead; and, knowing this, he shook his head and made the point that linemen would want no cannon-men over them.

Nobody is going to be over nobody, said Jim Holt. Over us is too many and too long.

Then let it be Jamie, said Jack Maloney, and I said:

To hell with that! Let it be you, for I tell you it shouldn't be any man of the 11th, which has had ten whiplashes for what any of you had—and tell me different!

But they looked at me out of the dark, hairy faces and said never a word.

... And ten wounded for each of yours; so they'll say, It's a good grievance the 11th has, but why should *we* thraw for *them?* And that's why it shouldn't be me, and maybe Jack neither, him being British; so what about Billy Bowzar, who can read and write to boot?

They agreed to that. Bowzar was a native man, quiet and not looking for a fight, but a good soldier and a way of talking that made folks listen. They voted him, and he climbed up onto the table and said:

I accept and I call you to order in a sober way, my good comrades. Now I say to you that we must bind ourselves together here and become like one man, for it's the way old Ben Franklin said now, and maybe now for the first time. If we don't all hang together, just as sure as there's a God in the heavens above, we will all hang separately.

He stood with his head under the peaked roof, his head

all dark and somber up there, but the edges of his red beard catching a glint from the tallow wick.

I pledge you together, he said. Take the pledge.

And we all of us raised our right hands and pledged that we would stay together and see this thing through, come what might, even if it meant that we must die together.

Then who wants the floor to speak? he said.

But since we were committed now, since we had all of us already done a thing for which many of our comrades had died in the past—spoken and plotted and organized against the gentry who led us—we fell to brooding upon our position instead of giving voice to thoughts and plans. Silence and cold crept over us. Rum would have loosened our thoughts and our tongues, but we had no rum; and thereby arose at that moment a danger point, where the whole thing might have simmered out, each running to unbraid the particular piece of hemp he wore as his own collar. Sensing this, I began to speak without having any clear orderly notion of what I would say. I only knew that someone had to talk, ease them out, start their own tongues. I knew no more than they did where we were going or what awful road we were preparing to explore; but I did know that as soldiers we had things in common, and soldiers we were, and maybe the best in the whole damned world, if the truth should be known; and I also knew that, as with so many of them, the whole of my grown life had been as a soldier and discipline was in my bones and mutiny was a dreadful thought to entertain. Yet I spoke, telling them:

It'll be me first, if you tolerate it, and I welcome you here to the magnificent hut I live in. Anyway, you know me, all of you: Jamie Stuart, sergeant in the 11th; and Danny Connell and Moses Gonzales have watched me since I was a little shaver of a lad, and now I'm a man grown, and all the years in between right here in the Line as a regular soldier. The others of you know me too, and you know what is true and false in me. If the gentry look on us as dirt—and dirty we are—I say the best thing in my life is the comrade in the Line, and I'm here because I want to be here. We joined up in York village before they ever wrote out the fine principles of independence, and I said to myself, shaver that I was, the fine logic of my life is the army of the Revolution. Where else was I to look for logic? Born out of slavery I was, my mother and my father in bondage, like so many of yours, and when I was six, turned into the fields to pick. And apprenticed at ten. And beaten, starved, driven, mocked at. I know not why the Yankee men fight, but I know how it was with us in Pennsylvania, and I know that when I fell in love with a sweet young lass called Molly Bracken, my master beat me and told me love was for the gentry. The devil it is! Love is for us. There are land and woods and iron in this place for all of the world, and this is what my musket says, me, Jamie Stuart. But where am I now? They sold me. My mother and my father they sold, and they sold me, and here I sit, ragged and hungry and worn out with the wild battles they made me fight out of their vanity and stupidity and their fear lest the Revolution should turn itself into something against the officer gentry. . . . And that's all. I've had my say.

Then it was Andrew Yost, the Dutchman, who rose ponderously and told what his father had said to him, one day when the Line encamped nearby to his land.

We hold on quits from the patroon, said Yost, and all his life my father dream of freehold. If we hold land in New York Colony, the patroon goes with the British. Instead, we are lucky. We hold land in Jersey, and the patroon has to go with the Revolution or lose his land. So he goes with the Revolution and they make him colonel. Now patroon is colonel, and the rents go up. On my father's land, every year since 1776, rents double, and when I go home to my father last spring and ask for food, he just look at me. He just look at me and say, you think I'm not starving too, God damn you to hell, and the Revolution with you. That's what he say, with barns empty and larder empty, and all the officers of the 4th, 6th and 10th quartered with the patroon and living on the fat of the land. Then he say to me, Lend me your pay. Make me a loan of your pay. I say to him, *Pay?* My God, old man, you're surely crazy as hell!

Then there spoke Freddy Goulay, who said, his voice singing like a drum softly beaten:

You all know me, I am Goulay, black man, African man whose daddy was sold into slavery for Quenten Soames, the Lord Schofield, who I never seen—only his name I know. But I know that, sure enough. When I eight year old, they put me in the field under the whip, and whip me in the sun and whip me in the rain. Whip me in the sun and whip me in the rain, and I ain't got no back at all, only the whip marks. Then there comes war for freedom, we hear, war for freedom, sure enough for us, for who need freedom more. Sixty-two of us work the fields out in Blue Valley in Virginia, and when news come, we rise up and slay the overseers. Seven of them, and us do like the Bible say, and put to death them who hold us in bondage. Cold and cruel we put them to death, for they whip us and hold us in bondage, and we brake the muskets over their heads. Then we go across to Pennsylvania, for them in Virginia would be wrought for what we done, and we enlist us here. Sixty-two black men from Lord Schofield's lands, and only me, Goulay, and Jim Holt and Kabanka is left. We is left, but the other all perish, for the gentry put them in front. All right—the gentry put them in front in Monmouth and eighteen of us is slain right there, and that all right, I tell you. You going to slay for freedom, you going to pay the price. We know that—but we know too that the gentry is turned around, and they don't want no freedom. Otherwise they don't take men who fight the war and make beasts of them and slaves of them, and starve them, and let them die away of the plague while they fill their bellies, and whip them and hang them, and gut them in, like so they did to Kelly, and make a mockery of them, and steal their pay and spend it on wine and women . . .

Like a drum, his deep voice beat, and the rhythm caught the upturned, haggard, dirty faces of the men, and set them to nodding a rhythmic agreement; for who was not hot with the memory of the fourteen thousand dollars pay money stolen and spent by Lieutenant John Bingham of the 5th and the four others who were with him, and the three thousand dollars spent and squandered by Captain Silas Greene of the 3rd, and how he said, when they tried him—not believe me, as they tried us—that it was better spent than on the lousy Irish and the heathen Jews? Who did not recall that his fate was neither death nor whipping, but six strokes of the cane and then a disgraceful removal of his name from the regimental rolls, a disgrace that paid him well enough? And who was not bitter with the memory of four thousand dollars more of commissary money—hard money and not the worthless paper—appropriated to the Philadelphia tailors to make fine winter woolen uniforms for the officers when all the while we starved in our nakedness? And more and much more; and the memories flooded over us and stiffened us and hardened us as the black man spoke—we who had once hated black men and had then learned to die with them and eat with them and live with them, which was more than our gentry could learn.

There then spoke Lawrence Scottsboro, master sergeant in the 1st, a bent, gnarled, bitter little man of fifty years—old, woefully old that was, in our ranks—toothless, professional soldier all his life, from the French wars; dirty profane; such a man as I would have shrunk from once, but whom I knew now—and knew also the core of hope and fear within him.

Naked, he said, naked into the world and naked out of it, and where will I lay my old bones when the time comes? A bounty of twenty dollars they promised me, nor paid it. Christ no! Nor paid my wages! I see them a nation! Gentry they are, but where is a tot of rum to warm my aching old bones? A shred of meat? A man wants a woman, a sip of wine, a bite of pudding! A man's entitled to his wages—I tell you so. What in hell's name else has he?

Else, much else, said the Jew Levy, in his piping voice with its Spanish accent, a skinny little man with black eyes and a thin, ragged beard. He has in him a soul which can also be whipped, and that can be whipped to death even if the body lives. We here—we are like huntsmen roving the world for some flowers to smell, but the smell, it has become a stink in our nostrils. For you it is the cane and the whip; but for me and my kind, it is dirty Jew bastard from dawn to nightfall.

Talk, talk, talk, said Emil Horst, chief carpenter in the train, but what does it lead to? It leads to the gallows, you benighted fools!

Will they hang all of us?

How many scaffolds have ye built, Emil? Will you carve us one?

Now who is that? Who is that? roared Horst, a powerful and bitter man, short and broad and powerful.

He leaped onto the table top and roared, Come up here with me! Come up here with me, you dirty outland rat, and stand up to me, and say it to my face!

Ah, quiet, quiet—or they'll be hearing us over in Morristown, soothed Bowzar.

Do I have the look of gentry? Has sense no place here? Are you all mad with hunger and the want of a little rum? I'd be a rich man and gentry myself, if I had a dollar for every lad who died mutinous! And frightened I am not—we pledged the oath, I hold with it!

And how many scaffolds have ye fashioned?

I'm a soldier, and I was ordered to build, and by God in heaven, I'll build a staircase to hell if they order me.

Then Jack Maloney leaped onto the table alongside the carpenter, and they stood there in the center of that stirring, murmuring, packed body, like two wolves centered in the circle of the pack, the one great and gross, the other small and dapper, and Jack Maloney, grinning, asked:

Will you call yourself a better soldier than me?

Shaking his great head, the carpenter answered seriously, No, no, there be no better, Jack, but you have betrayed the King what fed you.

Betrayed? For what pay? For what reward? For what gain? So that I will never lay eyes again on my bonny land and my native Yorkshire? You have never seen a pretty land, Emil Horst, until you look upon the green sward of England, but it's bitter for a man whose eyes open and who says, Only a butcher kills for pleasure or pay. From that, I move one step. One step! How many times have I told the raw recruit that fear is a matter of one step; the second comes easier. When I had said to myself, I will not fight against the rebels, I had to ask myself: Then will ye not fight alongside them? Only if I stayed in the pay of King George would I betray, and now if I bend my head to this mockery the officer gentry have made of good men who fight for freedom, then I betray. Don't betray me, Emil Horst! Get out now, and go to the Hardwick House where the gentry are swilling, and tell them that over here in a hut of the 11th, a lot of dirty curs are making a mutiny— or stay here and hold your peace, for they will never hang the Pennsylvania Line! Who will hang us? Who?

He addressed this to the crowd, and a low, animal roar of approval answered him.

Who? Who? Five years ago, when the Yankees ran like frightened hares in New York, their war would have been over if it were not for the foreign brigades—and it hasn't been different since. You ask who is the Revolution? We are the Revolution—we are! And if we should cast out the gentry who have made this noble thing into a pigsty, who is traitor to who?

No answer now, but a deep and thoughtful silence, now that the thing had been formulated, worded, made plain. Whatever thoughts are, whatever thoughts we had been keeping inside us, no one had ever spoken like this. My heart matched theirs; well I remember the stab of fear and pain and excitement and wild exultation that ran through me, as if a new sky were seen beyond black clouds, a sky that was more of a mystery than the secret of life itself, but glimpsed a moment. All the years I have lived since, all the pain and sorrow I have known, have not served to take away that one single glimpse I had that night, in that crowded, body-warmed, stinking hut.

Now stay or go, Emil Horst, said Jack Maloney, in a voice that was gentle and awful. And after moments, the carpenter answered:

I stay.

Do we all stay? asked Jack Maloney.

Then the Revolution is over, a voice spoke from the dark corner of the hut.

Ye are mistaken there, for it has just begun.

Then clear your heads and fuzz the cobwebs off your brains, said Billy Bowzar. The night is half over, and we have a matter of work to do.

PART THREE

Being an account of the events of New Year's Day, observations on the mood of the men, and certain details concerning the preparations for the rising of the Pennsylvania Line.

D AWN CAME, AND STILL only the barest essentials
of our work were complete, for we were trying to
remake not only the Pennsylvania Line of the Rev-
olutionary Army but, in a fashion we only vaguely understood, our lives and our destiny and the lives and the
destinies of all folk within our land; and that, you will
agree, was no small undertaking for a handful of wretched
and hungry soldiermen. So when it comes to what we made
and what we failed to make, you should measure the target
we shot at as well.

One of the first steps we took was to appoint a Committee, to act for the Congress of the Line, which had come
into being spontaneously and without plan or direction,
but simply out of grief and anger over the death of the
drummer lad, of the soldier Kelly, and of our own tired
hopes. A Congress of fifty or sixty persons could hardly
accomplish what we needed to accomplish before dawn
broke, and that was readily agreed to and understood; so
we created a Committee of Sergeants, which would have a

sergeant—or in some cases a corporal, since many of those were good men, held back by the hate they had earned from the gentry—to represent each of the ten infantry regiments, with an eleventh to speak for the artillery company. A twelfth was added to the Committee, and that twelfth was myself; the purpose was to ensure discipline and protection. First, I was designated provost, but the name itself was compounded out of such hate and fear and terror and misery, that it sat uneasily with me and with them as well.

We could not do as the provosts did. If we were not all of us hanged or shot down by noon of the next day, we would begin to bring something new into being; it would be a new army with a new discipline and a new law and a new hope, and it would have no officers, but a discipline out of itself—which was not a matter we understood too well, but somehow felt in the marrow of our hopes. All that long night and morning, we were changing, and somehow we had the assurance that all the soldiers of the Line would change too. Yet for all of that, we knew that in the first stages at least, there would be an iron hand needed—not I but a group, a Committee, to enforce decisions; and if they chose me first, it was because I was Pennsylvania and Scotch too, free but born in bondage, native yet bound blood and body to the foreign brigades. And another thing, if I say it—I was a soldier, and I would know my work. If they chose me, it was because the pattern of toil and trouble was rubbed into me—and they knew I would not leave them in the lurch.

So my committee was given the title Guard of the Citizen-soldiery, and I myself was called President of the Guard.

It may seem strange to you that everything we did was

done through committees and you may have heard folk who malign us say that we took not a step or an act without making a committee first; but it should also be remembered that, before the gentry took over, the Revolution arose from committees of the plain people; and for five years, the lesson had been driven home that war is not made by heroes or by gallant officers in blue and white uniforms, but by the men of the Line, standing shoulder to shoulder. It is true that we created committees for care of the women, the children, the ammunition, the commissary—yes, and we even had a Committee of Moral Purpose for Citizen-soldiers, and a Committee of Propaganda, and a Committee for the General Good of the Common Weal; and it is also true that few enough of these committees ever functioned; but that is not to say that what we did was wrong. We did only what we knew how to do, and that was little enough.

First the Committee of Sergeants was formed. Names were raised; they were discussed—some at length, some hardly at all. Billy Bowzar was elected from the 10th, Danny Connell from the 11th, Lawrence Scottsboro from the 1st. These were all unanimous, but there was a good deal of discussion over Leon Levy of the 5th. Many held that it was not right for a Jew to stand for a whole regiment, even as they held again that it was wrong for the black man, Jim Holt, to represent the 2nd Regiment. It was Jack Maloney, who was elected from the 6th over protests that a British deserter could not be wholly trusted, who said:

What kind of a mockery is it when we make foreigns among the foreigns themselves?

They were elected, as was Bora Kabanka, the giant African-born Bantu of the 9th Regiment. There was Dwight Carpenter from the artillery and Abner Williams, the gentle Connecticut-born scholar from the 3rd Regiment. Sean O'Toole stood for the 4th and Jonathan Hook for the 7th. Some thought it proper to have someone stand symbolically for the 8th, but since they were hundreds of miles away, guarding Fort Pitt, and since we had heard nothing of them for so long, it was decided better to let them be apart from us, until they could come to a decision of their own.

Before the Committee of Sergeants sat down to build an agenda and deal with it, a Commissary Committee was appointed by Billy Bowzar and myself, with Chester Rosenbank as its president, and they adjourned to his hut in the encampment of the 2nd, to begin to deal with the various and complex questions of supply.

Most of the night had gone by now, and most of the lads of the Congress had staggered sleepily away to their hutments. Built red though the fire was, it could not drive off the cold that crept through the chinks in the logs, and our tallow wick had burned out and we had no fat to replenish it. Katy Waggoner was huddled on the floor, close to the fire, with Mathilda's head in her lap, and as the mountain girl slept, Katy gently stroked her yellow hair and sang to her, so softly that it came as a kitten's purr: *Long is the night for sleeping childer, goblins dance in the redwat snow* . . . In the bunks, men huddled in the straw snoring hoarsely, for our heads were heavy and thick with constant sickness; and on either side the long table the Committee of Sergeants sat and planned, their bearded faces weary and gray. Billy Bowzar had a writing pad that he tilted to catch the fire gleam, and Jack Maloney was advancing an argument for speed and precision in getting under way.

Or you'll find a traitor among you, mark me, said Katy Waggoner, breaking her sad song and then picking it up again.

Angus MacGrath came in, beating the cold from his blue knuckles.

How is it? we asked him.

Caller, and much so. Cold and deeply so. But quiet.

Have ye a good guard of lads?

Twenty of the best. I took me the Gary brothers, who are tight on a scent as hellhounds, and I put me one at the Hardwick House and one at the Kemble House, and there they crouch in the snow for a whisper among the gentry. But they sleep the sleep of the just this New Year's, even if no other time, with bellies full of wine and pudding. And if I may trouble ye, Jamie, I'd be the better for a crust of bread in me to stave off the cold.

And wouldn't we all, smiled Danny Connell. Just tighten yer belt and come another day—we'll all of us be eating sufficient, or without any appetite to trouble us.

Jamie here—and heed me, Angus, and get it into your thick head—is now President of the Guard ... said Billy Bowzar seriously, his broad, flat face solemn and judicious ... and it's him we will thank for staying alive. We are a Board of Sergeants to deal with a rising up of the whole Line, so that from this moment on, we will fight a war for ourselves and for our own, and not for the God-damned officer gentry. . . .

The big Scot's jaw fell, and he rubbed his beard and

looked from face to face among the twelve stolid members of the Committee.

Well?

Give me a chance to swallow.

Are ye with us or agin us, Angus?

What in hell kind of a question be that to ask a man? Do I have the look of the fause?

True or fause, each man pledges here.

Be damned to ye, and I pledge, said the Scot sourly. Ye would mistrust your own mother, and me that has never been corporal even, for I would not put my head where some will!

And I'm a better man than you are, Danny Connell, he added. Or any other black Roman! Would you make something of that?

If I were not this tired, answered Connell wearily.

Button yer lip, MacGrath, said I, putting my arm through his, for you are my man now. We need a hundred more to the twenty fine lads ye have found, and then we will figure out the putting into action of all the fine plans they cook up here.

And I turned him to the door—

Come along, and if yer head rings a little, and if ye find your belly rubbing your backbone, it's but a temporary nuisance; for it seems to me that we're on the wildest jig a man ever danced.

And it's no pleasure dancing when the ground is four feet below ye, MacGrath said solemnly. Ye do not intend to go into that cursed cold at this hour of the morning, Jamie Stuart?

Indeed I do. There is no more sleep for us, Angus, until this is finished.

There is sleep for me, the Scot said stubbornly. I have done my round of this mad duty.

I slid my musket from the rack and looked at him. Then I said:

Well now, Angus MacGrath, this is a new hitch for me, but the skin of my neck is tight enough for me to play it out, and to tell you the truth, I don't much give a damn at this point. I have lived in hell too long, and I will not see my sweet Molly again, and the whole fact of it is that I'm past caring for anything but the one chance in a thousand we are playing for. So what do you say?

I leveled the musket at him; and from me he looked to the eleven grim-visaged men who sat at the sawbuck table, all of them watching us, but no one of them saying a word, and still Katy Waggoner in front of the fire, keening her plaintive lullaby.

What will I do? I thought to myself then. What will I do? Will I shoot down this great brave man, this large ugly Scotsman who is like a brother to me—or will I back out? And if I do back out, what then? What sort of a wild venture have I embarked on, that every step of the way it comes to a crisis that must either be driven home, like the peg into its wooden loin, or left to triumph on the ashes of our insane hopes? Are any of us sane? Or are we all mad with hunger and cold and humiliation?

Yet for all of these thoughts, I knew that I was sane—saner indeed than I have ever before been, in all of my life, and I also knew that I would slay Angus MacGrath or any other who stood in our path from here on. Something had happened to me, just as something had happened to the eleven at the table; a new fire had been lit, and the heat of its flame was still untested.

Well, I will be damned, said MacGrath. Here is Jamie Stuart, with the pap still wet on his mouth, and he holds a gun on me. By all that is holy! Well, it will take the gentry to slay me, not such a skinny lad as you, Jamie Stuart. So let us go out into that cursed cold night and do yer crazy business.

And I went out arm-in-arm with Angus MacGrath, and when I returned, as I said, there was dawning in the smoky air, and still hardly a beginning had been made by the Committee. I brought them an accounting of the Line, which was three thousand and fifty-two enlisted men, as near as I could reckon it with no access to the officers' records.

Just for a moment before I entered the hut, I paused and looked across the silent, flat parade ground, with its lines of huts and its tracked-over, dirtying snow. It slumbered in uneasy peace; but what, I wondered, would it be like a few hours from now? Would that pale, cold sun, nudging the mist so timidly, look down upon a sanguine plain of fratricidal horror? And would this be the end of all the best hopes that the ragged band of us had ever entertained? Yet I was committed, so what did it matter? And as for nightmares—had I not lived long enough in the midst of one?

The Committee listened as I made my report on the number of soldiers we had in the encampment. I spoke and blew on my hands alternately, edging to the fire to warm myself. Now Danny Connell rose and spread his ragged coat over the two women, who lay sleeping before the bed of coals, and old Scottsboro shook his head sadly, commenting:

A sight of men is three thousand and more, Jamie, and has any of us the head to lead them?

Cut that grumbling, said Jack Maloney.... How did you and Angus make out with the Guard, Jamie?

I reported that we had enlisted at least sixty more lads who pledged to stand by us; but that it was no easy work, crawling into bed with a man in the dark and persuading him with whispers. The call for the Guard was the refrain of the Yankee camp jig, to be sounded three times on the trumpet; and whenever that came, if there had been no further instruction, the men pledged to us would lead their hutments out onto the parade, with arms and bayonets fixed. But so far we had nothing to speak of among the 4th and the 2nd, and were particularly strong in the 10th and 11th.

And where is Angus?

Seeing to the guard over the Kemble House, and then to sleep, which I must have too, otherwise I will not be able to set a foot in front of the other.

I would sell me own sweet mother for a pot of steaming hot coffee right now, said Sean O'Toole.

Then heed me, Jamie, Billy Bowzar nodded, marking the words with his quill, and then you can turn in for two hours but not a minute more. We have made certain decisions, the main one being that a man on a gallows trap had best get off it or prepare to dance in the air. There is no more turning back from what we decided, and no more delaying it either. So we have chosen sundown this day to expel the officers and take the Line, and the Revolution too, into our own hands. There is our commitment; either we succeed tonight, or we will pay for it tomorrow.

But it ain't humanly possible to convince all the men before this evening, I protested.

And we don't want to, said the black man, Holt. If they all know of this, they will set to pondering it, and they will coddle right and wrong until they're tight in it as a worm in a apple. Let them do what they feel when we hail them. They do right—and we win. They don't do right . . .

It is the only way, Jamie, insisted Dwight Carpenter. Either the men are with us or they are not with us, and there is no persuading them with words, not if we had a fortnight to plan and plot. This is the only way.

Like casting dice . . .

Ye see it wrong if you see it that way, Jamie, for the hopes and dreams of men are not dice to play with. We have been too much played with already, and if this was just a wild adventure for our own hope and glory, why then there would be somewhat in your say. But we got a simple and unclouded stake in freedom, not in wealth and property and power as the gentry do, but for the right to hold up our heads a little and taste some sweetness in living, and don't you think that every lad in the line has a similar stake?

I don't know.

You are overweary, Jamie, said Billy Bowzar, and it's truly a miracle you wrought out there in the darkness. So turn into your straw and rest your head for a time.

This, I did. I was past thinking or caring, and the moment I had covered myself with straw, I slept.

It was that morning, during my short rest, I think—for I kept no journal then, being more concerned with remaining alive than with telling the tale someday—that I dreamed so sweetly of my lovely lass, Molly Bracken. I make note of this because I believe it helps somewhat to show the simple, ordinary nature of folk we were; which might be taken for granted, as you might take for granted that most men are wrought out of the same stuff as you yourself, were if not for the slander that every learned scholar places upon the great rising of the foreign brigades. But the learned scholars sit snug and warm; they never took a barefooted march of thirty miles in a day, and they never went hungry for weeks on end, and they were never called forthright with the earnest, Come and enlist in the army of freedom, for ten dollars a month and eternal glory! So they never took that glory apart to see what it was made of, and less they care what the men who found that glory were made of; and the most they give thought to is how passing strange it was that the great land of Pennsylvania, with its three hundred thousand folk and all its great resources, could never call more than fifteen hundred native born to its colors and had to enlist the remainder out of the foreign scum. But the native born and the foreign scum both dreamed, and I dreamed of the future and the past.

And in my dream of that past that morning, I sat at the cobbler's bench of Fritz Tumbrill once more: I, Jamie Stuart, an apprentice lad of sixteen summers, and for the grits and greens and fatback he fed me, and the patched shirt and trews he lent me, I cobbled all day, from the dawn to sunset. I swept the shop and blacked the boots and cleaned the panes and weeded the garden, and for all of this I never saw a minted penny. My reward was in blows from the huge, hamlike hand of the enormously fat half-German, half-Yankee master cobbler. And I stood it because until I had my trade, I was no part of the world of men. I gritted

my teeth and stood it until they nailed up the first enlistment bill, and then I stood it no more, but flung my apron
in the fat pig's face and told him:

I've a new trade now—and when I and the other lads
have driven the British back into the sea, take care, take
care!

And I walked off to the tune of his curses and abuse.
But it is of before then that I dreamed, of the first time I
saw Molly Bracken. I sat at my bench, alone in the shop,
for Fritz was out for a pint at the tavern and Tibby, the
junior apprentice, was over at the tannery, picking up a
hide. In my dream I worked at a set of buskins for a little
boy, awling the high uppers, when there came a tinkle from
the bell at the door. Come in, I called, and there entered a
slim reed of a girl, with hair so black it startled one, and
eyes so blue they fair frightened one—until one saw how
direct and open they were, how wise and knowing they
were. And those eyes looked at me calmly and appraisingly
as she said:

I have come to be fitted for a pair of walking shoes. I
am Molly Bracken, the daughter of the new parson at the
Lutheran Church.

To that point, my dream matched in a fair way with
reality, for it was much in that same fashion I had met
Molly Bracken. But in my dream I rose up and took her in
my arms and kissed her, for I knew her well and nothing
held me back. But in life itself, four months passed before
I dared to take her hand and set my lips to it. And in those
four months, she taught me to read and write and she
taught me to know the flowers of the field, the stars in the
sky, and some of the noble things men have done which
are greater than either—in a certain way. Her father was a

wise and humble man, and he took a liking to me and made his house my house. He unlocked his bookcase for me; he fed me, and he was as much a father as I ever had.

What a hunger I had for the things he gave me! As you will see, there was much apart from me in Pastor Bracken when I grew to manhood and had become proficient in the one trade I knew aside from cobbling, the trade of killing; but at that time of which I speak now, when I was a tall and stringy lad of fifteen years, he was the best and wisest person who had come into my life—the more so than my poor father, who had loved me but could give me naught.

In my dream, I dreamed among other things of my coming to the manse for the first time, where Molly Bracken brought me as she would bring a wild animal into a tame pasture, saying:

Never in all my born days did I see the like of such a boy as you.

Well, let me be, then. Let me be as I am. I ain't asking to be no different, so let me be.

You're a creature, not a boy, she said.

Well, you can go to the devil and be damned then, calling me a creature!

We were outside the manse, and she stopped and turned to me, wide-eyed and horrified.

Jamie Stuart!

What you asked for you got.

Then I'll leave you alone to your dirt and your nasty mind. You're a miserable little boy!

And she stormed into the house and left me standing outside alone, and there I stood, first on one foot and then on the other, and then on both feet, but unable to move, unable to go and unable to remain—in that wholly ambivalent condition that only a boy of fifteen, deeply and wholly in love for the first time in his life, can experience. And there I remained until Pastor Bracken came along on his way into the house, cocked an eye at me, prepared to pass on and then paused to question.

Waiting for someone? he wanted to know.

Nope.

You're the Stuart boy, aren't you?

Uh-huh.

Tumbrill's apprentice.

I nodded, feeling shame cloak me and run all over me. Evidently, he sensed what was going through my mind, and in any case there was visual evidence in the way in which my toes crawled for cover into my broken shoes, the way in which my elbows crawled from their holes, my knees from the gaps in my breeches. But mostly my toes, writhing over each other like terrified snakes, for what could be more incongruous or humiliating than a cobbler's apprentice shod as badly as I?

Why don't you come in, he said, and meet my daughter?

I know her, I answered, staring at my toes as I manipulated them.

Oh.

She don't like me, I said.

No? Well, maybe she could learn. That happens, Jamie Stuart. People start out disliking each other fit to tie a cat, and then they change. So why don't you come in and have a cup of tea with us? How about that now? Won't you come in? Come along now, won't you, Jamie Stuart?

And Jacob Bracken put his arm through mine and took me into his house with him, and of this I dreamed and of other things as well. How he made Molly my teacher, I dreamed; for he gave me a book to read and I pretended to read it. Yes, one fine day this happened, as I sat with them in their unbelievable kindness, and the man who wrote that book was a poet called Milton. And there in it was a picture of the splendid and awful turmoil of heaven and hell, so that my very heart ached to know what it meant.

Read it aloud, Jamie, said Pastor Bracken.

My head was bent and I would not raise it.

What is into the boy? asked Pastor Bracken. Molly, what is into the boy, do you suppose?

Leave him alone, she answered, God bless her. Then and there, I said to myself, God bless her for her kindness, for she is the best and sweetest lass in all the world.

Jamie! cried Pastor Bracken then, in the thunderous voice he used on a Sunday morning in the pulpit. Jamie! he cried.

And I raised up my head all covered with tears, and answered that I was as ignorant as a pup just whelped, and not a word of the English language could I read or write, and here I was, fifteen years and better.

So Molly taught me, and I dreamed of her teaching me. I dreamed of the ABC as I, a big gawking lad, learned it out of a hornbook, and I dreamed of the first little verses I put together. But such is the magic of words that I dreamed also of the first book of depth and beauty that I was able to make out for myself, and how eventually I lay before Pastor Bracken's fire, reading like a cat gone mad in the catnip, first from one book and then from another, all unconcerned with the beating these late hours away would earn me when I returned to the shop.

*　　*　　*

So I dreamed of this and that, of one thing and another, of my meeting Molly Bracken, of seeing her, of learning from her, of defending her once from a mad dog, holding the dog at arm's length, both my hands flexed around its neck until it strangled like that, and conscious for the first time of the strength in my long, lean body, and proud— proud as when I said to her:

There was a spark inside me once, which I always knew. But now it will burn, and you will not be ashamed of me. . . .

But the dream placed all together, and in the dream, after I kissed Molly Bracken, I took her hand in mine and we walked down the street through York Village and out to the meadows beyond. And as we passed along the street, everyone whispered:

See there, it is that worthless orphan lad, Jamie Stuart, but we must honor him now, for there is by his side the loveliest lady that ever lived.

We walked into a meadow all carpeted with daisies, and suddenly we were ringed around with fragrant pine woods, alone under the sun and the breeze. Oh, my true love, sweet Jamie Stuart, she said to me, and I answered, For all eternity, I will be true to fair Molly Bracken. We stroked each other's face and hair, and our happiness was so great that it seemed we must surely die of it, for it was too much to bear.

And then Jack Maloney was waking me, with:

Time's up, Jamie lad. Would you sleep away your whole last day of grace?

Let me go back to my dream, I begged him.

There is no going back to dreams, Jamie, he said, with strange tenderness. As a matter of fact, it seems to me that there is no going back ever, whether in dreams or out of them.

I resisted him and closed my eyes and tried to slip back into the pool of sleep. Weary enough I was, but he kept shaking me, and as he shook me the dream dissolved and I knew I would never regain it.

You have lost me the fairest maid in all of Pennsylvania, I said.

How, Jamie?

You have never loved, so how would you understand?

And do you think there is a man who never loved, Jamie, even a soldier of King George III who was put into the camps with the pap still on his lips? Let that be . . .

I crawled out of the straw and dropped to the ground. The hut was dark, as it always was, with just one narrow bar of light through a crack in the door.

Close the damned door! I cried.

You're mighty mettlesome, Jamie, nodded Maloney, closing the door. Then he said:

There are some of us who have had no sleep, Jamie, so sit on your temper. You've got a day's work ahead. The Committee wants a check on every hut in the encampment, and at least one member of the Citizen-soldier Guard should be chosen from each hut, if that is possible. Then, tonight, when we issue the order to stand to arms and parade, the guards can lead. We have also heard gossip that a ration of rum has been allotted and will be issued out in honor of the New Year—which is something, for all the officers' crying that they had no rum or food either. Also, it is a piece of madness, for that rum on empty stomachs will drive the men crazy. All the more reason for the guards to be good men and to keep their heads. Also, keep your foot down on powder and shot. The hotheads will want to load muskets, and to the Committee's way of thinking, there's more danger in that than in anything else; for if we pull this off, bayonets will be ample to deal with a hundred and fifty officers, and if we fail, there will be nothing gained by turning it into a blood bath. We have had reports from the Hardwick House and the Kemble House and from three houses in the village where gentry are quartered. They stuffed themselves last night and most of them are still sleeping, and unless I mistake their temper, they'll give the encampment a wide berth all this day. But if any officer seems to get wind of what we're up to, Jamie, you are empowered to place him under arrest, binding and gagging him. The old hospital hutment will be turned into a guard-house. Both barbers have joined us and taken the pledge to be true to the Line and the enlisted men.

I was out of my sleep and my dreams now, and I noticed that Billy Bowzar and the Jew Levy still sat at the table, scribbling away on paper in the light of a tallow wick they had obtained from somewhere. While Maloney gave me my instructions, two men entered the hut, spoke softly to Bowzar, received slips of paper, and left. And as the door opened, I noticed two other soldiers on guard outside.

The men of my command, who shared the hut with me, were all of them awake, which was strange since they had missed most of the night's sleep. Curled in their straw, which was the only place they could find warmth when they did not have parade or drill—neither of which would be given us on New Year's Day—they were oddly grave and quiet. From somewhere by some means, an organization was shaping itself, and the wild venture of the night before, which should have been revealed for all its lunacy on this cold, clear morning, managed to maintain itself.

Well then, I said to myself, swinging my feet down to the floor, here you are, Jamie Stuart, twenty-two years old, with a little reading and a little writing and a little cobbling, making a great uprising. And I bethought me of Jimmy Coleman of my own regiment, who was hanged here on this same parade in Morristown only May past. Nothing had Jimmy done or said that could match the distance we had traveled since the evening before; he had only talked openly and publicly of the gap between the punishment and food issued out by the officer gentry. He had written down in charcoal across a posted order of the day, *When Adam delved and Eve span, Who was then the gentleman?* And it was also charged that he fomented plots and had made insulting remarks to Colonel Chickering, of the Connecticut Line. For this, he was put on the gallows and hanged by the neck until he was dead. But I remember well his behavior there, how he was calm and easy as any of the gentry might be, fingering the rope as he said: A little bit of freedom is not enough, my friends, so mind you treat us better or you will find the tiny spark you struck a mighty flame—and it may be that flame will even singe an officer or two. So the officers cursed him and he swung out of this life, and the officers said: Good riddance to bad rubbish. When an apple is rotten, you pluck it from the barrel.

Well, here I was, Jamie Stuart, and that was that, and there was no use thinking about it any more, and Jack Maloney was saying:

Hop to it, Jamie. There is much to be doing, and after we have made an army out of ourselves and driven George's men into the salty sea, we'll clean house. So there'll be no rest for a long time to come, and you might just as well put that in your pipe and smoke it.

I had slept with my shoes, and there were needles in my feet as I moved across the floor to the musket rack.

As I passed the table, Levy caught my sleeve and said, A moment, Jamie. I am writing you our credentials, and you had best wait for them.

Credentials? What in hell's name do I want with them? Is there anyone in this Line who don't know me?

Know you or not, said Billy Bowzar quietly, every Committee man will have credentials from here on. And no order need be obeyed unless a man can show his credentials and his warrant from the Committee.

Yet if it peters out, I reflected, a man carries his death warrant in his pocket.

That's right, Jamie, said Billy Bowzar, regarding me evenly from his bloodshot, fatigue-ringed eyes. We are all in this together, you know.

But Levy smiled slightly as he handed me my credentials, a slip of paper I still have here beside me as I write, so many years later, the paper less mortal than the men who made and wrote upon it. On it, it says, in the fine, cultured script of the Jew Levy:

To all men who may examine this: Let it be known that this warrant empowers Jamie Stuart, Sergeant in the 11th Regiment of the Pennsylvania Line, to carry out all and sundry orders, desires, needs and complaints of the Committee of Sergeants, which is now and until the enlisted men of the Line shall rule otherwise, the supreme authority and the commanding power in the army of Pennsylvania—which power was invested in them by a representative Congress of the Regiments of the Line, notably as follows: 1st, 2nd, 3rd, 4th, 5th, 6th, 7th, 9th, 10th, 11th and Artillery.

Enscribed this Day of the 1st of January in the Year 1781, by LEON LEVY *and signed by* ... WILLIAM Z. BOWZAR *sec.*

This I took and wrapped in oilskin with a profile I had sketched of Molly Bracken, a testament of bravery given to me after the New York fighting and signed by Reed, three letters from my Molly, my Bill of Apprenticeship, and my enlistment and bounty papers. These constituted all that Jamie Stuart had gathered in twenty-two years of living, and for what they were worth, I carried them wherever I went.

Then I left the hut to undertake my duties as President of the Citizen-soldier Guard.

That day we began, after midnight struck, as a rude and unruly Congress; by dawn we had created and put into operation our Committee of Sergeants and certain other committees; and by nightfall of the first of January half the Pennsylvania Line was organized and prepared to move; and except for one incident, which I shall relate to you, not one breath of this came to the ears of the officer gentry. On that day when we worked to prepare the uprising, the feat we accomplished seemed not one half so remarkable as it does now, all these years later; but on reflection it seems passing strange that we, the enlisted men and noncommissioned officers of the foreign brigades, despised and reckoned as so much dirt, so many filthy animals, could have carried out in so short a time an organizational scheme never matched in all the history of the Revolution. It is a matter of record that no permanent encampment of the Continental Army was ever broken with so little preparation as we had for our uprising; and it was part of our plan that once we seized power to ourselves, we would break camp immediately and march through the night to another place. This was through the urging of Jack Maloney, who insisted that the only way in which we could consolidate ourselves and impose our new discipline was in the motion of a march.

Marching men, he said, are soldiers. Encamped, they are something else.

But that morning when I came out of my hutment, only the most tenuous threads bound us together. A credential in my pocket which was as good for the hangman as for anyone else; a few loyal and true comrades scattered through the encampment; and a musket in my hands which held one shot to smooth the path to glory. But I was young, and my earlier despair was transmuting itself into a mounting excitement, and my dreams of fair Molly Bracken gave way to dreams of a new army, an army which would sweep across the land, calling thousands to its banners, an army which would brush the British into the sea as a new broom flicks the cinders, an army which would call upon all of those who worked by the sweat of their brow and the strength of their hand to create a new kind of republic. . . . Yet there my dreams halted, for I knew of no way in which men could live except with the gentry above and such people as myself below. However, I shrugged that off, deciding that I was better for the doing, leaving the planning and the thinking to such men as Billy Bowzar, the Jew Levy, Jack Maloney, and Abner Williams, all of them men in their thirties, wise in all the ways of the world and full of the bitter wine of experience.

As I began to cross the angle of the parade, to a hut of the 1st where there were four good lads to start work with, a little group of officers, mounted and cloaked, came into sight on the road from Morristown. Strangely enough, I was the only one on the parade at the moment, except for a handful of men at the other extreme, a half mile away. There was no reason for me to be afraid, even though I carried a loaded musket—for I could bluff through that with a tale of guard duty—but the very sight of officers threw me off balance. They were the first I had seen since the day before; then they were my officers, the men who led me; now they were something else. Now they were ranged against me and I was ranged against them, and I carried a warrant in my pocket which would give any one of them justification to shoot me down like a dog.

I forced myself to walk along without changing my pace, yet I couldn't help glancing at them, and I noticed they slowed from a canter to a walk and that they were engaged in conversation—in the course of which one of them pointed to me. They must have come over from Kemble; for Wayne, the brigadier general, was among them, and it was he who nodded the agreement that detached one of them to my direction. The rest picked up their canter and went down the Hill Road toward Mendham, and in a few minutes they were hidden by the huts and the rise of ground toward the parade. The one who rode toward me, I recognized as Lieutenant Calvin Chester of the Artillery, the arrogant, pimply-faced son of a Philadelphia merchant.

He drew his horse up within arm's length of me, prancing it as was a habit with them, so close that I could smell the toilet water from his lace and see the brown drip of snuff from his nose. He wore a splendid greatcoat of brown, with yellow facings; his riding boots had yellow cuffs and he wore gauntlets of yellow pigskin.

Stand to attention! he shouted at me. What's your name and rank?

I presented arms, clicked my heels where there would have been heels had my torn boots owned any, and staring straight ahead of me, answered, Jamie Stuart, sergeant in the 11th.

From the corner of my eye, I watched the bobbing heads of Wayne and the others disappear beyond the hutments.

Sir.

Sir, I said.

And what are you doing on the parade with a musket?

Relieving guard, sir.

Now that's a damned lie, said the lieutenant, for I never knew a sergeant to stand guard where there was a private to do his work for him, and much less one of you damned, dirty scuts from the 11th. Let me see your pan.

I leveled the musket.

Primed, he nodded, and—with his affected, imitation-English lisp—'Od's blood, but we'd be better off if every one of the damned 11th was hanged from the hill. You're under arrest, Mister. Make an about-face, and we'll stroll over to the provost.

Oh, no, I smiled—hitching the musket around and dropping it on the middle button of his fine greatcoat—You are under arrest, and don't reach for a pistol, or I'll blow your fat ass out from under you. Just climb down from your horse and hook an arm through the reins, and lead it like you and me was out for strolling, and never a thought of who is gentry and who is dirt.

You'll hang for this, he began wildly, but I cut him short, telling him, I have no desire to converse with you or any of yer damned brethren. Just walk ahead until we come to the last of the 1st's hutments, and then knock at the door.

There was something in my voice that told him I meant what I said, and he did as I ordered him to. He led me and his horse to the hut and knocked at the door, which Sammy Gruen opened, rubbing the sleep from his eyes and staring in wonder.

We have a breakfast guest, I smiled, so make him welcome.

That was all Sammy needed, and the lieutenant entered the hut quicker than he warranted, and dropping the reins of the horse, I followed. There was an oil-paper window in the hut, and by the light I saw the dull, hopeless expression on the lieutenant's face as he watched the men tumble from their straw and gather round him. Dennis Sullivan, a good lad, but wild and marked for some sort of foolish fate, fingered the greatcoat, stroked the lace, and then pinched the pimply cheeks.

Do you plan to kill me? asked Chester hoarsely. For if you do, you will swing for it as sure as there's a God in the heavens above.

Now will we? grinned Dennis.

Pack that! I snapped. He was going to arrest me so I arrested him instead, and you can take off those nice clothes of his and gag him and tie him up, but no man-handling and no taking out grudges here and no talk. Tie him up and put some sacking over him, and we'll bear him to the hospital, where they're making ready for the sick.

This they did. We trussed him, wrapped him in sacking, and bore him to the hospital like a sack of potatoes, only of less use in any way. Sullivan and Gruen and a Pole named Krakower came with me, after I had warned those left in the hut to stay in the straw and keep their mouths shut. Two others, Kent and O'Malley, unsaddled the horse and then led it to the Artillery stable, with a story of a stray mount.

The old hospital hutment was supply dump and dispensary for the 4th, 10th and 11th Regiments. No doctors were assigned to it, since at that time we had only three doctors for the whole Line, and two of them were fine gentlemen with Philadelphia practices, which at the moment they were attending. The third doctor, a Jew from Charlestown in South Carolina, was brigade officer at the General Hospital, which was at the further end of the encampment. Some thought we might trust him, seeing that he was a Jew, but others said, Jew or not, he was an officer and gentry and would therefore best be left alone. Here at the dispensary were two barbers from Edinburgh, Andrew MacPherson and William Hunt, and they tended the odds and ends of hurts, distempers and minor sicknesses that took the three regiments. For all that theirs was a rough-and-ready practice, picked up as porters at the medical school and as staunchers on the battlefield, I would rather have had them than the cruel and offhand gentry; if you died, you died at least with a warm hand on your shoulder—and when one of our lads stopped a large-bore ball from a British gun, it was short odds that he died whether you had a physician or a barber to bleed him.

MacPherson opened the door for us. He was a tiny, wizened imp of a man, clean-shaven, a sharp, filthy tongue in an ugly little head, a randy goat of a little man and never without a woman, whether in camp or on the march. And not an old bag either, but the fairest lass in camp would be his, and how that was none of us could ever make out; except that his was a joy in life not matched in that grim and sorrowful encampment. Hunt, on the other hand, was a dour, unhappy Scot, dark and humorless, and slowly dying away with longing for the streets and taverns and fog of Glasgow.

Now welcome, Jamie Stuart! cried MacPherson. You would not think business to be this good when we have only set up some few hours past, but already the lads of the 10th have brought us two white-livered sergeants, and that's not bad for the first of a darg. Now what have ye there? . . . Not Chester, the dirty little dog!

Chester it is, sang Dennis Sullivan.

Then roll him in and make him snug and warm.

And like a sack of potatoes, we rolled the lieutenant to where two sergeants, trussed and gagged, sat against the wall. Already the hospital was crowded, and the day had only begun—and it was hot. A huge blaze roared in the hearth, and six women crouched before it, so close that the loose ends of their hair crackled, melting lead and spooning it into bullet molds. The hutment being supply depot as well as dispensary, a good third of the space was taken by bar lead, stacked as high as a man's head. Only the two barbers had sleeping quarters there; but in addition to them, the six women, the three prisoners and a white-faced lad from the 4th who was being bled for the shakes, there were Arnold and Simpkins Gary making a high bid for the girls, and with me and my four lads and the heat, and the

sharp smell of molten lead, the bitter smell of medicine and
the sweet odor of blood, the air was near unbreathable. But
no one seemed to mind that. The women gave the Gary
boys as good as they took, telling them, Now why don't
you take over this molding, if ye're so bright and strong
and free with affection? And as she worked, MacPherson's
lass sang: *The Bishop's wife, she looked me down, ye're
either fine or common, I got what ye can never match, and
sure it's far from common.*

And how is a man to treat the sick with this stinking
lead boiling? . . . Hunt wanted to know . . . Already, we are
cursed with committees, for the first Committee man comes
and turns this into a jail, and then comes the second snook-
ing for supply. The lead he spies, and orders it to be bullets
before nightfall come.

Come out a ye tout, laughed MacPherson. The less sick
we meddle with, the more will survive, and this is a fine
piece of organization. I tell ye, we got a natural bent for
committees.

But my heart was heavy as I left there. Suppose Chester
should be missed and a search made? And didn't all this
activity indicate that the gentry had a whiff of something?

From the hospital, we started a check of the hutments,
but already the thing was in motion of itself, and every
third or fourth hut there would be a black, cold silence
until I had shown the warrant the Jew Levy wrote out for
me. The men were in the straw and the encampment was
dead—a silence and withdrawal that would have been sus-
picious on any other day than New Year's.

Because it was New Year's Day, much went by that
would not have passed muster in the normal course of
things. There was no parade and no drill; and until mid-

afternoon, aside from Wayne and his orderlies, no officers approached the hutments; Lieutenant Chester was not missed, which was not so strange, for we learned afterwards that his mess had thought him to be with Wayne and Wayne had thought him to be back by now at the Kemble House. In any case, though the officers neither knew nor cared what we did that New Year's Day, the hutments were full of talk about how the gentry passed their time, once they had slept off their drunkenness of the night before. And they could not have better confirmed us in what we had decided to do.

There was, around our encampment, a ring of great holdings of the gentry, some of them patroons, some of them British quality, and all of them loyal to His Majesty, George III. We learned well the year before, when we encamped at this same place, to respect that loyalty, for eight men of the 4th Regiment who broke into Peter Kemble's grain bin were docked their pay and given thirty lashes each. The pay was nothing, for we never got it anyway, but thirty lashes is a cruel and terrible thing, and one of the lads, a boy of fifteen, died from the beating. Peter Kemble held over four thousand acres of land, with three manor houses upon it and sixteen barns, and for all that he was open and brash and defiant with his loyalty to the King, never a step was taken against him; instead, our own gentry snuggled up to him, for he was a true gentleman and hunted his hounds day in and day out, and in return for their respectful consideration, he quartered our officers, lent them his hounds to hunt with, and fed them at his board nightly. It was one of those things—as I came to know later—that are understood among gentlemen, even though they fight on different sides; but it was not understood by the buckskin men in our ranks, those who came from the Western counties, Scottish men with a century-old dream of an acre of land for their own, bound out to America to realize their dream—and discovering then that, far from their having land, they could never get enough hard money to own woven clothes or an iron tool.

So when word passed through the hutments that four musicians had come up from Philadelphia to play for a New Year's minuet at the Kemble House, and that two carriages of Philadelphia ladies had followed them—and that there were hanging for bleeding on the Kemble sticking rack two beefs and five fat pigs—you can imagine that our mood was not eased.

Angus MacGrath and I were going among the huts of the 7th, passing out instructions and arguing with faint-hearted men and family men, when we came into a hutment with a stew cooking, the first stew we had smelled in a long while. Chicken heads, they told us: a stew of two dozen chicken heads scrounged out of the garbage of the Kemble House; and did we want a pan?

I would die first, said Angus MacGrath. I am a simple man and not a prideful man, but I will see myself damned before I scrounge in garbage for the leavings of the gentry.

It was no way for him to talk, for these were hungry lads and hunger is a great leveler, and a man wants a taste of meat after he has lived a month on corn mush.

Toward midafternoon, there was a flurry of alarm in the hutments, for we beheld a company of at least thirty officers coming toward the parade at a smart canter. Angus and I were at a hut of the 7th then, and we and the men inside it charged our muskets and determined then and there that if this was a stroke to cut the head from the rebellion, we would go down under bullet and bayonet and not stand trial for any shameful hanging. But the crowd of officers turned off down the road to Whippany, and we learned later that they were guests for a great dinner given that evening at the castle of the patroon Van Beverhoudt. Van Beverhoudt was a mighty Dutch lord who held two hundred black slaves and lived in peace with both the British and the Colonials. In '76 and in '77, when the flame of the Revolution burned hot and fresh, one of his barns had been raided and burned, but after that he went to Philadelphia and had certain dealings with certain folks there, and from then on he was not molested.

So with one thing and another, the men became more sullen, more bitter, more willing to attempt some wild and foolish enterprise, and their bitterness increased as midday passed and the promised ration of rum, the one note of joy for the New Year, was not dispensed.

I recall how Angus and I faced at least forty of them, packed into a hut of the 7th, answering their questions, fighting their wild, random moods.

By now, I had spoken to hundreds of men, and I came to realize that the dream I held, the dream held by Billy Bowzar and Handsome Jack Maloney and the Jew Leon Levy—the dream of turning the still, stagnant current of the Revolution into a mighty new stream; the dream of a whole population of farmers and artisans and bond servants, serfs and slaves, rising up and sweeping the handful of redcoats into the sea like so much rubbish, and then making a true new land where there was freedom and equality for all—I came to realize that this dream was no commodity for sale or conviction. The men were with us; they were for the Committees; they hated the officer gentry as much and more than we did; their cup of sorrow was so full that they no longer cared for the consequences of some wild venture—but they could not be lured with dreams.

We must be paid, they said. That's a simple matter, a plain matter. If a man enlists him at ten dollars a month, he deserves that money, not in paper, but in hard metal. If a man is promised a bounty, he has got to get it. Now what of that, Jamie?

It is not a matter of money, I tried to tell them. There is a reason why you have not been paid, and the reason lies in the very nature of how the gentry lead this struggle. That is what we must change.

But how will *you* pay us, Jamie? How will the Committees pay us? It is all very well to have a fine dream, but a man wants a dollar to send home to his wife and kids. And whatever you say about the gentry, it's them as has the hard money, not us. Not any of us. Can you deny that?

I could not deny it. There was a simple truth in the fact that the gentry had the money, the wealth, the food, the forges and the looms. That they had it out of our blood and sweat, I knew, but what other way there was, I didn't know.

Now me, says a lad out of the German country along the river, I enlisted in '76, and they told me for three years, but I cannot read nor write, as you know, Jamie Stuart, and it seems I put my mark on articles for the whole of the war, with the right for them to hang me, just as they hanged Hans Forst and Emil Guttman. If the war lasts twenty years, I got to fight and grow old and gray and get my death of a wound finally, and all for a twenty-dollar bonus they swear to pay when peace is made.

And how many a good lad is dead and never lives to see the peace!... cried Johnny O'Brian.... And the dirty militia cowards that come up now for a six-month enlistment, they get a bonus of one hundred dollars in hard cash, while the heart of me at nineteen years is worn out with fighting and marching and starving. If Jack Maloney and Billy Bowzar are making a rising, I will follow them to hell and be damned, for I care no more for this kind of living. But I will not go on fighting. For what, Jamie?

For the Revolution, I answered.

Be damned with the Revolution! It's one set of masters for another, and that's the way it has always been. In the old country it was the chief of the clan, and here it's the cursed squire; and it will always be that way and no different, and if you think otherwise, Jamie Stuart, ye're just a feckless young idiot. You know what they say in the old country—for a dog there be always a shangan, and we are dogs. Look a-here at Johnny Burke, sitting beside me. Eleven years old he is, and already two years in the ranks and not knowing of anything but foul language and blows...

A lot more I know, and the hell with you! the child squeaked.

Now shut your damn mouth, Johnny Burke, and let me speak. When they bring up their whores from Philadelphia, they are lasses and ladies, but the women who bore our bitterness and our children in the camp and on the march, they are whores and are whipped monthly for the morale of the regiment. No, Jamie Stuart, we have had a stomachful of the Revolution! We will drive out the officers with you; but then, down arms and go home!

Where is home? a tall, broad-faced Pole asked slowly.

I was racking my brains for what to say, when Angus MacGrath rose and told them:

If I thought living that dree and no hope but to be a lousy gillie all my days, then I'd blow out my brains and be done with it. Give it up, Jamie. I will not argue with these scuts. To hell with them!

We left together, but there was no comfort in the Scot's words. We walked along the hutments, and already the early winter evening was upon us, cold and dreary.

At the houses of the 10th, rum was being poured from two hogsheads on a cart, an ounce to a man, and the muttering of the soldiers began to grow like a drum beaten heavier and heavier. White-faced, the two rum peddlers sat on the seat of the cart, their lips trembling, their eyes cast down. Captain Oscar Breddon of headquarters straddled a hogshead, pistol in hand, glaring his hatred but keeping his mouth shut, while the sergeants measured out the ration.

As we reached the cart, a soldier, his rum in his hand, walked forward to the driver and said: You profiteering Yankee bastard, look at me!

And when the driver turned his head, the soldier cast the rum in his face, spat in the snow and walked off.

PART FOUR

Being a true narration of the great rising of the Pennsylvania Line, with details and incidents not hitherto revealed.

WHEN I REPORTED TO my hutment an hour past sunset, it was like the heart and brain of an army in battle. Candles and two lamps had been found, and the hut was filled with light. Five of the Committee of Sergeants sat at the table, each engaged in some separate task, and there was a steady stream of men coming in and out from the various regiments. Messengers delivered messages and sped away with the answers. Also, food was being found and stored, and already the bunks were crowded with sacks of grain and corn meal and frozen sides of pork and lamb.

Most of the food had come from the central commissary, for the whole guard there was with us and were already removing whatever could be taken without arousing the suspicion of the officers; but somehow, already, news of the rising had leaked out to small farmers nearby, and the meat was a gift from them—and this heartened us more than anything, since not only were most of us foreign brigades but even those of us native to our country's soil were foreign here, to the land of Jersey. The years of our campaigning over the roads and fields of Jersey had wasted much of the country, and those who had suffered most were the tenants of the patroons and the great lords. They were filled with hatred for the army, so it was a wonder now that they too should make a separation between us and the gentry and that they should aid us instead of betraying us to our officers.

I had to push my way into that hut, for at the first glance it was like a madhouse; it was only when you looked a second time that you found a scheme in the madness. A giant, yellow-haired German shouted at Levy, who ignored him and went on speaking to the black man, Holt, and to Prukish, who loomed over the table, a pistol in each hand. A delegation of women demanded to know what Jack Maloney expected to do with the children, while he strove to give a messenger an answer and to dispatch him with it. Bowzar roared for quiet every so often, and Sean O'Toole, in his high-pitched voice, screamed across the table at Levy:

Ye damned Jew, if ye will not give me warrants for the two hostlers, how in hell's name am I to find horses to move the four cannon I have already laid hands on that are standing exposed like a cake of ice in the pit of hell!

And background to this was a wild hammering which came from my own bed and berth, where the hated Captain Jack Auden of my own 11th—and how many marks I bore from his cane I cannot count—lay trussed like a turkey for roasting, his face in a side of pork, his heels drumming madly on the wall. I saw him, and the strain I was under snapped, and I stood there in the doorway roaring with laughter fit to break a gut.

Shut up, ye Dublin dung digger! cried Jack Maloney at O'Toole, and to hell with yer cursed hostlers!

And at me:

Jamie! Jamie—have ye gone mad or maybe gotten the pint ration of rum we was promised? Get in here and make a disposition!

Now here is Jamie, shouted Billy Bowzar. Will you shut your mouths or get to the nation out of here!

But three more men crowded in behind me, calling for Connell.

We were sent to see Connell, they insisted, and that we will. We will see him or be damned. We will not be taking our orders from a black Nayger man, and here we stand until we see Connell, or you can take yer rising and be damned with it!

So you see, Jamie, said Bowzar, when I stood over him finally, the Romans and the Protestant lads and the Naygers and the Jews are all at one another's throats; and this is what we have, with two hours left before the rising . . .

He had not slept, and his broad, flat face was lined with fatigue, yet the square cut of his curly red beard and the bald spot on top of his skull gave him a whimsical turn of humor, and there was a blaze of suppressed excitement in him, the more unusual for so stolid a man. From somewhere, he had obtained a big silver watch—it was a wonder, the things we discovered about ourselves now—and it lay ticking in front of him, while alongside of it there was a big sheet of foolscap entitled *General Orders and Instructions for All Regiments on the Night of January the 1st.*

So make a disposition, Jamie, he said. Have you covered the hutments?

The noise dwindled. We were like that, with waves of confidence, and then with waves of fear. We were sure of ourselves, and then our certainty went away, and we stood in terror. We had been beaten and starved too long; we were criminals or madmen or heroes or wild adventurers who were embarked on a road no man had traveled before: and do not imagine it was easy for us to know, or that we were all of one mind or one piece.

Talk up, Jamie. And where is MacGrath?

He went over to the old Connecticut huts where the 5th and the 9th lie, and that is where we will have trouble as sure as God. They took the Nayger Kabanka, because he was asked to polish the boots of Major Quenton, and Quenton was in the boots and said, Kneel down, you black dog. And Kabanka answered, That I will not do, nor be called a black dog again. So they put him under guard, and now MacGrath is over there to see how bad it is.

A plague on this bloody pride! snapped Maloney. Are their noses up?

At those regiments, I answered. They have turned out all the lieutenants of the two regiments, and they are in and out of the hutments, filled with fury that they should not be swilling with the others; and if a man turns up from another regiment, they drive him on his way. Angus is on it now, and as for the other brigades, they are secure, or as secure as anyone can hope with a day to prepare, and they are sitting now with knapsacks strapped and bayonets fixed—not with one mind, but our lads have the better of it in the disputes. And all I would say is, for Christ's sake, do this soon, for a man can go mad with waiting!

Ye wanted much more waiting before.

Well, I don't want it now.

His neck itches for the rope . . . a pock-marked buckskin man remarked.

The lot of ye shut up! cried Danny Connell. Christ, to make a rising with this lot!

And I never saw an Irishman that wasn't expert on matters of rising!—I shot back at him—But to put two and two together, yer land is under the redcoat heel and never was else; and I'm sick of the talk of them that think this is a tea party. Ye sit here, but all this cursed cold day, I was in and out o' the hutments—

Now, easy, Jamie lad.

In and out o' the hutments, and this one wants wages and that one wants to go home and this one wants his bounty, and is Billy Bowzar going to pay it, and is the Jew Levy going to get gold from the Philadelphia Jews, and they've all had enough of the bloody war and want no part of it again, and they've heard there are Nayger men on the Committee and will not be led by Nayger men . . . and here ye sit like Jesus Christ was going to walk on the earth and make a miracle!

And it may be that He is, Jamie, answered Billy Bowzar—quietly, but heard because all the rest were so quiet now; and in that deep silence the Jew regarded me quizzically, his narrow, pinched face puckered up, his dark eyes probing as he said:

Now, then, Jamie Stuart, you are an impatient lad who wants a thing answered that can't be answered. But since the olden times men have risen up like we are rising up to throw off their hurts and sorrows.

But in the hutments they tell me, *There have always*

been gentry, and always them who are bounden under. Will Bowzar be gentry now? Will the Jew Levy or the Nayger Holt?

No.

What then?

I don't know, answered the Jew. Maybe the Almighty God knows, and in time He will reveal to us what to do. And maybe not so. But there is a will on our part to assert ourselves and to cast out those who make a mockery of our dreams, and that we must do—because if we turn back now . . .

Flatly and matter-of-factly Billy Bowzar said: Go to work and stop this business of trying to be a gypsy, Jamie, which no Scot is any damn good at. There's not much time left, so get out in the cold again, which is better for your hot head, and turn out your guard. Let each man committed and pledged tie a white rag around his arm above the elbow. The left arm, Jamie. Rouse them up, and when Andy Swain begins to sound the camp jig on his trumpet, all files are to parade before the hutments, bayonets fixed, knapsacks on, but no powder in the pan. I don't mind if they load them their guns, but keep the powder safe from hotheads. We want no killing of the officers, Jamie—and you others too!

Now Bowzar rose and looked from face to face.

No killing, no murder! This Committee stands as a court of military citizen justice from here on, and every crime will be punished. Before tomorrow night, we will have arranged and set down the discipline of this new army; meanwhile, we will make it a simple and elementary justice, such as anyone can understand. When the officers come running, cast them off! Drive them away! Tell them we do not want them in the sight of our eyes! But no one retorts and no one speaks unless he carries a properly executed warrant of this Committee. We will be no rabble tonight, Jamie, but a credit to the honest folk of this land. And if shameful things are done, we will hold you accountable. Mark me, Jamie Stuart.

I mark you, I said, and then I saluted. It was the first time a sergeant of the Committee had been saluted. And then I went out to prepare.

I saw Angus coming across the parade, a dozen lads with him, and I joined him. We tore cloth from our shirts and neckcloths, and made our badges, and the moon rose and lined our shadows out across the trampled snow. Low lay the huts, like sleeping hounds, and fanged like hounds too, and far across the white expanse of the parade were the bare trees and the belly hills of the fat Jersey land. Here and there, a light gleamed as the door of one or another hut opened, and, dim on the other edge of the parade, we saw the shadows of men running but could not make out who they were or what they ran for. The sentries were out, and in their cold loneliness they paced back and forth, wrapped in God knows what dreams—for that was a cold and uncertain night, a night for dreams and fears and the inner coldness that freezes the heart of a man who cuts the ropes that bind him to his past. For whatever it was and however it was, this army was our life, and many of us knew no other life or remembered another life only vaguely and indistinctly. We were parts of a body organism that was mother and father, and the tissue of our lives and the logic of our lives was the army of the Revolution. So I do not recall that we had a great and burning certainty; there were forces that moved us and drove us, and there was a spark of glory somewhere; but in the cold matter-of-fact, we moved because it was intolerable to remain as we had been.

We formed the lads in twos, Angus at the rear and I to the fore, and I smartened them and whipped for a marching gate and fancy arms. We went from hut to hut, checking the mood of the men and passing the word on the time, and the way the sentries walked their beats and saw us not at all gave us a strange feeling of disembodiment. At one point there, two officers galloped their horses madly across the parade, but either they saw us not at all or wanted not to see us; and after that a hutment door flew open and men poured forth, but back they went as if the hut had blown and sucked in one spasm. And the minutes passed and the moon traveled; and then the time was upon us, with the shrill, taunting call of the Yankee camp jig.

Now the two officers came riding back, whipping their horses madly; and as they reined up near us, I saw that one of them was our regimental commander, a bitter, sallow-faced man, and one of the very few human souls I have known who never showed one spark of warmth or graciousness. He had a high-pitched, rasping voice, which shrilled out to know why the cursed damned trumpeter was playing that fool tune.

To awaken the dead! roared MacGrath.

I'll have your hide off for that, MacGrath, he screamed back. And you, Stuart, what in the devil's name are you doing with that file?

Drilling them! I shouted back.

With him was Captain Purdy, who claimed to be the

first son—and a bad one, he always added—of Lord Purdy of the County Mayo, and he spurred on us; but Angus fired a musket over his head, and his horse bolted with him. Meanwhile, the trumpet kept on shrilling, and all up and down the regimental hutments, doors popped open spilling light onto the snow, and men poured out and began to fall in. From the area of the 6th, a rocket hissed up, and a roar of sound greeted it. The colonel whipped out his sword and spurred his horse at the 11th's hutments, screaming a string of foul oaths, the only printable words of which were *Back to quarters! Inside with you!* But the men laughed at him, and Katy Waggoner flung a handful of snow at him as he went by.

I ordered my men on the double with bayonets for attack, and we made a smart sight as we ran down the hut fronts, with Angus and me shouting:

Fall in! Fall in! All troops out on parade! Fall in! Fall in!

It was amazing how much discipline was shown there, for hardly had the bugle finished its call when at least a thousand men were forming in parade order, muskets in hand, knapsacks on back. A ripple of musket fire came from the direction of the redoubt; and then, square down the center of the parade, hanging for dear life onto a big white horse, came Sean O'Toole with four fieldpieces and their ammunition carts thundering after him. A wild roar of cheers greeted this, and O'Toole, for all his difficulty in maintaining his seat, managed to wave back and grin and bow his head. Most of this, and most of what followed, I saw in only the most fragmentary fashion—for I was moving on from hut to hut, shouting at stragglers, calling them out, and putting the parade into marching order as I went along. What became of the colonel after that, I do not know, but at least twenty minutes went by before any officers appeared on the scene, and then it was too late. By then, better than half of the Pennsylvania brigades were under arms and in marching order, with the Committee of Sergeants as the acknowledged authority.

It was our plan to march across the face of the hutments and over to the separate quarters of the 5th and the 9th Regiments in the old Connecticut huts. From where I was and in the darkness, it was impossible to see what had happened over there; possibly they too had gone out—possibly not. In any case, we felt that the moral force of our own column of men, in perfect discipline, with fifes playing and drums beating, would sweep them along with us.

In the telling, and more so in the telling after so long a retrospect, what happened up to now seems simple indeed, as if the men had moved with one mind and one heart; but things are not done in that way, even though the wise scholars of our Revolution would have it that the rising came about of itself, born and executed in that same evening, as if three thousand men all at one moment felt the need to rise up and cast out their officers. But in my mind's eyes there is a memory of that chaotic night, of hundreds of men running here and there and shouting all at once, of little clumps of men locked in struggle, of a five-year-old child standing in the snow and crying, of the disorganized groups trying to maneuver the cannon into position to cover our advance, of the frantic fool who touched a match to one of the cannon, and the roar of grape as it screamed across the parade, of O'Toole beating the man into insensibility, of the twitter of the fifes as the drummer boys and the fifes from all the regiments formed at our head, of the group of Germans who barricaded themselves into a hut of the 6th Regiment, screaming that they would die there before they joined the rising, and of Andrew Yost standing before the hut and addressing them in Dutch in a mighty voice that carried over all the noise and tumult.

We had reached the space between the huts of the 1st and 2nd Regiments when the baggage train appeared, led by an ox-drawn freight wagon, with the Gary brothers riding astride the lead oxen. The freight wagon was filled with the youngest children, and women and older children were perched all over the baggage carts. I recall that moment well, for it was then that the magazine was broken into. I heard the flurry of musketry and wondered whether we were already engaged in a fratricidal combat with troops who held back, but the shooting stopped as suddenly as it began, and I learned later that we had taken the magazine easily enough and that only one young lieutenant had been hurt with a bayonet wound in the thigh. But the children in the big wagon began to weep in fright, and Arnold Gary had to shout at the top of his lungs to make himself heard, as he called:

Well, here we are, Jamie, and where in hell do you want us to put these brats and sluts?

Olive Lutz climbed down from the wagon and ran up to him, crying, You big oaf, sitting there so one cannot tell which is ox and which is man—there's children behind you and keep your tongue decent. We're not in this to take from you what we take from the gentry!

She's right and this is no rig, said Angus. So shut your dirty mouth, Arnold Gary.

Where the baggage train was to go I had not been told by the Committee, but it seemed obvious that the best place for them would be somewhere in the middle of the column; and acting on that, Angus and I led them along between the huts and the parading men. The men cheered as the women rode by, and the older children watched everything open-mouthed, this being such excitement as they had not experienced before.

Now, for the first time, I ran into Billy Bowzar and Jack Maloney, and they seized me and pulled me outside the line of men.

How is it, Jamie? asked Bowzar.

There are still men in the huts, but each one needs a great argument and persuasion, and I would say, To hell with them.

I am with Jamie, agreed Maloney. We want to march.

While we spoke, other committeemen ran up and down the files, trimming them into order and dressing them up. Never before in the history of the Continentals had a permanent camp been broken thus swiftly and with such dispatch, and there was a new air about the men, a smartness in the way they addressed their lines and ordered their arms.

By now, the musicians had arranged themselves into one compact group, and the two dozen or so little drummer lads were stiff and proud as peacocks, not wholly understanding what had come about, but knowing well enough that they would no longer be sport for any officer who wanted to exercise his cane. Chester Rosenbank started the music, leading the men so that they would all play together, and the first song they struck up was that sweet Pennsylvania air, *Oh lovely hills of Fincastle, for thee my sad heart yearns.* Afterwards I asked Chester why he had chosen that air instead of marching music, and he answered that marching songs were only partly ours, but this song of the buckskin men something all ours and calculated to take the hot bitterness out of the men, yet leave them their resolution. The fifes played sweetly if somewhat raggedly, and the drummer boys tapped their sticks lightly.

The shouting had lessened and now with the music it halted entirely. At least fifteen hundred men were on parade now, and Sean O'Toole had finally arranged his cannon to flank the column head. Angus was laying out the baggage carts alongside the center of the line; and there, but outside the men and facing the expanse of the parade, I stood with Bowzar and Maloney. We were joined by the Jew Levy and Danny Connell and the Nayger Holt; and it was then that we saw a body of mounted men sweep up the road from Morristown and drum across the parade toward us.

So here are our officers, said Danny Connell.

We stood side by side, waiting, and the Line dressed like grenadiers. The music finished and there was no other sound than the drumming of hoofs as the officers rode down upon us and drew up their horses a few yards away. I counted them; there were seventeen of them, many of them regimental officers, with Anthony Wayne, brigadier general of the Line, among them and voice for them. He, with Colonel Butler, stepped his horse forward and demanded:

What in hell's name is the meaning of all this?

As if he didn't know—and that was to be the way it was, at first, as if none of them knew. Billy Bowzar glanced sidewise at us, and his look said, Keep your mouths shut. Let me talk. If more than one talks, we'll be talking against one another. . . . So Billy crossed his arms and looked at the general a lot more coolly than I felt; but I stepped back and waved at Angus, and when he ran over I told him to dress up ten lads of the Citizen-soldier Guard directly behind and alongside of me, and for them to prime their muskets. While this went on, Butler reared his horse, a trick our gentry knew better than the leading of men, and roared out at the top of his lungs at the Line:

Undress! Stand at your ease!

I think of all the moments we faced, that was the hardest, for it was in us and in the marrow of our spine and our bones to obey a command hurled at us that way; so that while my mind said, Keep cool and stand still, Jamie Stuart, the muscles in my legs twitched of their own volition. I looked at the Line, and a good half of them had dropped their muskets to butt the ground and were falling out of parade position. But their sergeants and corporals were snapping, Dress it, dress it, ye dirty white scuts! And once again the Line pulled itself into tension.

Who gave these men the order to parade? Wayne demanded.

The Committee, answered Billy Bowzar quietly, yet loud enough for much of the Line to hear. He was square and small and rocklike, and to this day I recall the pride I felt as I watched him that night. There was a solemn, unruffled truth about him that few of us matched. He had been a ropewalker before the war, in the Philadelphia cordage house, and, as with the ropewalkers in Boston, he and the men who worked with him had formed a Committee of Public Safety and armed themselves, and when the question of independence hung in doubt, the whole shop laid down tools and paraded a show of strength before Carpenters' Hall.

What Committee? Wayne wanted to know, his tone high and disdainful. Many of the other officers, I could see, were afraid, but there was no fear about Wayne, only a wild anger he could hardly keep from dominating him. The man had courage and little else; and courage was not enough to make us love him; for along with the courage went a cold streak of contempt and disdain and unmitigated cruelty that had earned the undying hatred of all too many in our ranks. A general they loved or a general they didn't know might have won over many of them right there, for what we had done was yet unresolved, and the light of fear had begun to burn in us—and we had no certainty, even now, that an army could remain an army without officers; but we did not love Anthony Wayne, and we knew him all too well, and what we had done for him in the past, to give him such glory, we did because his gut was the gut of a reaver. His gut won no respect for him here.

The Committee of Sergeants, answered Billy Bowzar, still in the same tone.

The Committee of Sergeants, said Wayne. The Committee of Sergeants!

And he raised his voice, hurling it into the cold and rising night wind:

Disband, I tell you!

But it was too late, and we stood on our ranks, and we stood silent except for the wail of a little child that lifted over and above the men and mingled with the winter winds.

Butler said: I know you, Billy Bowzar, and I know you, Jack Maloney, and I know that dirty Jew Levy and that black Nayger Holt, and you too, Jamie Stuart, and well indeed do I know that slaister Connell who was swept up with the dung from the streets of Dublin—and I have a long memory!

We are not hiding our faces, answered Billy Bowzar.

Then well you should, cried Wayne, for this is the dirtiest picture of a mutiny I have ever seen, and I'll go down to my grave if them that fixed it don't swing for it!

We are not mutineers, spoke Bowzar firmly, but loyal and good soldiers, as you should know as well as the next man, General Wayne, and it is not for the sake of any mutiny that we stand here in the winter cold.

And what are you loyal to?

To the name of freedom and to the deep hopes of Pennsylvania folk.

Enough of this sanctimonious gibberish! cried Butler. Either disband or prepare to take the consequences!

We are well prepared, for this is not anything that we did lightly, and we are no strangers to your consequences—

What kind of damn fools are you? cried Wayne. How long will this rabble last when we bring the brigades up against them?

What brigades? said Billy Bowzar softly.

I tell you, cried Wayne, loud enough for the whole Line to hear him, that if you go back to your hutments now and lay away your arms, and go to sleep as honest men should, then no more will be made of this, except the punishment of the rascals who lead you! I tell you this now!

There was a mighty urge in me to turn my head and see how the men of the Line took this, but Bowzar and

Maloney and Levy and Holt and Connell stood as still as though they had become a part of the frozen ground they occupied, and, for all the cold that seeped now from my skin into the marrow of my bones, I would not do otherwise. But when I heard not even the crunch of a lifted boot, I was filled with a heady pride, as if I had suddenly become drunk, and my earlier dreams of a great movement and rising returned. Now Butler sided his horse to Wayne, and moments went by while they whispered to each other. Then Wayne dismounted and walked over to us, so that he, in his elegant, booted, spurred, cloaked height, his thin, handsome, clean-shaven face thrust forward, stood almost up against the square and ragged rock of Billy Bowzar, yet a whole head higher—like some chief facing a bearded, work-hardened crofter. It was later that they came to call him "Mad Anthony," but even now there was a touch of madness about him, and fame and glory had touched him, so that he would never forget what it was to wed either. He was imperious, but without the humility that could have made him a great leader whom men would love as well as fear; and when years later I watched Junius Brutus Booth play out Shakespeare's tale of *Richard III*, I thought immediately of this young, wild, arrogant general officer who crunched toward us through the snow so fearlessly; but again it was only years later that I could place myself inside him and understand that much of the courage came from hopeless desperation; and that, for all of his proud and violent talks, there that night his world crumbled about him, and all the vainglory of his belted boots, his fine doeskin trousers, his powder-blue coat and his deep blue cloak surrounded a crushed man. No better picture of the relationship of this officer gentry to us can be shown than through their surprise at our rising; not only did they not anticipate it, but, now it was here, their only means of treating it was as another cause for caning or whipping. But you do not cane or whip a line of the best and hardest troops in the New World, standing motionless to arms in the bitter cold of night.

Yet Wayne carried it through in the only way he knew, and he walked up to Billy Bowzar and faced him boldly and asked more quietly:

What do you intend to do?

We intend to march away to our own encampment.

Where is your encampment?

That is in our own orders, General Wayne, and not for the knowledge of you or any other officer.

Are you the leader of this mutiny?

This is no mutiny, and it doesn't profit you to call it that; but I am spokesman for the Committee of Sergeants.

And what does your Committee propose to do?

To reconstitute the army of the Revolution.

That is talk, said Wayne, and you know that as well as I do. Tell me what you want, and it may be that I spoke hastily before. But if you will state your demands and I can satisfy your demands, I am willing to forget that to-night ever happened and no measures will be taken against any man—including your Committee—and you can go back to the hutments and sleep out the night. Things will look better in the morning.

We can never forget that tonight happened, said Bowzar seriously and reflectively. If I did as you say, I would be hanging from a tree in the morning...

You have my word!

...But it is not the hanging that stops me. I am not so

almighty fond of life that I can't look at a rope, even the way my good comrade Jimmy Coleman looked at a rope last year when you hanged him until he was dead; but tonight is something you can't blow away like a handful of snow. Look at them—

He turned and flung a hand at the Line.

When have you seen the men stand to parade that way—with the cold so bitter that it freezes the juice in the bones? They would not heed your command, and I have little doubt that they would less heed mine if I ordered them back to the hutments.

What are your demands? insisted Wayne stolidly, but biting his underlip until the blood smeared through, his fists clenched, his cheek twitching. I have given you my word as an officer and a gentleman. What are your demands?

We have no demands of you, General Wayne. There is nothing you can do for us. Our demands are to the people, and the Congress.

If I can right them—

And can you right them, my general? asked Billy Bowzar, grinning bitterly at the handsome young man before him, taking a fold of his cloak between his fingers. Will you cover all our rags with this? Will you feed us with the slop from your New Year's dinner? Will you pay us, who have not been paid these six months past? Will you bring back our children, who died of disease and hunger? Will you put shoes under our bleeding feet?

His voice raised; he still held the fold of Wayne's cloak, and Wayne stood rigid as steel while Bowzar spoke, ever more and more loudly and bitterly, with a passion I never knew the man to own.

Or will you scrape together our bloody tracks over five thousand miles of road for five years? Will you give us back our honor, we who have been beaten and lashed as foreign scum—or will you take one man out of the ranks, one man who talks the English a little less finely than you do, one man without property and wealth, and raise him up to be an officer over us? Will you honor us with even one of our own to lead us? Will you stop the ache of hunger in our bellies, so that while you fatten yourselves in the houses of the God-damned patroons and the cursed British gentlemen, we must watch our little drummer lads die for want of a shred of meat? Will you march us against the British enemy, instead of leaving us to rot in these cursed encampments—because you have not the guts to risk a fight that might bring a frown from that rotten, betraying Congress? Will you bring all the Lines together, so that they will stop plotting against each other and go against the enemy? Will you make the Declaration of Independence the law of this army? Will you give us equal bounty and equal pay? Will you hang every officer who kills one of us in his anger, who cheats us, who sells our food, who gambles away our pay, who speculates in the Philadelphia market with our clothing, who insults our women, who kicks our children? Will you do that, General Wayne? Will you declare that the Jersey and Pennsylvania farmers who hold their land in tenancy from the patroons and the lords now have it in freehold forever? Will you tell them that if they give us food, we will fight to the death for their freehold? Will you guarantee a hundred acres of land for every man in this army? You can do that, General Wayne—for there is land without end or limit in Pennsylvania, and no one owns it but the lords in London. Will you take it from them, and give it to us? Will you give us a stake in this? Will you now? . . . Come now? . . . The Line is standing to arms in the bitter cold, and you would not have them stand in the cold the whole night through! You would not have that—for then they would think that this is another evidence of the ways of the gentry and the disregard they have for what a simple man feels. So speak out, General Wayne!

In a fury, Billy Bowzar finished, and he flung away the general's cloak as if it were dirt. But Wayne didn't move, and there came a sigh out of the paraded men; and then Wayne said softly:

These are not demands I can satisfy, as well you know.

Then you can satisfy one other demand of ours, said Billy Bowzar. Get on your horse and ride out of our sight, and take your damned staff with you. The lot of you are like an abomination!

Now Wayne was rage incarnate, his face flour-white and every muscle along his cheeks trembling and quivering, and like a man made out of clockwork, tight springs and bent metal rods, he mounted his horse, hesitated just one moment, and then walked his horse toward us—with the other officers following him—spitting out words that were like molten spots of metal.

I command this Line! Do you hear me? All of you! This is an order: Break your ranks!

It was just before and during this that Angus MacGrath returned and whispered to me. For Christ's sake, Jamie, there is hell to pay in the old huts—and breaking into the Scottish—an' a deil gaed o'er Jock Webster, and the situation is dour, I tell ye, with the 5th and the 9th standing to arms, all cosh with the officers; and will ye tell the

Committee to get us to hell out o' here before we shed our blood and die in this damned place?

Where are they? I asked him.

Parading over yonder, behind the Connecticut huts.

But then Wayne was riding his horse down on us, and his officers less confident, less brave, but with him at the moment, and as the Committee was pressed back, it was touch and go; so I did what I felt should be done; I addressed the citizen soldiers and told them to let a volley into the air. The muskets roared over the horses and a harsh shout went up from our men, and the horses broke and bolted, the riders not fighting them but letting them bolt across the parade and into the darkness in ten directions, riding with relief to be away from that long file of grim and bitter men. But the truth must be told that Wayne alone fought his horse as it reared and beat it back onto the ground, his face contorted, tears running down his cheeks; and then he ripped open coat and vest and shirt, ripping the clothes and buttons, tearing at his undershirt to bare his breast and revealing it with the red marks of his nails across it. And he screamed at us:

Then kill me! Here is a mark, if you want a mark, you dirty, mutinous bastards! Then kill me here and now, and have it over with! God curse your souls, kill me!

There was a trumpeter standing by, and Bowzar ran to him and had him play the advance. We left Wayne screaming and weeping, alone on his horse, while we ran down the Line to its head, where the drummer boys had picked up the beat, and Rosenbank was already marching and keeping time for the shrilling fifes. As we ran, I told Bowzar and Maloney of the news Angus had brought, and they questioned Angus as we ranged ourselves across the head of the Line. Somehow, we had failed with these two regiments: the officers had got there first, and now five hundred men were standing to arms and ready to bar our path—yet the way they had remained behind the Connecticut hutments, out of sight and sound and a good half mile away, it was plain that they would avoid a struggle and leave us to march out of camp if we wished to.

And they got six cannon, said Angus, by grace of Emil Horst who sold us, the dirty smaik . . .

We will go up against them, nodded Billy Bowzar wearily, for this is either all of us or no part of us, and it's better to die here than to split the Line. If we split the Line, then it will be civil war and not war against the enemy, and I would rather hang now than have it that way.

Then it's war now, muttered Danny Connell.

Is it? If our brothers will cut us down, we are damned wrong, and we should know it.

And Billy Bowzar waved his arm and swung to the left— and the whole long Line of the Pennsylvania regiments moved across the moonlit parade toward the Connecticut huts. We marched slowly, four abreast, a long, dark ribbon across the entire parade, and the shrill of our fifes and the beat of our drums woke the countryside for miles around.

It was a wonderful moment, that in which we crossed the snow-swept expanse of parade, for the beat of the drums was matched by the beat in our hearts; and when I ran down the Line and back, I saw in the faces of the men, cold and reddened and wrapped in rags, an indication of the fierce exultation of our strength—our power, inevitably—for nowhere on the whole Western continent was a force that could come up against us; we were the heart of the Revolution, and now we had suddenly translated the

Revolution into ourselves and our hopes and our angers. Many, many times before, I had seen the Line go out, sometimes on parade, sometimes on one of those interminable marches up and down the Jersey pine barrens, sometimes against the enemy, sometimes in the lonely, broken way of retreat; but I never saw the Line as it was then, like a fierce old eagle whose clipped pinions had suddenly discovered once again the power of flight. The men could not keep still, and they picked up the march, so that their voices rang out with:

In freedom we're born, and like sons of the brave, will never surrender, but swear to defend her, and scorn to survive if unable to save....

One deep, rich voice picked up the verse—joined then voice by voice, while the fifes lifted it and shrilled like a wild and savage Highland fling. It was then that the two regiments came forth, marching in an opposite direction to ours, so that the two files crossed and faced each other, while a thousand throats roared their defiance in a song we had not sung these many months past—and were heard in every house and hamlet for miles around, and heard by the men of the two regiments as we chanted:

> The tree which proud Haman for Mordecai reared,
> Stands recorded that virtue endangered is spared;
> The rogues, whom no bounds and no laws can restrain,
> Must be stripped of their honors and humbled again!

The 5th and the 9th moved to cut us off, their officers riding behind them and shouting at them above the wild chant we maintained; but as we continued, the two regiments halted, and then a field gun was pressed through from behind, officers straining at the big, iron-bound wheels that men would not move, and Emil Horst holding a lighted match. Billy Bowzar and Jack Maloney and the Jew Levy ran toward them, Bowzar waving both his hands for silence, and Angus and I ran after them, and the lighted match waved back and forth like a torch. The singing died away, and the sudden silence was cut by a shrill voice screaming:

Fire on them! Fire on them!

We halted before their ranks, but MacGrath ran on, his musket clubbed, and as Horst dropped the match, he struck him on the side of the head and felled him like an ox.

Fire on them! Fire on them! The voice shrieked.

Now what in hell's name are you doing there, Bowzar cried at them, when the whole Line is marching?

This was heard, and a roar went up from our ranks, and our men called them out by name, and suddenly a thousand voices were calling:

The Line is marching! The Line is marching!

The two regiments broke; they went mad and wild, and when their officers cursed them, they pulled the officers from their saddles, beat them; and some they bayoneted; and the rest ran away, whipping their horses through the night. Two officers were slain there, and many more wounded, whereas in our own rising there had been no bloodshed at all. But it lasted only a few minutes; then it was over, and Bowzar's great voice was heard, crying:

Make room for the 5th! Make room for the 9th!

The Line parted to allow the regiments to form in their places, soldiers embracing soldiers, laughing, crying, shouting—and presently the drums picked up the march again.

I saw fleetingly Emil Horst staggering along, his hands bound, his face covered with blood. I saw Bowzar running toward the head of the Line, the tears streaming down his face as he ran. I saw Captain Oliver Husk lying face down in the snow, in a pool of blood.

And then I joined the Line, which was marching off to its own strange destiny.

PART FIVE

Being an account of our first march, and of the fate of
Emil Horst.

W E MARCHED ONLY FOUR or five miles that first night, to a place nearby where two Virginia brigades had encamped the winter before. What huts they had built were made slovenly, in the way of some Southern folk, and they were rotted and of no real use, but there was cleared space and a stream for drinking and plenty of firewood; and the only tactic we had worked out for that first night was to get away from the Morristown encampment. Once we did that, we felt that sleep was the first item on the agenda; although all in all it was little enough sleep that we of the Committee got ourselves, then or later.

In this march, there was only one incident of any importance, and that happened when we came to the first fork of the road; but already Billy Bowzar and the Jew Levy and Jack Maloney and Danny Connell had dropped out of sheer exhaustion, and they lay on a baggage cart, sleeping the sleep of the just, for all the rocking and lurching of the cart. A platoon of the 1st Regiment had intercepted a herd of cattle, a gift or a bribe or a sale from a wealthy patroon of Amboy to the officers; we left six beasts for the officers, and the rest, almost a hundred, we drove with us, and though they milled around the cart where Bowzar and the others slept, all their mooing disturbed them not at all. In the same way the women and children slept, but the little drummer lads stumbled along, keeping their rhythm going, and the men swung out their legs and sang as I had never known them to sing before.

Abner Williams and I led the column, and directly behind us marched Angus MacGrath and the Citizen-soldier Guard, which now numbered about one hundred men, and which was finally stabilized at exactly one hundred, in ten platoons of ten each with a platoon leader who bore the title of citizen-protector. Many of these names might appear pompous today, for it is a different time and a different era I write this in, but they were neither strange nor pompous to us; and we were filled with a mythology and a folklore of freedom, in which such names loomed like giant symbols. Each member of the Citizen-soldier Guard had a white rag of some kind knotted around his left arm; and later these became white arm bands, six inches wide, sewn into the sleeve above the elbow—and to this day I have the band, sewn onto my old, ragged coat, yellowed with age, but not the least, I think, of the few honors I retain from that ancient Revolution. Also, the members of the guard carried primed muskets, held at advance position with bayonets fixed.

Behind them, Chester Rosenbank led the musicians of the Line, the fifers and drummers and trumpeters, and now two Scotsmen from the 5th Regiment, who had unearthed from somewhere kilts and pipes and who marched along, one on each side of the drummers, making the night awful with their wild Highland music—nor would they desist or keep time with us, for all of Rosenbank's pleading.

It is a night for the pipes, they said, and if you want harmony, tell yer damned drummers and fifers to hauld off!

Behind them, came the regiments, flanked by the guns and interspersed with at least two hundred carts and wagons, and at the very end, a dozen of the citizen-soldiers to whip the stragglers into position.

I do not know of any other occasion during the entire war when a camp was broken like this, during the middle of the night, with no prior preparation; yet for all of that, we marched well and the discipline was good. We had cast out all of our officers, but the sergeants knew their jobs; and the long and short of it was that we were, almost without exception, tough and hardened soldiers who did not have to think twice about doing a thing.

When we came to the first fork in the road, the only incident of the march happened. There was a clearing in the woods with the moonlight flooding through, and on the branch of the road that led to the coast and toward the British, Wayne and a handful of the officers had stationed themselves, mounted, their haggard white faces set in desolate determination. We had planned to take the other fork anyway, but when I saw them, I halted the column, and Abner Williams went forward to speak with them. In the course of this, they asked him his name and rank, and that was how it came to be that in so many reports of the rising, Williams was mentioned as the leader. But in all truth, the whole Committee led the rebellion, and if credit should be given, Bowzar and Maloney and the Jew Levy deserve more than either Williams or myself.

My rank is sergeant, answered Williams, and we are in no mood to stand here in the night chatting with you.

Can ye stop that cursed skirling? Colonel Butler demanded.

We have little to warm ourselves with, other than the music, said Williams, and if you would talk, talk over it.

We have come to hold this road! shouted Wayne. Here we are, and you will have to shoot us down before you march here!

Why should we march there?

To join the British!

A roar of anger went up from the men who were listening. Now the drummers and the fifers stopped, leaving only the skirling pipes; and MacGrath, all in a rage, advanced toward Wayne, crying:

A plague on yer foul dreams! Ye would bespatter all with yer own dung!

Grasping his arm, I pulled him away, telling him, Easy, easy, Angus—we have no truck with them and we have no words with them, and they will go their way and we will go ours.

And I waved my hand for the march; the musicians picked it up, and the column went down the road toward Vealtown—and we marched without another halt until we came to the old Virginia encampment. There we made a quick, rough camp, letting the women and children sleep on in the carts, building a few fires for warmth—for the cold broke that night, and it was almost balmy outside—

and raising tents only for the sick and wounded. I divided
the Citizen-soldier Guard in half, and placed them on two-
and-two sentry duty, and then, like most of the Line, I
scraped the snow from a bit of ground, wrapped a cloak
about me, and fell asleep so quickly that I have no clear
memory of the process.

I have a better memory, though, of being awakened in
the sad, wet fog of the early dawn, with the feeling that I
had only slept a moment, and with the feeling too of a day
lost somewhere; for here it was but the morning of the
second day of January in the New Year, yet in twenty-four
hours I had lived lifetimes; and the old Jamie Stuart, the
lad from the Western hill country, the cobbler's apprentice,
the gawking, freckled lad who had dared to love the Parson
Bracken's daughter—all of them were gone, and I was
something else who was awakened by Billy Bowzar and
told, as he shook me:

Now come awake, Jamie—come now, Jamie! Would you
be sleeping the whole blessed day away?

Just an hour of it, I pleaded.

You have had five good hours, Jamie. Come, lad, there
is much to be done. We have a tiger by the tail, and it will
be dancing and prancing all over us—and maybe a little bit
of clawing too, and we on the Committee have become
such theoreticians and such great ones for planning and
scheming that it will do my heart good to know there's a
soldier standing by to do a soldier's work, if it need be
done.

So spoke Billy Bowzar, who was a better soldier than I
ever could be, and a better man too, as he showed in the
end. But that was his way, and he could make you love

him as I loved him that morning, standing up with every muscle in my body aching and throbbing. Yet the cold had broken, and the morning breeze was soft and mild, and from far off across the meadows came the screech of roosters and the doleful *caw, caw, caw* of the crows. The mist lay low in the valley where we had bivouacked; its smoky tendrils shifted over the men where they slept, and on every side, as far as one could see in that gray morning, the men of the Line lay haphazardly, a clump here, a single man there. The few tents raised the night before floated like strange boats on the sea of mist, and the cattle wandered among the men, nosing in the snow for grass. Far off, the sentries moved like ghosts, and somewhere a baby whimpered with that plaintive insistent sound that seems to have more of the crux of life in it than any other.

Now come along, Jamie, said Billy Bowzar again; and I followed him, picking our way among the sleeping men to a large brigade tent which had been staked directly in the center of the encampment. The Stars and Stripes had been raised over it, for it seemed more fitting to the Committee that we should use this new banner, which had only come to us during the November of the past year, than any of the old ones, marked as they were with memories of whippings and hangings and the shame of our eternal retreats from the enemy; the two striped flags we had were never flown before, and, unless my memory fails me, this was the first occasion that Pennsylvania troops ever flew the flag of the United States.

As we entered the tent, we were saluted by two members of the Citizen-soldier Guard, who were stationed on either side the doorway. I had a moment of shame, for while I slept much had been done; yet I realized that there was still enough for the doing. In the tent, three camp tables had been set up in a row, and a crow's nest of candles ringed the tent pole. Around the table sat Jim Holt, Abner Williams, Leon Levy, Danny Connell and Jack Maloney. This time, it was Williams who was writing a long document, and as I entered, he laid down his quill and smiled wanly.

Greetings, Jamie, he said, in his mild and cultured voice.

He was a slim, soft-voiced man, college-educated, the son of a Protestant minister, strangely out of place among us, yet strangely liked and respected by the men. About thirty years old, he was a thoughtful person, holding matters inside himself, not easy to know, but coming out occasionally with strange statements indeed. He was a nonbeliever, not passively as so many were in those times, but militantly, as if God were a personal antagonist of his. At a later time we had a long talk, which I will put down in its place. Now he went on to say:

Here are the orders of the day, Jamie, which we have decided upon. It will be up to you and the Guard to see that they are carried out.

Read it aloud, said Jack Maloney.

Billy Bowzar dropped into a chair to listen, and Jim Holt stuffed a corncob pipe with a mixture of grass and dried sheep dung, with a little tobacco to flavor it. Levy seemed to be dozing, and Danny Connell sat with his eyes closed, his legs sprawled, rubbing and scratching at his beard. I remained standing as Abner Williams read:

The first General Orders of the Pennsylvania Line, issued by the Committee of Sergeants on this date of January 2nd, in the year 1781, in their names and also in the names of the citizen-soldiers of the Line ...

So it began, and when it was all finished, as you will see, Abner gave me a copy which I have preserved. Not the paper I took then, which fell apart from usage, but a copy which Abner gave to Billy Bowzar, who held it until we were together in York village and which I left with my sweet Molly Bracken and which I have before me today. Thus I am able to copy the words exactly rather than from memory, yet they are the same as Abner read in the tent that morning. There were twelve Orders, as follows:

1. The expulsion of Officers shall be maintained, and all authority is vested in the Committee of Sergeants, until a representative Congress of the regiments shall decide otherwise. However, any regiment shall have the right to recall its representative sergeant and appoint another in his place. No member of the Line is to hold any converse with an Officer, and such converse shall be regarded as grounds for expulsion from the Line.

2. The Committee of Sergeants shall have the power of court-martial in all offenses against the security of the Line or the People of the United Colonies.

3. Any foreign regiments of the States of the Confederation shall have the right to join the Pennsylvania Line. Upon such action, they are entitled to representation upon the Committee of Sergeants.

4. All soldiers of the Line are to conduct themselves in manner becoming a citizen-soldier and worthy of the aims of this Line of musketmen, that is, the Freedom and Welfare of the peoples of this Continent. They shall strive

sedulously to win the affection of the inhabitants, so that we may look forward to a future where we become one with the people.

5. The following offenses are punishable with expulsion from the Line and with whatever additional measures short of death the Committee of Sergeants shall see fit to impose: Looting; inflicting of damage upon any property other than enemy property; the use of vile language to any comrade citizen-soldier or to a woman or to a child or to a civilian citizen; neglect of weapons; infractions of general disciplines imposed by these orders.

6. The following offenses are punishable with death upon just and considerate court-martial: Dealings or converse with the British or any of their agents; rape; murder; desertion in the face of the enemy.

7. All citizen-soldiers of the Line shall regard their appearance as a part of their solemn duty. All citizen-soldiers are to shave daily and to see that all extremities of their bodies present a clean and wholesome appearance. All arms are to be cherished. All sergeants and corporals will be held solemnly accountable for the enforcement of these regulations.

8. All pay shall be equalized, regardless of rank. But bounties shall be determined by length of enlistment and battle service. All citizen-soldiers who present to the Committee of Sergeants adequate and sworn testimony to the expiration of their enlistments, shall be released from further service ten days from the date of such presentation. All enlistments and re-enlistments shall be voluntary.

9. All food and liquors shall be divided equally among all ranks, but first preference shall be given to women

and children, and then to drummer boys and other enlistments under the age of thirteen years.

10. All citizen-soldiers shall have absolute freedom to practice the religions of their consciences. No measures shall be taken to discriminate against Jews, Romans, or Naygers.

11. All foodstuffs and beasts for slaughter shall be turned in to the central commissary. The commissary shall allocate the food and the liquor to the extent of four ounces a day when available.

12. All disputes in the practice of these General Orders shall be referred to the Committee of Sergeants or to a duly authorized Committee to be set up for that purpose. The only authority in any and all instructions and commands shall be the authority of the Committee of Sergeants, through a duly issued and inscribed warrant. This authority shall be binding until such a time as the Committee of Sergeants disbands itself or is disbanded by the regiments of the Pennsylvania Line.

Such were the first General Orders, which Abner Williams read that day in the tent. What discussion had gone into the making of them, I do not know, but they were plain and clear and simple, and they expressed well enough what the men wanted.

But where does it begin? I wanted to know. Look at us here now, dirty, unshaven—

And here it begins, Jamie, answered Billy Bowzar, smiling gently. We are still in the manner of rubbing our necks, but it has come off, hasn't it, Jamie? And for some of us it is like a dream, with an army on our hands...

His voice trailed away, and weariness and wonder

passed across his face; so that looking at him and looking at the others, I began to realize the enormity of what we had done; and we were so immersed in our own thousand-fold detail that we had never paused to think that the sound of this was rocking across the world, that the great Pennsylvania Line of the Americas, those same soldiers whom Lord North had called "The ragged watchdogs of the gates of Hell," those same soldiers who were not only the heart of the Revolution but the Revolution itself—those same soldiers had taken the power and the glory into their own hands, and, for what it was worth, the American Revolution now sat in this torn tent, black man and cursed Roman and hated Jew sitting down with the Protestant to go where no one had ever been before.

So I folded the General Orders, put them in my pocket, and went out once more into the foggy morning, waking those who had a white rag around their left arms, until there were six of them, and while they still rubbed the sleep from their eyes, told them:

Now we will shave ourselves and clean ourselves, and begin to make a new army.

Yet the words were as strange to myself as to them, and the affronted wonder in their eyes must have been matched by the doubt in my own. However, we shaved; without mirrors and without soap, we cut off our beards and scraped our skin and scrubbed our dirt away with the melting snow; and those of the soldiers who woke and saw us laughing, and then crying with pain as we cut our flesh, thought we were mad—as perhaps we were.

The encampment was coming awake, but I could not wait. I was eager, like a boy again, and it made me feel like a boy to finger my smooth face. I ran through the sleeping men, shouting for the trumpeter, and after me ran the six guards, whooping and laughing. Then the trumpeter sounded and the camp came alive, and there was never such a reveille as that one. The sun was breaking, warm as a winter sun rarely is, and everywhere the snow was becoming slush and dirty pools of water; but to me it was all beautiful; and it must have been beautiful to the men as well, for never before in all the history of the Line had they laughed this way, romping with each other as if they were children again. We picked up the guard as we went, and I found Angus sleeping under a caisson, and I dragged him awake and told him to shave and clean himself up, so that he would not be a disgrace to us.

Are ye daft? he asked me.

But then his eyes opened wider as he noticed that seven of us were shaven already.

Pawky, pawky, he grinned. And what in hell are ye up to, Jamie? Women?

Angus was well onto forty, which was old for me and old for most of us, so I told him:

Shut your mouth, you dirty old goat! I want them paraded in the brigades, like they never was before!

The men were crowding around us, and they doubled over laughing with what I said to Angus. Old goat, roared Stanislaus Prukish, old goat—and Angus caught him by the shoulders and threw him like a tenpin. That was how we felt that morning. I sent Angus to lay out the order of the parade with the guards, and then I was off to find the Gary brothers, so that they might organize some sort of scouting line for our march. I saw none of the Committee, but I felt that if they left it to me, it would be well done; for this was my own meat and not one of those fine theories of where the Revolution was off to—a bone they chewed day and night, filling paper with little script and burning every bit of tallow in the Line.

To hell with their theories, I thought. I am twenty-two years of age, Jamie Stuart by name, and the blood in me runs quick and free.

Already, the commissary was distributing mixed grits of buckwheat and corn, and here and there a pot was bubbling. Voices followed me with:

Hi, Jamie, what goes today?

We did not do bad, eh, Jamie?

Stop and have a bite, Jamie!

The smell of porridge touched my nostrils, and I realized all in a moment how famished I was; so I sat in with a group of lads from the 4th, and they filled a great bowl for me, a spoon of molasses upon it, and the whole topped with a fine lump of gribbled lard.

Now this is eating like I haven't seen in a nation of days, and where in hell did it come from?

From the Dutch crofters, and before God, I think me they broke open the bins of the stinking patroon!

Ye don't say?

I do say it. They must know of this rising now in China, for before the sunrise the woody-shoes were clumping in with the provisions. We ask them why? Because ye will burn down the patroon's castle, they tell us, and hang him high as Haman.

So see that ye do it, Jamie, another added.

Laughing, I stuffed myself, and the sun rose and splashed us with its light and warmth, and the sparrows sang as foolishly as if it were spring already. The women of the brigade were primping and cooking and scolding the children and singing: *The squire came along the road, he saw the huntsman's bloody load, and Mary Jane will weep but sing no more. Heigh-ho, heigh-ho...*

I wanted no better than this, to be here with my comrades all around me and to see the love in their faces because they trusted me. So I ate me my breakfast and finished my rounds and went back to the command tent to make my report. By then, the parade was forming and Chester Rosenbank was marshaling his drummer lads and his fifers to beat to station; but the two Highland pipers were walking their bags in a circle of delighted men and children, skirling the Devil himself awake.

Entering the tent, I saluted; but here was more than I had been prepared for. The candles were gutted, yet the weather-worn tent gave light enough. At one end stood Emil Horst, with Sammy Green on one side of him and Dennis Sullivan on the other, each standing like a ramrod, with musket in line from navel to chin; and Emil Horst looked like the very Devil, his face all stained with dry blood, his head swathed in cloth, his lips as white as the skin around them. A few feet away, the Reverend William Rogers sat upon a camp stool, his long, thin face fixed on the ground in somber meditation. At the camp tables were the Committee, shaven and cleaned and somber as the Reverend Rogers, but starker in their look and grimmer in their aspect.

So you are here, Jamie, said Jack Maloney as I entered. Is this a wake?

A court-martial, he said flatly. And how is it outside?

The men are parading for a reading of the Orders. We

will have them read up and down the Line, so that all may hear. And then?

And then we march, answered Billy Bowzar. But wait here, Jamie, for you are a part of the Committee, and it's fitting and proper that you should have a vote.

So there I stood, while Abner Williams arose and spoke, apparently continuing what he had been saying before.

We have seen a peculiar treason, he said, for this man Horst has betrayed his comrades and nothing more, and when has there been a punishment for that? He claims loyalty, and I must defend him, for it would not be fitting that he should have no advocate.

You are his advocate, Billy Bowzar nodded. He needs no accuser since we have all seen what he did.

Yes, he did an awful thing, Abner Williams agreed, more thoughtful than angry. . . . He had a lighted match in his hand, and he would have fired a cannon loaded with loose grape, sending his own comrades to their deaths. For this he should be slain, which is what the men would ask if we brought him before the Line and demanded their will. That is what they would ask, but he must be defended.

I did what a loyal soldier does! cried Horst. I stood by the colors when you all had betrayed them! That's what I did!

Ye had better shut up, said Dennis Sullivan, or it will be me duty to tie a bayonet atween yer God-damned teeth.

This question of loyalty, said Jack Maloney tiredly, is the strangest of all questions. I have thought about it too much—too much to know the answer.

He rubbed his bloodshot eyes with both clenched fists, shaking his head as he did so; then he laid his hands, so small and dainty that they might have belonged to a woman, flat upon the table in front of him, staring at them and examining them as he spoke. He and Billy Bowzar and the Jew Levy were the only ones among us who seemed to have been marked for greatness; but Jack Maloney more than the others, for he was a man racked in perpetual combat with his destiny; and because he struggled against wrong, as he saw it, as if it were embodied like Lucifer the Devil, he had a great and sometime splendid dignity. To the very end, he had that dignity, as you will see; for it is my intention to pursue this narrative to its ending, making a whole thing of it.

Now, however, he spoke searchingly and painfully:

What is one loyal to? he asked. That German—and he nodded contemptuously at Horst—is loyal to the colors, as he puts it, but there are other colors too, and the blood of all men is tinted the same. When I wore a red coat, I read a book by a man called Thomas Paine, and I decided that I had been loyal to the wrong things. I was born a bastard and weaned on gin, but I was told to be loyal to my sovereign liege, George III, for that mighty privilege. And when an officer of the King took me as a drummer lad and did terrible things to me that are best not even spoken of, I was told to be loyal to him. I was in the regiment the half-witted Howe marched against the fishermen at Pelle's Point, and only I and eight others lived from the regiment; but we marched, because we were loyal—the way a whore is loyal to her pimp. But after Pelle's Point I said, Since I am destined to die with a bullet in my belly, let it be for freedom; not for Wayne, not for that cold Virginia farmer, not for that craven Congress in Philadelphia, not for the fine Pennsylvania ladies in their silks and satins, not for the property of every dirty lord and fat patroon in Jersey, not for the tobacco plantations and the merchant fleets of Boston and the warehouses of New York—not for that, but for freedom and a little bit of dignity for them that was born like me and raised like me. For this, do you see. I talk pretty and sweet, but I not only can dance like an ape—I got an ape's ear to mock the talk of the British officer gentry who turned me into a servant to black their boots and shine their metal. So there's a variety of loyalty, and a complexity to it also, and sometimes I think we are all the accursed, who are loyal to a dream and no more. But I take no talk of loyalty from him!

So spoke Jack Maloney and without bitterness, but only tiredly.

Yet I must defend him, said Abner Williams stubbornly, and the Reverend Rogers raised his head and nodded.

That is so. His is a different kind of loyalty. Don't scorn it, Jack Maloney, for some of us are loyal to God as we know him, and others are loyal to a piece of rag—and some are loyal to the Devil.

At this point, the reading of the General Orders began, and through the open tent-flap we could see the Line drawn up on parade, and though we could not see him we could hear plainly the booming words of Angus MacGrath. Five or six little boys and girls, flaxen-haired Dutch children from the neighborhood thereabout, raced past to see this great wonder of men and guns and wagons that had come down upon them during the night, and I bethought me of how strange it was, the way life and death mixed themselves; for we who were subjects for hangmen so shortly past were now debating the life or death of this dull and obstinate man, Emil Horst, and still children played and laughed under our noses—and soon they would be listening to the great lies and tales of the children of the camp, and thus were legends born and thus would one of these children someday remember how the Pennsylvania Line, the terrible, savage foreign soldiers, had come into their valley and drawn up on parade, so that documents might be read to them.

. . . To ask for his death, Abner Williams was saying, would be an evil thing. We are not such an army as the officer gentry would have made us. Somewhere in him, fat and dull though he is, there is a streak of the gentry, so let him go to his own kind without stripes and without caning.

And anyway, I said, without any by your leave, this is one thing that was not in the General Orders. We made no provision for those who betray us.

Horst stood still and eager, mouth open, for somewhere in the words he scented life and freedom; and he cocked his head as the Jew Levy said:

True—true. You can see the gentry in him.

Ay—ay, and that you can, said old Lawrence Scottsboro, twisting his wrinkled neck and spitting over his shoulder. And Danny Connell broke the spell for fair, leaning back and laughing as he said:

Gentry or me eyes have never seen it.

But on no grounds of loyalty, said the Jew Levy softly and meaningly. He is loyal to nothing, that animal.

There was no courage in Horst. He stood there and hung his big head and stared at the ground.

Remember, cried Sean O'Toole, that the blood in you is blue—blue blood of gentry! Go to them and tell them that you are like they are—and if ye doubt it . . .

Like a flash, like an animal, the little Irishman was out of his chair, knife in hand, and the knife flicked and left two crossed cuts on Horst's cheek.

Damn you, O'Toole! Billy Bowzar cried; but O'Toole stood in front of the cringing Horst and laughed, and then wiped his knife on Horst's overalls, sheathed it, and spat on the floor.

Do it yer own way, he told the Committee. Me own gut is too sick with him.

Yer gut is like your head, said Jack Maloney, and you're too damned quick with a knife to satisfy me. But get Horst out of here because he stinks the place.

Sure, get him out, said Jim Holt, and Bowzar nodded and the others of us nodded too. But still the man stood where he was, cringing and weeping as the blood ran down his cheek. The Reverend Rogers rose and took his arm and led him out, and as he went past I severed his bonds with a stroke of my knife; but I felt sick, sicker than I would if they had killed him, and my sickness increased as he walked across the fields, away from the parading soldiers of the Line, across the fields and into the woods.

PART SIX

Wherein we discover that roads must be made before
men may travel.

IT IS SAID THAT certain officers remained near us, and others watched us in great danger of their lives; but of all that I know nothing, and until the sun set on Wednesday night, we saw not hide nor hair of any officer. It is true that late on Tuesday afternoon, we had word that one hundred and twenty officers were massed ten miles away with two thousand militiamen, but that proved to be nothing but a wild rumor, and so did every other rumor of militia being massed against us dissolve in smoke. For the militia could only come out of the countryside and the town, out of the crofter on shares and the tenant farmer and the little freeholder, out of the artisan, the carpenter, the cobbler, the weaver and the ropewalker, out of the hatter and the barber and the saddler and the cooper and the soaper and the tinker and the staymaker and the vintner and the silker and silverer—and they were with us, and would make no militia to go against us and shed their blood and our blood. And how much they were with us we learned on this very morning.

I must tell you of the weather, for unless you have lived in the Middle States, you will not know how it is that so often, early in January, winter turns into summer for a spell; the sun shines warm and sweet; the snow melts and the ground dries, and the foolish birds come out and sing as if there were no long and dreary months of cold ahead. The sky is bluer than even in the summertime, for there the cold, metallic sheen of winter persists, and when the sun sets, there is a riot of wild color, as if nature were upset and distraught at this topsy-turvy inversion of the seasons. This was the weather we had on Tuesday and Wednesday as we slowly marched through the Jerseys, with our fifes playing and our drums beating, but with more than that too.

We changed. It wasn't merely that we had new General Orders and no officers, for the change was as much inside of us. I felt it in my heart, in my stomach, in my limbs— and the others felt it too. For the first time in the five years since 1776, the regiments of Pennsylvania shaved them- selves and cleaned themselves in the wintertime, and that was done on that Tuesday morning before we moved out of our bivouac. I remember well the camp that Tuesday morning, for it was different from any camp we made be- fore that, or after that either. For one thing, it was alive— and in a manner of speaking we had been dead for a long, long time. The cold of winter was gone, not only from the air but from our hearts, and we exploded into life and noise and song and heady exuberance. And the women caught it, and the children too, running and laughing and shout- ing. There was such a time of cleaning and mending and patching, and rubbing the bayonets and muskets with lye and soap until they gleamed in the sun, and polishing the cannon and scraping the mud from the carts and carriers, and more mending—for we had a sudden lust and frenzy to look like an army and we carried this on until we were strangers to ourselves, and I remember how men stopped to look at each other and to grin or hoot or laugh until their sides shook.

And we had an audience. First, when the Jersey folk began to gather around our bivouac from all parts of the countryside, we were reserved and wary—for we were still the foreign brigades, and this was the land where winter after winter we had starved and sickened and died on all the endless miles of road we had marched, from Morristown to Newark to Trenton to Princeton to Basking Ridge to Chatham and Pluckemin, north and south and east and west, year after year, and here too we had fought and fought, on the Palisades and in the lonely reaches of the flats and at Monmouth in the pine barrens and along the rivers and on the coast; and always we were strangers and always we were hungry.

But not now. Let those who lie about us and malign us explain how, on Tuesday morning, the farmers came from all over the countryside with their gifts of food, with grain and pigs and sheep and sides of beef and chickens and bags of apples and potatoes. More and more of them came, until our commissary wagons were loaded full and piled high, and still the people came until a solid circle of them ringed our whole encampment. I doubt if there was one man or woman or child for ten miles around who was not of the gentry and not bedridden who did not come that morning to watch us and cheer us and bring us some gift.

They came out as if it were a holiday occasion. There

were fat Dutch housewives holding little children, who shuffled uneasily in their wooden shoes, Dutch farmers with their clay pipes, Westphalians in their colorful costumes, the women with their high hats, the men with their blue vests and silken tassels, Saxon peasants who yawked open-mouthed at these terrible foreigners who had cast out their officer gentry, even the way it was whispered their own ancestors had done so long ago in their own revolt, which ran away in the distances of time in a river of blood. There were tall, raw-boned Yankee tenants, Connecticut men from the paper works, wagon drivers, bearded, dirty leather-clad men who for years had driven their Jersey produce to the coast, where it was picked up by fishing smacks and sold at the wharves of British New York. And there were children of all ages and all kinds babbling away in all tongues, so that it occurred to me again, as it had so often before in Jersey, that we of the brigades were no more foreign than this strange assortment of folk who lived in the land. Little enough they had of Scotch and Irish, but sufficient of everything else—although today you would never know it to travel through the Jerseys as they are now. But it was different then, and the folk were simpler, and in their simplicity they saw much in us that we did not see in ourselves. Many of the women came with loaves of bread and baked herrings and potato pudding, and if we were wary of them, at first they were warier of us; for even their own hatred of the gentry could not entirely overcome the legend of our wildness and wickedness. But in a little while, all of these fears broke down. The drummer children were fed as they had never been fed before; the fat Westphalian women clucked and sighed over our skinnyness, and the wagon drivers handled our British muskets, which we had taken from the enemy in the course of the years, our long British bayonets and our shining bronze cannon. Children worshiped open-mouthed at our strutting pipers, who had such a wind as was never seen in America before, and tirelessly went on and on with their outlandish Highland music. Farm girls giggled as they helped our lads to patch their clothes into some sort of order, and reticent close-mouthed farmers became loquacious and snorted over the condition of our animals.

And for our own men, this was the strangest thing that had ever happened in all our years of warfare; for we were the foreign brigades without home or kin; we were soldiers without discharge; we had been whipped and beaten and herded like cattle; and for us there was no discharge—as there was among the New England and Southern troops. Where would one of us go if he deserted? Never before had we known such a sense of the people for whom we fought, and never before had the people known us—except as ragged, ugly strangers who marched endlessly up and down their roads, who stole their stock and broke their fences, and who did the will of our officer gentry. Long ago, in the first flush of revolt, they had welcomed us as we marched north to Boston, but already when we fled from New York, in 1776, their doors were closed against us; and never thereafter had either party done anything to endear him to the other.

With Abner Williams, I watched this that morning, after Emil Horst had been driven from the camp like a leper; and I was filled with emotion and sadness and joy all at once, as a cup is filled with water that laps over the edges—and I felt above all things a loneliness and wanting for the one maid whose lips had been sweet to me; and as I watched

Abner Williams pick up a little child and pet it, I tried to make some order out of my thoughts. I pointed to the loose, eddying throng of our men, and I asked Williams:

What has happened?

I don't know, he answered, stroking the hair of the little girl as she laughed at him.

But you see that something has come over us.

I see it, but I don't know, and he put the child down, and it ran between his legs and then onward, twisting this way and that way.

Why did they hate us yesterday? Why do they love us today?

If I knew that, I would know much more, answered Abner Williams.

And what has happened to the men?

What has happened to you, then, Jamie Stuart?

What has happened to me? How should I know what has happened to me when I am sick a bittock and mighty a bit-tock, and I want to put my head to the side and cry, and I am filled with shame for every time I was drunk or wild or laid with a whore, and I feel pure and close to all these hard and godless men. But I am only Jamie Stuart who knows a little cobbling and a little bayoneting and you have had yerself education and college and learning of all kinds.

Of all kinds but the kind that would tell me what has been done here in our awful despair of yesterday.

And where do we go?

I don't know, Jamie, he said, and I said nothing to that, but stood in the warm sunshine, looking down at my broken boots, my torn, mud-stained leggings, my coarse overalls, so big and rough over my bony knees and legs—and

I remembered back to the springtime after Valley Forge, when we came out of our stinking clothes and all of a sudden became thin-shanked lads frolicking in a brook. So we were young again now, and there was the strange and frightening discovery of youth in all we did.

A woman came to us and asked was there anything she could do?

Do me a favor of sewing, I said so softly, and took the rag from my arm.

They had come with needle and thread. Here were men who wanted mending, and this was a needle for the soul as well as the cloth; and it is never those who fight the wars who reap the glory. She was a woman of forty or so, buxom and round and yellow-haired, and Dutch I would say, from the manner of her speech, with little blue eyes like buttons; and just to look at her made the man in me rise up and beat against my stomach and chest. So she stood by me and sewed and asked me:

What is your name, son?

Jamie, I said. Jamie Stuart.

A foreigner?

I was born in Pennsylvania, but my folks were bound out from the old country.

As were mine, she sighed. And will you be going home?

I have no home, I answered, my voice all thick with emotion and longing. I have no kith and no kin.

You are an orphan boy?

That I am, I told her, but I am not so much of a boy as you think.

And I moved closer to her and touched her round, full breast, not boldly and wantonly, but so timorously that she smiled instead of being angry at me. But fires raced through me and all over me, and she saw in my eyes what I was thinking, and asked me:

How old are you, boy?

Twenty-two years, if you count the years. But if you measure the sorrows I have seen, I'm older than you are.

And all the while I stroked that fine, full womanly breast of hers, and she did not tell me nay, or make any other kind of play with me, but kept looking straight into my eyes.

I'm old enough to be your mother, she said.

That, you are not!

What do you want of me, boy? Marching in you come, and then you will go marching out, and you are hard as nails and strange as the moon, you men of the brigades.

Why am I strange to you, when you are nohow strange to me?

What do you want of me, boy? she asked.

And I knew what I wanted. I wanted to go where she was and lie next to her and put my head on her bosom and soak up the fullness of her and the warmth of her and feel the comfort of a bed and a woman and an end to this marching into nowhere.

Marching in, marching out, she said.

Put your arms around me, I begged her.

With a thousand folk to see?

Let them see and be damned to them! Put your arms around me!

And that she did, holding me tight and tender. And then she let me go and began to sew with quick, nervous stitches at the dirty rag that was my badge of rank, saying to me:

It's a bitter thing to be a soldier.

Bitter indeed, I nodded.

But now we are sib, she smiled, using a Scottish word as the needle raced.

Sib, I nodded, sib, and the tears rolled down my cheeks. She finished the mending, and Williams returned and said harshly:

Blow the horns, Jamie, and get them to marching! What in hell are we doing here?

He was right. Without looking at her again, I left and found the trumpeters and had them blow; and Chester Rosenbank rounded up his drummer lads, their bellies so full they stuck out, and while the drums rolled and the fifes twittered, the men ran from all over the broad meadows, falling into ranks.

It was a heady thing, the way the men moved; it was full of pride and confidence and strength—and never did a sergeant or a corporal have to raise his voice. Regiment by regiment, they fell in, until the regiments and the artillery company were lined up across the meadow. It has been said often and too often that through all the time of the rising, we were drunk; but if we were it was not with rum but with this fine new freedom we had found for ourselves. Drunkenness was made a reason and excuse for every action we took, and it was said that the whole countryside sold us rum; but we were men without a bit of silver coin among us, and I do not remember any case of drunkenness in the first days of the rising—nor did we have rum to drink.

And drunken men never paraded and marched as we did. We set off down the road to Pluckemin with our drums beating and our flags flying, and we raised our voices to sing:

Captains, once more hoist your streamers,
Spread your sails and plow the wave,
Tell your masters they were dreamers
When they thought to cheat the brave.

The Committee marched in front; then the band; then the first six regiments of the Line; then the artillery; then the wagons with the women and children and sick and wounded; then the last regiments of the Line. We covered a good deal of road, and often the head of the column was out of sight of the rear, but we never broke pace or order; and all along the way, the road was lined with village and country folk who cheered to see us pass.

The hundred men of the Citizen-soldier Guard paced the files and skirmished the front and rear, and I ordered the head of the column with Angus at the end of it. The men were in fine spirits and as proud as peacocks, and at every halt they did things to give them a uniform appearance. Though some regiments of some states had uniforms, we of the Pennsylvania Line never had more than our yellow canvass overalls and our brown coats to mark us as soldiers; but all the uniforms in the world could not have made any other troops on the continent march as we did. How well I recall it, when I ran up and down the files, the shoulders backed, the lines of four rigid and holding, the muskets swinging in tempo and unison—and there a wild longing came on me that we could meet the enemy as we were, in this mood and this heart.

Yet my courage was threaded with fear and born out of the sick loneliness I had after leaving that woman. She stayed with me and inside of me, and my stomach was sick and tight until finally I had to go to the roadside and retch out the morning meal. Now where would we be going, if all the men were like me? I knew how I was. Home, I wanted, and that more than anything else, and my home was in the town of York with the lass I left so long ago. And what kept me here, I wondered. What kept any of us here?

But you, Jamie Stuart, I said to myself, are a man, and they have given you the trust of a man.

That, too, is a damned lie, I said to myself, as I marched on. . . .

When we halted for our midday meal, two of the guard brought us a deserter who had stolen a chicken from a widow woman in the neighborhood. I mention this, because this was an incident that became known in many places, and when more than usual lies were told of us, sometimes someone might say, And what of the chicken of the Widow Brennen? So it became the case of the chicken of the Widow Brennen, and of fame too; for of all the chickens and hogs and lambs that had been stolen in the Jerseys in the course of the war, this was the only one that became a symbol of something.

The looter was Dennis Finnigan of the 3rd regiment, a man who was full of tales and with a talent for setting one of his comrades against another; a great one for talk of rising, he had run away when the rising actually came, as some two or three hundred men did, going over to the officers or going into the woods and the back lanes to watch their own skins. Already, he was something apart from the rest of us, bearded, dirty, frightened and cursing the fact that two men of the Line should drag him along for doing what any Pennsylvania soldier would have done had the opportunity come his way. He twisted and struggled and swore, and the two guards had practically to carry him, and behind them came the Widow Brennen, a mild and anxious little woman who was bewildered by this great turmoil she had raised, and would have stolen off and dropped the whole matter had we not insisted that she remain.

Then and there, the Committee of Sergeants convened themselves as a court-martial. The road was sunken in that place, between two stone walls, with an apple orchard on either side and a big stone barn making a backdrop for where we set our stage. We of the Committee seated ourselves upon the wall, and the men of the Line packed into the sunken road, and children climbed the apple trees and hung over us, and the people of the neighborhood pressed in to find places where they could listen and watch. The farmer who owned the place and his friends climbed into the big open loft of the barn, and our own women and children stood on top of the baggage wagons.

The guards told their story, briefly and to the point: They had heard someone scream, and they met Finnigan running with the chicken.

The Widow Brennen held the chicken now, a bedraggled little bird, and she said, I have my chicken, so let him go. I hold no grudge against him. The man was hungry—

And what are ye, dragging me around in this damned way? cried Finnigan. Are ye so damned virtuous now?

There are two counts, said Billy Bowzar. You have deserted from the Line and you have looted from the people.

Are ye the law now—you that are mutineers? What if I stole a thousand pieces of gold! I need no thief to read me the morals of me own thieving!

There was a roar from the men, and they surged toward

him and would have taken him and done badly with him, if it weren't for the guards holding them back. We waited for silence, and then Bowzar went on:

The morals of your thieving are something for you to ponder, Dennis Finnigan—we don't stand alongside of you. When we cast out the gentry, we became like the people. We are not bandits. If we take one ear of corn out of a field, we have nothing left, nothing—and then we are truly bereft.

There was a whole and absolute silence now; you could hear the breathing of those packed men; you could hear the wind in the leafless trees; you could hear the beating of your own heart, too, as I did, as Finnigan did the way he stood there staring open-mouthed at the Committee. And Billy Bowzar sat on a rock of the stone wall, a little man, smaller now that his beard was shaven, swinging his feet and contemplating them seriously and troubledly. His square face, his snub nose, his broad full mouth all reflected the inner conflict and doubt that beset him. When he spoke, he chose each word carefully and slowly, and marked them out with his hand, saying:

You make a great mistake, Finnigan, if you think of us as thieves. I think you are not much good as a man, and I don't give a damn what you think, but it is a mistake all the same; and the people all around here and back where we were encamped made no such error. We are a mighty force, for we are good soldiers and hard men, and I would lay the Line against any troops on earth, be they equal man to man or five times our number, and we could fight anywhere in heaven or hell or in between, and sometimes it seems that we have too, God forgiving me, for I mean no blasphemy. But what kind of force would we be if the people were against us? Just look around you, my lad, and tell we where all these folk have grown from—since all the winter days we marched this land and saw no soul are fresh in my memory. And how did they know that what we did was right? It is a staggering thing we did, to rise up and cast out the gentry who led us so long—and not to become bandits or thieves or animals to blunder the fields, but to hold our ranks and to make a better discipline than the gentry ever forced out of us. And this is what the people knew, before we ever knew it ourselves. Even before we rose, they knew it, and they came to Mt. Kemble with food, so that we should not march away hungry—and this morning they came to our bivouac and embraced us. Do you hear! They embraced us! How was that? We are the dirty, outland foreign brigades, and even our officers are afraid of us and paint us as devils, but the people are not afraid, and that is why we will not take a blade of grass out of their fields or a grain of wheat from their bins. We are no rabble; we are their army and their shield, and you brought disgrace on us and you deserted when we faced the gentry. So what do you say to that?

I did no worse than you did, muttered Finnigan.

Worse ye did, God damn ye! cried Connell. If ye looted, that was one thing, but ye crawled away into the darkness when the little drummer lads stood and beat their drums and faced the gentry!

Ye got no right to punish me! Ye got no right to whip me!

Bowzar looked from face to face and so did Finnigan, but there was no hope to be found in the Committee.

We are going to hang you, said Jack Maloney.

Jesus Christ, have ye gone mad?

The Widow Brennen fell to the ground and lay there sobbing as if her heart had broken, and here and there a man expelled his breath like a windy sigh of pain, but there was no other sound except the high-pitched screaming words of Finnigan:

Then what are ye hanging me for? For me poor belly that hungered? Four years I served in the Line, and did I run away when we battled? Is me hunger different from yer own hunger? Is a chicken exchange for a man's life? For Christ's sake, what are ye hanging me for?

For betraying yer own comrades, said Sean O'Toole.

And did ye hang Emil Horst who tried to fire a cannon at ye?

He was loyal to the officers, but what in hell were you loyal to?

Ye are not going to hang me! Ye cannot hang me! Me old mother in Ireland would know, and she'd die of the shame of a son who went to hell on the gallows! Ye look at me like I was a dirty traitor, but I swear to you by the holy Mother of God that I never betrayed you! Ye must not hang me! Four years I walked in this Line, and took with ye the bad and the good, and ye are not going to take my life away from me for a chicken—ah, Christ, Christ . . .

He put his face in his hands and wept, and here and there through the crowd a woman wept too, and the Committee sat like stone.

But after a long moment, the Nayger Holt said, Let him live. We that strong, we can let him live, and I never going to sleep if I see a man hanged by my hand. Make him go away, and we can spit in the dirt where he walks.

Billy Bowzar looked at me, and I nodded. Let him go, said Scottsboro slowly. I seen many a man hanged, but we don't need to hang men for crimes the gentry only whipped us for. Let him go.

Let him go, said Levy, and Jack Maloney nodded too. No whips, no canes, let him go. And Abner Williams said, Let him go. . . . And let him go far away from us, said Bora Kabanka.

So the press of people opened and Finnigan walked through, his head hanging, still weeping, and he climbed the stone wall and went away across the fields.

Then the trumpets blew, and we put on our knapsacks and marched away.

This was the chicken of the Widow Brennen, and while it is not much in the telling, it was much indeed to us and to all the folk in the countryside. It became something apart from the details of what happened, something that wholly transcended the simple fact that a chicken was stolen, and that the rank and file of the Line had dealt justice to thief and plaintiff. For no one who witnessed that strange and brief court-martial was not influenced in some way, and the men who marched away from that resting place were not the same as when they came there. And even to this day when I write, among the whole welter of lies and bitterness and awful accusations, it is still remembered that on this matter the Line was just.

Yet we were just on other matters too, and day in and day out the Committee met to pass on the slightest infraction of our General Orders; and if the truth is known, no army of that sort marched in America before then—or since then either.

But I must take up the tale of how we left our resting place and marched on toward Princeton. For the first time since the earliest days of the war, there marched along the Jersey highways an army that was light in heart and ready in spirit; for all of our doubts and fears, we marched as though we were returning victorious from some decisive battle. All morning and all afternoon the skirling of the pipes mixed with the drums and the fifes, and over and above it we sang every song we knew. With all good heart, we sang the Yankee song, *Come out, ye Continentalers, we're going for to go, To fight the redcoat enemy, so plaguy cute, you know.* And then our fifes picked up, *Why came ye to our shores, across the briny water? Why came ye to our shores, like bullocks to the slaughter?* But soon we had enough of Yankee songs, and all up and down the Line the regiments began to sing a strange and wild melody, the old Scottish air which was sung, they say, by the clansmen in the long past when they marched south against the false kings of England, and which was called by us "The Song of Revolution," but by others "The Song of the Foreign Brigades," for only we of the Line sang it. It is a low and moody song, mounting and savage and bitter:

> And his fate is now sealed and his power is shaken,
> As the people at last from their slumber awaken!
> For their blood has run freely on green grass sod,
> And no power now rules them save that of their God!
> Death to the tyrant, torture and shame!
> Death to the tyrant, faggot and flame!

Thus it was that we marched through the Jerseys and let our voices sound, so that the people would know that the Pennsylvania Line was coming; and as I said, in all that time, we saw no officer—and when we came to one of the manor houses of a patroon or a squire, the windows were barred and shuttered; the stock was driven away and the fields were empty.

Yet that day, too, it began to dawn upon us that men did not march without going somewhere, and again and again it was thrown at me:

Where are we off to, Jamie?

Where is our destination?

What is the Committee thinking? Where are the officers? What are they up to? Where are the other Lines? Where is the British enemy?

It was only curious now and only inquiring, for the men were still flushed with the ease of the revolt and with the rare sense of being their own masters, and with the knowledge that each and every one of them could become a part of the general flux of committees that we spoke of setting up. Also, the march was southward toward the Pennsylvania border, and that was as good a way to go as any other, and they were led by good men whom they had trusted before—but whom they worshiped with a singular reverence now that the revolt had come off so well and cleanly. Still, they had to have answers; so I took my place with the Committee, between Billy Bowzar and Jack Maloney, and told them:

The men are asking where we're off to?

Are they, Jamie? And is there a man in the Line who doesn't know every lane and bypath in the Jerseys?

That's tomorrow, and what comes the day after tomorrow?

And what do you think, Jamie? asked Billy Bowzar.

I've had no time to think. I've been on with the Citizen-soldier Guard since my waking hour—and that damned music takes the sense out of my head.

The music's good for the men, said Maloney. What are they saying and thinking?

This and that and everything. Some of them think that we should march straight into Philadelphia and put our demands to the Congress.

As if the Congress did not know that we are a bitter and angry file of men?

They might know it better if we stood on their doorstep.

And then what, Jamie? asked Billy Bowzar, as much to himself as to me. Do we take back our officers for the promises of Congress? Or if we get no satisfaction, do we take over the power of the Congress? Then we fight the country, eh, Jamie? And we fight the British enemy, and the country fights us and the enemy—and what will the people say, Jamie? And what of the men who enlisted for three years and served for five? Do we let them go away, Jamie? And then where do the foreign brigades recruit from?

If I knew the answers—

If *we* knew them, Jamie ...

We walked on then for a time in silence, and then I said, Then why did we rise up?

Have you forgotten, Jamie?

Christ, no! But you have forgotten, it seems to me!

Go slow, go slow, laddie, said Jack Maloney; we've been eating our hearts out with this.

I say again, why did we rise up?

Because it was intolerable to remain the way we were, answered Jack Maloney.

But this is madness, I insisted, and the more you turn

it in circles, the more insane it becomes. We have cast out our officers; the men are with us; we have the best line of troops in all this continent—and we are citizen-soldiers who have felt the whip enough to know better than to pick it up ourselves. All the dreams and hopes of men who were fed on dirt and scum for a thousand years add up to this. And when I ask you two where we arc going, you can only tell me that you don't know!

Because we don't know, Jamie. We will sit down with the Committee tonight and talk about it.

And talk and talk and talk.

That's right, Jamie.

We talked for five years, but in one night of action those of us who know a little about doing and less of gabble turned the world over.

Not the whole world, Jamie, said Billy Bowzar gently, taking my arm as I strode along beside him. Not the whole world, but just the Pennsylvania Line. And meanwhile we are marching to Princeton, where we will rest awhile and patch our boots—

And you'll have use for a cobbler, since I have no brains in my head to match yourself and the Jew Levy!

Easy, Jamie, and cork your bung a little. We got a great appreciation for what you did. I am no general that I can pin a medal onto you, Jamie, but I also have no crystal ball to peer into and find the answers. Maybe if we had waited a month or six months before we rose up, we would have known. But if we waited, we would have lost our guts, for we are still like men in a dream, and it was only last night, Jamie, that we did what we did.

Then Danny Connell drew me aside into the drain of the road, so that we stood against the hump of hedge and

rut while the columns marched past. The men came swinging by, grinning at us, and one and another said:

Ho, Jamie! Ho, Danny!

What bird pecks in you? asked Danny Connell, his
pinched, drawn face anxious and warm, an old man in a
lad's body, like so many of us.

No bird.

But the answer was fear, I knew; and I was asking myself, *Why, Jamie Stuart, why?* even as the 10th marched
past, singing *Erin's sons are weeping sadly, they will see
her sward no more* ... I wanted to know *Why? why?*

They got an affection for us, said Danny Connell, and
me damned heart is glad for that. We lead them, and they
got an affection for us, Jamie. There is the whole world
turned upside down.

And again, we stood and watched. Across the road, on
a shoulder of a hill, was a wooden stake fence, and a family
of nine or ten children were there, German or Dutch from
the look of them, all of them like peas from the same pod
with corn-thatch hair and blue eyes, a dog next to them—
all of them staring open-mouthed and silent at this endless
line of men, marching four abreast, playing drums and fifes
and pipes and singing outlandish songs.

Then the wagons came, and on one of them was Connell's Mathilda, and when she saw him, she dropped off
and he caught her up in his arms, laughing as he rocked
her back and forth.

To hell with that! I cried at him. We are on the march,
and you are of the Committee, and this is a hell of a thing
to do!

What pecks in him? asked the Irishman.

But I ran off to catch the head of the column again.

* * *

We bivouacked that Tuesday night in the old encampment at Middlebrook, where we had hutted for a time two years before. That was the way it was then in the Jerseys—for you will remember that for five years we had fought and marched over this ground. There was almost no stream of clear water where we had not bivouacked at one time or another, if not the Line, then one or another regiment of the Line, and there was no lane or bypath with which we were not familiar. And all over the country were our huts, or the huts of the Jersey men or the Connecticut men or the Massachusetts men, the abandoned parades, the forests we had clipped for our warmth, all of it brief, a quick erection that began to rot almost as the sound of our drums vanished; and I know of nothing more melancholy than an old encampment, filled with the ghosts of dead comrades and dead dreams—and in the same way have our deeds and sufferings vanished in the rush of years, to be replaced by a pleasant fairy tale for little children and old women, with no little memory of what the flesh and blood men were and what they wanted and what they died for.

So we came back to Middlebrook as the sun was setting on that mild, uncommon winter afternoon, and we encamped ourselves on the parade. We had no desire to put the hutments to use, for they were filled with all the old wickedness and suffering of the past—and dirt and refuse and the foul smell of long disuse. The weather was mild enough for us to be comfortable in the open. We raised up all the tents we had, built our fires foursquare, twenty to a regiment, and laid triple pickets around the place; that is, at no time in the night did we have less than three hundred men standing guard, and our cannons were loaded with small grape and short powder and set to sweep every approach. This was the trust of Angus and myself, and it was amazing how, in the short space of a few hours, the hundred men of the Citizen-soldier Guard had become expert at the business of organizing and provosting a bivouac. I can say without boasting that though I have seen many a display and bivouac of soldiers since then, I have never seen the discipline or the co-ordination that existed in the Line during the time of the rising. Each Committee we had created was functioning in part at least, and small though that part might be, it was better than the bitter hatred which had prevailed under the officers, the discord and resentment.

Meanwhile the Committee of Sergeants, augmented with other committee heads and leading men from the regiments, had begun to meet in an old stone barn which stood at the end of the parade.

MacGrath and I, and the Gary brothers with us, did not come to the barn until well after nightfall; by then at least forty people were present in the big, drafty room, which had only half a roof and was lit with pitch torches. Two logs had been dragged in for the men to sit on; the rest sat on the floor or on the old feed trough. It had turned cold with nightfall, and the men were wrapped in scarves and in their threadbare blankets, bulked up with shoddy goods and looking strangely small now that their beards were gone, like sheared sheep. When Angus and I entered, old Lawrence Scottsboro was speaking, and it took a while for us to get the drift of what had gone on. Sometime—my memory lapses here, and I cannot recall whether it was after or before we came—they raised the thought of a march westward; yet it was on that the old man spoke, that ever-present dream and refuge and last stand of the army of the confederation, ever since the confederation had come into being. Always in the past, when matters were so low that no one believed they could sink lower, when our nakedness was past nakedness and our hunger was past hunger, when the other Lines of the other states had shrunk into skeletons of a few hundred men each, when no army and no resistance was left but the foreign brigades of Pennsylvania—when that came to pass, the last card was brought from the deck and it was said that we would march westward over the mountains into the wild and lonely land of Fincastle, as we called it then, and make a new republic there, and war on from there if need be for a hundred years against the British enemy. But this was always the kind of dream that desperate men make for themselves, and it was like smoke, blown away by a close examination or even a puff of wind. Yet this was being spoken of now, and the old man Scottsboro was recalling how he had marched with Braddock in the great destruction that the Frenchmen and the Indians had brought upon them, and this and that about how it was to fight in the dark woods. And as we listened, a colder chill than the weather crept over us.

You may not understand now what a deep horror we had in those times of the dark and awful forest, where the trees were seven feet through the trunk, and where a man could walk a fortnight and never see the sky or properly know when it was daybreak or nightfall—and where a child could go out of sight and never be seen or heard of again, and a grown man too. You are town bred and country bred. But we had with us in the Line many, many of the lonely Scottish buckskin men from Fincastle, who had been driven there because not an acre of open land existed but was pledged to a man of property who had the King's guns to shoot down those who poached on it; and yet these men shook their heads somberly at talk of a retreat across the mountains.

Yes, we could lose us, said Scottsboro, choosing his words slowly and painfully, and the nation would lose us too. And we would not set up a republic, but only a company of lost men who would turn bandits in that bitter land.

Lawrence Scottsboro was an ancient among us, a small, knotted man, wrinkled, with only four teeth in his whole mouth, and on and off racked with the rheumatic pains which were the special reward to each and every one who followed the soldier's trade. He, like Jack Maloney, had no father, no mother, no kith nor kin. He had licked and scraped from a camp kettle when he was seven years old, and he had not the slightest notion where he came from or who he was or of what blood. Scottsboro, as you know, was the old wooden fort the British built on the upper reaches of the Hudson River, so long ago—and now not even a stick of it remains—and that was the name he took, since it was the first place he could root out of his memory. And he had grown up in the camps of the British regiments, lickspittle at first, serving and scrounging and running to heel with a fist at his forelock—until he was old enough to beat a drum and then to carry a gun. Often I have heard him remember the endless marches he made, the uncounted miles from garrison to garrison, fort to fort, post to post—in the dirty, miserable, meaningless life a redcoat Regular lived, the cane on the shoulders, the filth, the loneliness, the depraved practices among the ignorant, hopeless, undersized men who sold their souls and their lives for the mess of pottage King George served out. He became a corporal and a sergeant and then a master sergeant, and you would have said that there was never a thought or a dream in his obedient head; but the bitterness had made a score, and when the farmers beat the British into Boston in 1775, he and two others cut off a redcoat captain's head and brought it to the Yankee farmers as enlistment papers. But he was an army man and nothing else, and in the great rout of 1776, when the Yankees ran away, he saw that the foreign brigades remained to fight, and he joined the 1st Regiment of Pennsylvania—which was my regiment then, until they took me out to be sergeant in the 11th.

This old man, such a hard and bitter old man, now spoke with gentleness and wisdom and said:

Because we are not a folk, but an army. We be soldiers, and of soldiers and soldiering I know something, laddies, for I was under the weight of a gun before the lot of ye were born. There is no good in soldiers except what comes from the folk they soldier for—and if you soldier for that bastard King, as I did so long, what are ye but a buffer, a pimp, a bruiser, a blower, a hooker, a prigger, a whipjack— and it don't matter ye wear a red coat on your back. Now, what virtue is in us? I been rolling that round and round in this old head of mine, for we are as hard-bitten and scraggy a lot of men as there are in this whole world over, and I know, I tell you. I seen hard men a-plenty, but I seen harder in these foreign brigades. But I look around at my comrades, and I find them gentle, so gentle I got to go and put my cloak over my face and cry, which a grown man shouldn't need to do. I ain't but a simple man, as ye know, but I think there is a deeper virtue in freedom than we sense—and that is why the country folk come with food. That is why. We are their soldiers for freedom, but we got no virtue apart from that. I don't know how to say that to make it plainer, because it ain't too plain in my own head. But if we go away from them, from the Jersey and Pennsylvania and York and Connecticut and Massachusetts people, we become something else, and all what is bitter and hard in us will erupt like a boil that breaks. When ye come down to it, that is why we let the gentry cane us and whip us and starve us these five years—we got a deeper attachment than them. But if we do like Connell and Carpenter says and go into the deep woods, then God help us indeed. I don't know what we can do, but not that.

He's right, said Billy Bowzar then. We are in a war because people have suffered and people struck back. If we go to a place where there are no people, we are all through. It would be better to lay down our guns and go home.

And where is home for the foreigns? asked the Jew Levy. Here is my home.

Me thought is this, said Danny Connell, that Scottsboro is an old one, and the heart is out of the old ones. Me old father he said, If ye are going to make a rising, then go through with it and be damned!

Christ, when I hear an Irishman talk! cried Jack Maloney. Do ye make a rising for the sake of a rising? Then ye would rise all alone, ye damn fool! We made a rising because the men wanted it, and now we have cast out the officers—but what the old man says is right, and don't make mock of him. I tell you, I will not run away to the mountains! I will lay me down and die first! I will crawl first to Wayne and tell him, come back and lead me again!

I am sick to me belly of hearing ye talk about the Irish,

began Danny Connell, but Billy Bowzar cut in and held them.

You have neither of ye the floor, and hold your peace. This is a Committee meeting, and that it will be. If you want the floor again, put up your hand and ask for it, and when your turn comes you can speak. But I'll not have us shouting back and forth like a gabble of red Indians.

He then recognized Abner Williams, who remained silent for a while before he began to speak. There had always been a little of mistrust in our attitude toward Williams, not only because he was a Yankee with the long, narrow, aloof face that so many of the Yankees have, but because he was a man of college education, strange with our women, apart from our jesting, and had made such remarks as to the effect of his believing as little in God as he did in King George III, except that one was there and you could put a hand on him and the other had a residence unknown. While this wasn't taken well by the Protestants, it went even worse with the Romans, who pointed out that it was logical for the Yankees, who had cast out the true God, to make the next step and defame their own false God as well. Also, he spoke a different tongue from us, a different way of the English; yet he stood for us, and from him the officers took much that they would never take from us. He too had come to us in the great rout and had remained with us, and we knew that he, like the Jew Levy, was full of many books and many mysteries. So we hearkened when he spoke and studied his words, always conscious that we were ignorant men, most of us by far knowing no letters and few numbers. And for all our dislike of the Yankees, they were like the Jews in this matter of reading and writing, scrounging for it, even if they were just common folk like ourselves.

We are a people of committees, said Abner Williams. It's in the blood, and for ten years we've made a Committee for everything, and everything we have done has come through a Committee, even the Revolution itself—and my father used to tell me that more hours than he slept, he spent at committee meetings. I say this because perhaps a Yankee is more patient with the Committee way than someone who has not bitten his teeth on it. When I first began to hear and speak, a Committee of Resistance met at our house, and then a Committee of Liberty in the church cellar, and then a Committee on Stamps and then a Committee on Tea and then a Committee of Correspondence—only we couldn't run our army with committees. We tried, but it didn't work. Well, here in the Midlands, it is different, and you have a gentry of a kind we don't have in Connecticut, or in the Bay Colony either—or I should say that those of them we had, some we hanged and some we tarred and feathered and the rest we drove away on the British ships. Not because we are more knowledgeable about gentry, but because it is a different world in the North than here with the patroons and the lords and the squires—and the cheating of a man out of his little bit of land to make him a tenant, and binding men like slaves to apprenticeship, and the kind of officers who rode a saddle on us, and the kind of a war they are fighting. But they're not all of it, and that's why I want to talk as a Yankee, as a stranger among you, although I've eaten and slept and marched and fought with the foreign brigades for five years—and never seen my own home or my own blood in all that time. I lived under the officers as you lived under them, and to me they and what they represent and what they believe and hold are like a disease—and here for a moment the disease joined the body to cast off a greater danger; and sometime—a year, ten years or a hundred years from now—the disease must go or the body will die. That is why I rose against them and that is why I will do whatever you do and go wherever you go, even across the mountains—although I hold with Scottsboro that such a way is wrong and bad. But I've brooded over this and brooded over it, and I know no way, no other way. If we turn out the Congress in Philadelphia—and they have no force that can prevent our doing so—then we will plunge our confederation into civil war, and there is still the British enemy sitting among us and waiting. If we call for the other Lines to join us, some will, but some will march against us. Jersey is with us, and I think Pennsylvania would be with us—but I don't know what the Yankees would do, and I am a Yankee. And what would Virginia and the Carolinas do, where the gentry are worse than here, and where their own slaves have run away to fight in our brigades? And if we lay down our arms and go home—where is our home? Shall I go back to Connecticut and say, This is no more for me, this Revolution, for I hate the Midland gentry worse than I hate the British? *But I don't hate the British. I love liberty*—and not a word, but a way I've dreamed where there would be a little dignity to men, and not for the most to be like beasts driven by a few. And that we've won, here in the Pennsylvania Line; and we've had twenty-four hours of it, and, God help me, I don't know where we are to go with it!

Then Yankee, take the damned gentry back! Andrew Yost snorted. Or go to them!

Fairly—fairly: ask for the floor, several shouted.

I had the floor—all I want to say. I ain't got words like him! cried Andrew Yost.

Keep your order! shouted Billy Bowzar, pounding the floor with a stick of wood.

And I can tell ye where to go, cried Angus MacGrath, though I no be one of the Committee. Has a kemp a right to speak, Billy Bowzar?

I have not enough of the Scottish to know if that's a good man or a dirty scoundrel, but say your piece, MacGrath. This is a forum for the regiments. Say your piece.

I'll tell ye where we can go, providing ye got a little bit of courage. We can go up to York city and dad them—if ye got the guts—march north, and cross the river, and hit on them!

The British?

I mean no others, answered Angus, standing straight and proud, throwing his deep voice against the back wall of the barn.

There are fifteen thousand of them in York city! someone cried.

And when there were fifteen thousand dirty redcoats on the border, was it my own father afraid to come down and faught? The hell he was!

Ye got a fine notion of the Scottish, and too little of the English, a lad in the hayloft laughed.

I got a notion of the Line. And if ye want to fight for that notion—

Angus! cried Billy Bowzar, spreading his arms. I gave you the floor, and you said your piece. Now keep a still tongue! There is no doubting your courage or the courage of the Line, and I'll have no fighting unless you want to fight with me. And I'm no Scottish and no Irish either and half your size, but I'll take you on, thick head and all. Now listen . . .

We were laughing now, and wrapping deeper in our rags; for a cold night wind blew through the openings in that ruin of a barn; and the laugh was all surface, for there was a memory of the cold of winters past, and there was the beginning of a realization that we were embarked on a road no one had traveled before.

Now listen, said Billy Bowzar, if you are so short of memory that a day of sunshine can wipe the winter from your mind. Today we marched in the sunshine, but tomorrow the snows can begin again, and our tents would not even make good foot wrappings. That is why the Committee chose Princeton as our destination. The college buildings there are empty and waiting, and we can make something in them and in the hutments the British set up there. So Angus MacGrath says, *March on York city where the British are* . . . ? With enough leather on our feet to sign our tracks in blood? With twenty thousand loads of powder to the whole Line? I am not impressed with the fifteen thousand of the King's men, laying with their whores in that rotten city—give us the support of the country and the people, and we can take the Line against *them*, and cut them up too, and drive them shrieking and screaming and howling from York city the way they drove us out of there in '76—but I don't live in dreams. We have food for three or four days, and we will have more here when that is eaten, too, because the Jersey folk know us—but who will feed us when we march into the doxy-hole of New York?

Who will shelter our wounded? Who will give us powder when we have shot away what we carry?

The British, someone called.

Ah—yeah? And if it snows, and we must wait five days to feel the bottom of the roads before we can march?

Let me speak a word, Billy Bowzar, said the Jew Levy, standing up and walking over to where Bowzar sat on an old cider keg. He put his hand on Bowzar's shoulder, gripping it—and Bowzar smiled self-consciously, pulling off his woolen cap and running his fingers through his curly red hair. He nodded and pursed his lips, and the skinny little Jew said:

We are lucky for having Bowzar. Such men there aren't too many of.

No one's against Bowzar, said Simpkins Gary.

That's right—no one's against Billy Bowzar; but he hasn't slept for two days. He's never stopped for two days. It shouldn't be thought that this revolt just happened. It had to be organized and led, and it still has to. And if men should lead it, they got to see over the heads of the soldiers of the Line. A thousand times since it began, we said to each other, What will we do next? Where do you go with a thing like this? What is the rest of the army doing? What is Washington doing? Does he know about this? Does Congress know? And if we elect new officers—can we fight alone? You heard Billy Bowzar: Who will feed us? Who will arm us? Today the Jersey folk, but what about tomorrow? The people will not trust foreign bandits who have cast out their officers—this is not what we are, but this is what the officers will say. I know—I know what the people think about Jews and Romans and black men. Ask Jim Holt!

He is right, said Jim Holt. My God, we ain't criminal—we be good men, but who going to believe that unless we show it? And how we going to show it? The Nayger should be no slave, because we fight for no man to be slave, but if we sing out *No Nayger slave*, the whole Southland going to turn against us! We say, *No rich man, no man with a million acres*. But how you going to live without rich man? You hang them all, and then it just take a little time: there be rich man again. You going to turn them against George Washington, who is rich man with many Nayger slave . . . ?

Thus it went, on and on, with one and another and then still another speaking, and round and round and round it went—in a weary, awful circle, with the wind blowing colder and colder through the open gaps in the barn, with more and more men from the regiments coming to listen and shiver and watch our leaders butt their heads against a wall that had no openings.

Guns we had, and powder and shot, and almost three thousand of the best troops in the world—but we had nothing to fight for except what we had fought for under our officers.

It was the tail of the evening—well on and well under, when sleep had mixed with cold and many had gone and I no longer heard words but only voices—when Mac-Pherson came and shook me from my doze, and said softly, Come outside, Jamie.

I went out with him, and there was Allen Gutton, a barber from the 3rd Regiment who had dropped away in the rising, as men had here and there—and what with one thing and another, we were not able to brood on those who were gone.

So ye lost yourself, Allen, I said.

No, Jamie: I chose to stay.

Like similar filth.

Say what you like, Jamie. I followed my own conscience.

None of ye got one; but, anyway, what in hell are you
doing here?

I come with a message from the general.

I would have kicked him to the ground and driven him
from the camp on his hands and knees, with a stick across
his shoulders, but MacPherson was watching me out of his
somber eyes, and I nodded and said, I will get someone to
talk with you. My own stomach is too delicate.

Go to hell and be damned, Jamie. I come with a message
from the general, and I don't have to take your gabble.

Not now, you don't!

I went into the barn and called Billy Bowzar aside and
talked to him. He turned the chair over to Danny Connell,
and then nodding at the Jew Levy and Jack Maloney, he
motioned for them to follow. We went outside, our feet
crunching the hard ground, and Gutton handed him the
letter, which he read in the moonlight then and there. I had
wanted to make a copy of that letter, but I neglected that,
and it is gone and lost now, but I remember that it stated
matter-of-factly enough that Wayne and two of his staff
would appreciate a conference with the Committee of Sergeants of the Pennsylvania Line. It was polite and gentle
and somewhat coaxing, not the way gentlemen talk to dirt,
but the way one gentleman talks to another.

He wants to meet with us, said Bowzar.

He looked at me and I stared at him emptily, and then

he looked at Maloney and Levy—and they made no move nor gesture, but they did not have to.

Tell him to approach our pickets at Princeton tomorrow, said Bowzar tonelessly. The Committee will discuss any matters he wishes to bring before us. Now take him through the lines, Jamie.

With that, I escorted Gutton through the sentries and onto the road where he had left his horse. When he turned to mount, I kicked him in the butt and then ground his face in the dirt.

That's reward for your conscience, Allen Gutton, I said.

And something to remember in the future, Jamie Stuart, he answered, rising and climbing on his horse.

Remember and be damned! Geck on ye!

With no other word, he mounted and rode off; and I went back to the barn. The meeting was over now. The Committee and the Reverend William Rogers remained; the others had gone.

Well, Jamie? asked Danny Connell.

I sent the little rat on his way. But I been thinking to ask you something, you gentlemen of the Committee. What in hell have we got to say to the officers?

We don't know, Jamie, Bowzar answered.

Well . . . , I began, but Dwight Carpenter interrupted me with:

Close your yap, Jamie, and let us get to bed.

To hell with them, I thought. To hell with them and their theories and their wisdom; and I turned around and walked out. But before I had taken ten steps, Jack Maloney was after me with an arm around my shoulders.

Jamie, hold yer hot head. We are in a profound and frightening thing, and we got to feel our way.

And take back the officers!

We are not taking them back, Jamie. We are going to look at this and that, and try to understand what we have done. That is all. We got to find a future, because, as sure as God, there is none facing us now!

Then I went to my blankets, rolled close to the fire, and slept. And once more the morning was warm and sunny, and as we marched down the road to Princeton, the men of the Line singing as they paced, the drums beating and the fifes shrilling and the pipers blowing with all their might and main, my fears of the night before went away, and I knew only the great and massive comfort of the Pennsylvania Line, the strong and tried men who alone of all the armies in the world had no officers, but ruled themselves and marched for their own freedom.

PART SEVEN

Being an account of the events at Princeton.

ON WEDNESDAY, THE 3RD of January, about two hours after the sun had set, I was summoned by one of the Citizen-soldier Guard to Nassau Hall, where the Committee of Sergeants had established the general headquarters of the Pennsylvania Line.

In those times, the Prince Town, as many of the native Jersey folk still called it, was a village of some thirty or forty houses, almost all of them built on the main pike that ran southward and across the river to Philadelphia. It was a pretty and quiet little village, which Jack Maloney said reminded him of the Sussex towns in the old country, and it was dominated in its center by the hall of the college, which was not in those days called Princeton, but the Old School of the Jerseys. We were no strangers to Princeton, for one or another regiment of the Line had marched through there at least a hundred times since the war began, and at least four times the whole Line had made a bivouac in the broad meadow behind Nassau Hall, and so had the British on one occasion or another. And at least four regiments of the Line recalled well and vividly the wild and terrible battle we had fought with the British, hand to hand, butt to butt, knife to knife—when they first tasted the difference between the foreign brigades and the Yankee militia. Four years ago to the day, that was, on the 3rd of January—yet how many lives had we lived since then, and how many good comrades had died, and how many things had changed!

In more ways than one had things changed, for Nassau Hall, which had been such a fine and lovely building, was gutted and wrecked, with not a window left in it and not a stone in reach that wasn't defaced by those gentle advocates of culture, the British enemy, who had stabled their horses in one part of the hall, while the German mercenaries used another part as an outhouse. Also, the war had raged closer to this village than to many; some men had fled to York city; others had died or gone into the Jersey Line; and here and there among the houses was a little tyke who would never know that he or she had been sired out of the foreign brigades, and was none the worse for it either. So it was a good welcome the regiments found in Princeton, with the news gone ahead of them that they had thrown out the gentry, and with the brigades marching down the street between the houses like redcoat grenadiers, and with the two Scottish pipers taking their place on either side the big hall and skirling us around it onto the camp grounds.

My own work, along with that of Angus and the Gary brothers, was to lay out and order the encampment, and this time we set to work to repair the old huts and get them fit to live in, and it was from this that I was summoned by the Committee of Sergeants.

They were already at work around a long, mutilated table that had been rescued from the debris of the ruined hall. It was set up on the first floor in a big room, lit with candles and hastily made as habitable as possible. Old shutters and boards had been nailed over the smashed windows to keep out the draft, and a good fire was roaring in the hearth. Odds and ends of boxes and kegs had been put to use as chairs, and the tavern keeper from the crossroads had presented to the Committee, as his own peace offering, a big pewter jug of hot flip, which now filled the whole room with its delicious smell.

As I entered, Danny Connell dipped into the flip and poured me a measure.

Drink hearty, Jamie!

To the Committee of Sergeants, I said sourly.

What pecks in ye, me lad? grinned Connell.

My whole lousy, worthless twenty-two years of life, and my one glimpse of glory.

Then hold onto it, Jamie, nodded Jack Maloney, for I wish to God that I was twenty-two again, glory or no.

And when this evening is done, added Dwight Carpenter, go find a village lass, Jamie; for ye are a fine, upstanding Pennsylvania lad and winsome too—

The devil with you!

Old Scottsboro here, he is sour and old, but it is not natural, Jamie, to be sour and young.

Leave the lad alone, said Bowzar sharply. It's one stinking taste of flip, Jamie. Tell me, how are we covered?

It would not be covered at all if it was left to the great discussions of the Committee. At least, what I do, I do.

Jamie, Bowzar broke in, stop yapping of that. We gave ye a task because we thought ye could do it—and do you want a certificate for every time ye leak? Now, Jamie, how are we covered?

I got forty men of the Guard out, and another fifty beside.

That is not enough, Jamie. We want a picket around this place that a rabbit could not squirm through—and no picket is to yap—and I mean no gabble whatsoever. If anyone comes up to the guards, they are to turn him over to you or MacGrath. Turn out three hundred men on two hours—

They have had a day's march.

We know that, Jamie, and let them go guard tonight, and we want them out and on parade in full gear at seven o'clock in the morning.

I have no watch, I said.

But I have, and I'll turn you out, Jamie. So get that under way and leave Angus to do it, and then take one of the Gary lads and ten of the best and most likely lads you have got in the soldier guard, and go across the road to the inn, where you'll find the general and two of his staff waiting. Bring them here.

How do you know they'll be there then?

Because they there now, said Holt.

They are there, Jamie, but let them cool their heels a little.

They'll be raging.

Then let them rage, lad. They have done their share of raging, and it should not take too much out of them. Bring them here gentle, but very firm—very firm, Jamie. Polite, but very firm indeed.

Drums? asked O'Toole.

To hell with that, said Scottsboro. They have drummed

us sufficient, and we'll not drum them back.

I saluted.

That's a good manner, to salute, Jamie, said Levy. This is not the end, son.

I went out thinking of what the Jew had said, and I was thinking of it as I repeated to Angus MacGrath the instructions for guarding the encampment.

I want it proper, I told Angus, with a devil of a lot of rigmarole and saluting.

But I chose my ten soldiers for the honor guard out of sheer bitterness, five white and five black, knowing how the officers hated to see a Nayger or a Jew do more than die—or less. Three of the white were Roman, with the Irish thick on their faces as well as their tongues, and the other two were the Gonzales brothers. The black men were big Bantu, none less than six feet tall, big-muscled as well. From here and there, we scraped together the best clothes we could find, and I set the drummer lads to scurrying among the huts to turn up cocked hats, since the scarves and home-made woolen caps we wore were hardly of a soldierly appearance. Katy Waggoner and Jenny Hurst showed up at the command hut of the 11th, where we were, and set to work with needle and thread, sewing on the men as they stood around, self-conscious and grinning; and meanwhile a drummer lad blacked their broken boots and the toes as well, for I considered that in a dim light that might give the appearance of a whole shoe. When they were done up as well as they might be, I formed them in two columns, and we marched smartly across the road to the inn.

* * *

The Hudibras was kept by a Dutchman named Jacob
Hyer. I knew him from the past, a big-bellied middle-aged
man, with a gift for gab and a fund of stories of battles he
had never seen. Like a thousand others from the Jerseys
and Pennsylvania, he had once paraded with some local
folk, and that made him a colonel of militia or something
of the sort, but he was a smart man and a born diplomat,
and he blew the way the wind blew. When the British were
in Princeton, he, like the others, became as loyal to the
crown as a man could be, and the half-dozen barmaids he
employed for other purposes than drawing beer served the
King with all their will and might and main; but when
Continentals marched in, he was a mighty patriot indeed.
But we of the foreign brigades now occupied an uncertain
category in his mind, and when he opened the door for me,
after I had smacked it once or twice with a pistol butt, his
face, usually so pink and pleasant, was dead white and
earnest and apologetic—as he said:

Why now, it's Jamie Stuart, it is, and welcome here to
the Hudibras.

It is indeed, I answered him, and where is the officer
gentry?

Now, Jamie, I always been a good friend to you, and I
never have no trouble in my house. You come in by yourself, huh?

The hell I will. I come in with them—motioning for Gary
to lead the guard in, and standing there as they filed past.

And if there's one little bit of dirty play, Jacob, I added,
I'll ram this pistol up your fat ass.

Jamie, you know me as a good friend . . .

We went into the taproom, and from the blazing hearth,
the smell of roasting pork and lamb, and the fullness of it,

the steam of smoking flip, and the way the wine and the beer and the rum were flowing out of the taps and into the well-padded bellies of well-clad travelers from Tory New York to rebel Philadelphia and back again, you would never know that there was a war and a few thousand men in rags and bare feet trying to fight it. There were tradesmen there, and commission men from the shipping and corn agents and meat speculators and military contractors and subcontractors and overseers from the big holdings and prosperous farmers, and quiet, sharp-eyed men in black broadcloth who asked no questions and answered none, who minded their own business and did it with both sides in lofty impartiality—and there were women serving and having their behinds pinched and giggling; but the giggling stopped and the talking halted and the motion froze as the dozen of us stalked into the room.

They were afraid. How many times in the past had I come into this same inn and walked past the taproom to the kitchen, because officers were here and fine gentlemen in the fine clothes and I was a dirty sergeant of the Line in my patched overalls and my broken shoes? And as I moved through the taproom, close to the wall, no one had even looked up from their roast or beer—since I was something they paid no mind to, only one of the rabble that was foolish enough to carry a musket in the war. They looked up now; they looked up with terror and their chairs scraped and the scraping stopped—and there was silence until a barmaid dropped a pewter mug.

Where are they? I asked Jacob Hyer.

Even the motion of the candle flame seemed to have halted, even the reflection in the copper pots and mugs that lined the walls and the polished pewter trays and pitchers behind the bar.

Now, Jamie, my lad . . . began Jacob Hyer.

God damn it to hell with *Jamie my lad!* Where are they?

Let your boys go into the kitchen and wet their throats, and I'll take you along, Jamie.

Where I go, my men go—and we want none of your stinking brew!

He sighed and shrugged and nodded, and we all went up the staircase, and every eye in the place followed us, but no word was said. We marched up the stairs, the great Bantu Naygers bending their heads to fit themselves to the place, and down the short hall to a door, upon which Jacob Hyer knocked timidly.

Come in, a voice said.

He opened the door and entered, and I followed—Gary behind me, and then the ten men crowding into the room—and there was Wayne with Stewart and Butler, two colonels of the Line and men close to him.

In full uniform, they sat around a small mahogany table. Two candles in silver sticks burned on its polished surface, and a bottle of port stood there too. Each had a partly finished glass which he held and fingered, but the ease of it was too contrived even for the unknowledgeable lad that I was. I realized very certainly that they had been waiting for us impatiently enough, and had only taken up this pose when they heard us downstairs. The gilt was gone off them, and not now and never again would I see in these uneasy gentry even a touch of the greatness that I found resting so simply and softly in my own comrades. So I stood there calmly and deliberately, while the ten men marched into the room and around the table.

Whatever Wayne and Stewart and Butler thought, to see us, they concealed well enough. They looked at me and my men coolly, sipped at their glasses, set them down and flicked their cuffs. They were turned out in buff and blue without a wrinkle or a speck of dust—only a little fall of powder from their wigs onto their collars. Butler and Stewart were florid men, fleshy and healthy and big of head; in my mind, men, as against the lad that I was; well-turned out, well-cared for men who had always enough to eat and drink, always a bed between sheets, always a woman for their assured, commanding manner, always an arrangement to take care of any contingency—except this one. They were not, perhaps, identical with the old-country gentry, but they were very close to it nevertheless, good horsemen who had callused their asses driving over honest men's fields to kill a fox, good drinkers, good eaters, not overconcerned with politics but only with what they liked to call a soldier's task, and seeing nothing at all wrong with lying down in a Tory or patroon house, as long as it was with men of honor that they consorted.

Now they faced no men of honor at all, and they remained stiff and silent as Wayne demanded:

What is all this?

A guard of honor for you, Mr. Wayne—which I said deliberately, the lad in me playing it loose, which was something I paid a fearful and terrible price for, as you will see. Yet I do not know if I could have done it any differently, even if I had known well ahead what the accounting would be. I was a wild and headstrong animal—and not ashamed of that, even now, for the piece of truth that was in us was a firm thing.

Since when do you address me as Mr. Wayne? . . . he

asked—quietly, for all that his voice trembled with anger.

I have no orders to address you otherwise.

And who gives you your orders, Sergeant?

The Committee.

He didn't answer that, although he made to, and I realized that he had swallowed down what he intended to say. He sat in silence, and the two colonels with him were silent too. Now I noticed from the corner of my eye that the landlord still lingered, so I said:

Get to hell out of here, Jacob!

The door closed behind him, and still the three officers sat grimly silent around the table. Anthony Wayne was never a very brilliant man; courage he had, and loyalty to his own lights, but not the rapier mind that belonged to Hamilton and Burr and Reed and some others. His inner conflict was visible to us who watched, and when he spoke again his voice was hoarse and dry.

We will go along with you, Sergeant. We need no guard. Dismiss them.

My orders are that the guard takes you into our lines.

Damn it, Sergeant, he cried, his voice rising, you seem to forget who you speak to!

I have not forgotten.

To hell with you and be damned! We will not walk among you like dirty criminals!

Very well, I shrugged—and started toward the door. But he called me back, as I knew he would.

Wait a minute, Sergeant.

Without turning, I halted. Wayne spoke like a man with a bullet in his lungs.

Are these your orders?

They are. I'm not in the habit of lying, Mr. Wayne.

Very well, he said softly, so softly that I scarcely heard it. I never turned around—and this they remembered well, and for this too I was repaid in their own peculiar coin. The cobbler's apprentice led them out, and the guard formed on either side, and Gary brought up the rear. Into the corridor we went, down the stairs, through the taproom, outside into the night, across the road, through our lines, and up to Nassau Hall—and never a word was spoken.

Angus MacGrath was in command of the guard there. Ten of the citizen-soldiers, their white armbands showing in the night, their bayonets fixed, were lined up on either side the doorway, Angus opened the door, and inside were ten more of the Citizen-soldier Guard, a good, solid show of discipline and strength, a better show than they had ever managed themselves.

It made an impression on them, all right, even as the pickets had made an impression, standing so tight that a rabbit could not crawl through. We brought the three officers into the ruined and desecrated hall and led them over to the long table, where the eleven men of the Committee of Sergeants sat. Three seats had been left in the center of the table, and as we approached Billy Bowzar rose and said:

Will you and your companions be seated here, Mr. Wayne?

I think, sir, answered Wayne, we had better clear up this matter of address before we go further. I demand that we be spoken in our military rank.

Your military rank is in terms of the Line, sir, Bowzar said quietly. We admit you no rank in the Line now. Let me be square and clear about it. We are the Governing

Board of the Pennsylvania Line, and no officer holds a commission here today.

I hold my commission from the Congress, Wayne said.

Is that your feeling?

That is my feeling, Sergeant, answered Wayne, his fists clenched, the knuckles white, his whole body rigidly under control.

Then we'll address you as General Wayne, but we'll give no title to these two men—nodding at Stewart and Butler—who were regimental officers and are no longer. You can take that or leave that, General Wayne.

This time, I had a feeling that they would walk out; but they must have agreed in advance that under any circumstances, they would enter into discussion, and after a moment of silence, Wayne nodded shortly. They removed their hats, opened their coats without removing them, and sat down in the seats Bowzar had indicated, each with his big three-cornered hat in his lap. In their heavy, faced regimentals, wearing epaulettes and dress swords and large powdered wigs, with their ruddy, well-groomed faces, they made a strange contrast to the eleven men of the Committee. It is not only that five years of starvation and exposure will take their toll—a toll had been taken from us long before, and placed against the gentry we were undersized, as well as undernourished—wizened, with gaps where our teeth should have been, and the lasting marks of scurvy and the pox planted well upon us. A wig is a master's thing, for it sits on the head like a great crown, snow-white and beyond the damage of years, making the face and head very imposing indeed—as against little Jack Maloney, or Bowzar, who was five feet and three inches tall, or the Jew Levy who was a tiny, skinny man who could blow away

in a good breath of wind—or as against Lawrence Scottsboro, a wizened gnome of man, or Danny Connell and
O'Toole and the rest; all of us shrunk, except the Nayger
Kabanka; all of us patched—all of us, except the Yankee
Abner Williams, separated from the three officers by a
thousand years of demarcation between the squire and the
crofter, between the merchant lord and the broken-nailed
laborer, between the white master and the black slave, between the English Protestant and the Roman Irish, between
the Christian world and the hated Jew. And we felt it and
they felt it too.

Yet with all that, Bowzar was fine and soft and easy as
he introduced each man in turn.

These are the representatives of the regiments, he ex-
plained. We speak for the men, and every man in this Line
who executes any task or gives any command carries a
warrant from us. So when you speak to us, gentlemen, you
are in a way talking to the whole of the Line, and we can
answer for them too.

During this, I dismissed the guards, telling them to wait
outside, and then threw a few logs of wood on the fire,
which blazed up bright and cheerful—but no real warmth
against the winter wind, which crept into the broken room
from twenty different holes and openings. The table was
well lit with candles in sticks and bottles, but the corners
of the big hall stayed in darkness, and every now and then
one could hear the scurrying of a rat.

Instead of seating myself, I stood at one end of the
table, near the fire; and even with that measure of heat, it
was pleasant enough, and I would find myself becoming
drowsy now and then. For that reason, my memory may
not be too exact on these conversations, but I recall well

the tenor of them, and the picture of Wayne and Butler and Stewart as they sat there will remain with me as long as I live. How different it was from any pictures I have seen of that almost forgotten war!

Billy Bowzar finished speaking and waited—and there was a long silence until Wayne said:

Concerning the uprising and all that has happened in the past three days, I have the power to say this. If you agree to a return of the officers, no soldier will be punished. I give you my word on that.

We rose up against the officers, Billy Bowzar reminded him. Why should we take them back?

Because you are no army without them, Wayne said shortly.

Were we an army with them?

That's neither here nor there.

But it is, said Jack Maloney, because as sure as God, we are an army now.

Looking straight at him, Wayne said, You deserted out of one army, and now out of another.

Damn you, whispered Maloney, I am a truer man to the republic of Pennsylvania than ever you were.

Shut your trap! cried Stewart, and Bowzar broke in, cold as ice:

You come here as our guest, Mister.

You make a great score for yourself, Billy Bowzar.

Yes, and I have made great scores in the past, and paid them too, Mr. Stewart, and if I have to pay for this one, you render the account when the bill is due. Until then, you sit in our house at our table—and however such things are ordered with the gentry, they are ordered decent with us. We did not ask this meeting. We cast you out—every damned one of you—and you beseeched us this meeting. If you cannot sit and talk as gentlemen, then go back to Jacob Hyer's whorehouse!

I had never seen Billy Bowzar like that before—his face dead white against the red hair, every freckle standing sharp and prominent, all of him in a cold, awful anger that had its effect on the Committee as well as on the officers. His nostrils dilated with fury; the muscles bunched all over his square face; and his tiny blue eyes became narrow slits. If a bird pecked in me, it pecked deeper in him, closer to the soul of him that had been scarred by God only knows what. He reached in his pocket and drew out the silver watch that had become the official timepiece of the Line, and laying it on the table before him, he said:

You have one minute, gentlemen, to decide whether you will stay and talk decently—or whether you will go.

And then there was silence, the watch ticking away the seconds in a large and painful silence—louder and louder it seemed, or perhaps only in the memory is it that way; for I have often recalled those seconds and wondered whether our lives and the lives of many others would have been different had Wayne waited through the whole sixty seconds and then left. But that is idle fancy; the matter was a matter of power, and we were the Line and the power— a sullen, proud, angry, aware power that no force on the Continent could challenge, and Wayne was a general without an army, even as Stewart and Butler were regimental commanders without regiments, and all of them had gone through three terrible days—each of them no doubt contemplating a pistol at one time or another and debating a question of blowing out his brains. For the whole fabric of the thirteen states was hinged on the Pennsylvania Line, and whatever the result, they would have to answer; we were the power, and they were, at the moment, only three men alone. So they stayed, and Wayne said:

We will stay and talk.

As you desire, gentlemen . . . Bowzar nodded shortly, and then waited—as we all waited.

Wayne groped with his thoughts; Butler leaned over and whispered to him; Stewart sat stiffly and proudly, the bitterness congealing within him like a souring curd.

Well, said Wayne—well, we must discuss this. I recognize how hard it was for the soldiers in the Line. War is not a gentle practice, but it may be that it was too hard. On the other hand, I have stood for the men: I pleaded for food; I pleaded for clothes; I pleaded for money . . .

His eyes traveled from face to face, but none of us said anything. He placed his three-cornered hat on the table in front of him, as if that was a symbol of concession, but a muscle near his mouth twitched and twitched and his back was like a ramrod. Swallow and chew, I said to myself, as the scene blurred before my eyes and then returned again to focus—swallow and chew, my friend, my general . . . And then I held my own conversation with myself: Ask him for my youth, Bowzar, before you sell me. I am wise in the ways of men who lead; they are all alike, men who lead, and the tears were in my eyes for the woeful, lost hopes of my comrades back in the huts. But, I said to myself, leave them here to discuss, Jamie Stuart, and back to the huts and sound the trumpets, and march off.

Myself—said Butler, speaking for the first time—am in agreement with the general. The patience of the men was tried too sorely, so they rose up and hit out at what they could see, the officers. We are agreed that this is not a criminal matter, but an orderly and peaceful disposition. But under all, there is a fervent faith in my heart, and in the heart of the general and in the heart of each and every one of my fellow regimental commanders, that we and the men are of one mind and one heart concerning the basic principles and program of the Revolution, as set forth in that document we have lived by, the Declaration of Independence.

That we are, answered Bowzar.

Then it is possible that we should make progress.

Ye sit facing the men, said Danny Connell suddenly, which is not a common thing, and every word brings up another matter of reality. Ye make the Declaration a blanket to cover both of us; and we, who are such ignorant clods, by and large, that we cannot write out our own names, nevertheless know that document by heart—which is more learning than the gentry have studied lately. Therein it says, word for word, that when a long train of abuses and usurpations, begun at a distinguished period and pursuing invariably the same object, evinces a design to reduce them under absolute despotism, it is their right, it is their duty, to throw off such government and to provide new guards for their future security. Have I quoted correctly?

We do not deny that the men had certain just grievances, Wayne said.

But you deny that those grievances were in the province of the officers, countered Bowzar.

We have laid aside our pride—said Wayne—to come here and discuss these matters for the common good. If you would lay your grievances before us—

You know our grievances, Billy Bowzar interrupted him.

Look around you here at the leading Committee of the regiments, and see how we are clad and how we are nourished
and how we are provided. Out there in the hutments, the
men are fed and their bellies are full for the first time in
months. Have you fed us? But you fed yourselves. Did you
share what you ate? You clothed yourselves, and we went
naked. Without pay we went, without drink, and our share
was blows—blows until we cringed like a pack of dirty dogs
instead of free soldiers of the republic! And even dogs have
rights, for dogs are loved, and if they get a kick, they get
a caress too; but our lot was unbroken by any consideration, and you abased us until we were worse than any dogs
ever were. And when an officer shot down a man of the
brigades, there was no court-martial for that officer, no
trial, no demand that cause be shown—yet how many of
our own good comrades have been hanged by the neck
because provoked beyond all reason, they struck back?
How many, General Wayne? How many, Mr. Stewart? How
many, Mr. Butler?

The three officers looked at him, their handsome, ruddy
faces controlled now, their anger stowed in the proper
compartment, wherefrom it would be taken at the proper
moment. This bitterness, this recitation of grievance—this
was familiar and common and a part of their memory since
the war began. This they could handle. This was different
from the snarling, defiant anger of before. This was the
beginning of something—and this I knew, and I wondered
whether the others of the Committee knew it as well.

There is the matter of enlistments, Dwight Carpenter
was saying. A man who has made his mark for three years,
and served five—he said—is kept like a slave for his lack
of reading . . .

*   *   *

But I was no longer listening. It was the end and over, and two days of glory had finished. We had marched through the Jerseys and become something noble if brief, but now it was something else again. They went on talking, and I dozed, and some I heard and more I did not hear, but watched the fire and dozed and dreamed of how in my childhood in the warm summertime—so I had been told—I played in the little creek that ran by the house where my mother once served.

I played there because sometimes they gave me a sweet or some cold crust off the roast of the day before, for I was "the little one of Annie Stuart," and what a good, loyal servant she had been, not like those born and bred in Pennsylvania, who knew not their own place and standing!

Sick as my mother was after carrying me, with the seed of death planted inside her and planted to stay and take its toll in two short years after my birth, she nevertheless had gone each day to the house of Elder Simpkins, who was toll agent on all the roads through town and clerk as well, to do the service that his strong wife and his four strong daughters could not do, for they aspired to be quality as the fine ladies in Philadelphia were. All day, day in and day out, she had labored there, and her pay for a day's work was fourpence—fourpence for the price of a life!

So there I was allowed to play after she had paid her full price of one life for fourpence a day, and I was too much of a babe to even think of what was right and what was wrong, but knew only that there was a bit of a sweet or a crust of meat to be had for the memory of the strong Scottish lass who had served them.

One has a debt, said the wife of Elder Simpkins, later

on, for me to hear—loyal folk they were, and humane too. Poor lad—she said with such sympathy—poor lad!

Let the poor lad play, he feels safe here, she said ... One doesn't find girls these days such as his mother was; for now they're born and bred in the Pennsylvania land; they are spoiled, that they are, and not like the ones who had tasted a bond—they were the grateful ones.

You are grateful for charity, Jamie Stuart, she said to me, and the good Lord rewards those who are.

I am indeed, said I, *whose mother was a girl when she died, and a fine, strong worker ...*

And then back to today I came, and the hall in the college at Princeton and the fire and the fine figures of the bewigged officers. They were finishing their conversations now. I shook sleep off me; I listened to the Committee.

They agreed to meet with these three gentry the following noon, and then my guard and I marched Wayne, Butler and Stewart back across the road to the tavern ...

Early the next morning, I found Jack Maloney and Danny Connell, as they were going from hut to hut, talking with the men; and when I would have passed them, Connell called out:

How there, Jamie Stuart of the black puss and sour heart—what in hell eats you that you give me a look to make me stomach crawl?

When an Irishman betrays me, do you want me to lick his God-damned ass?

It's mighty quick that ye are for learning the Irish language, said Connell, but it is not myself that has betrayed you, and if ye want to take off that dirty jacket of yours and fight on it, why I am as willing as a lad could be.

I will not fight with a miserable, undersized Hooley that I could break in two with one hand.

Because ye lack the guts.

I said some words that are best not recalled, and Jack Maloney demanded:

What in God's name is eating you, Jamie?

This, your honor—the sweet pledges of the officers and the sweet pledges of the Committee. That's a start, and I can see damned well what the end will be; but I swear to God, I will never go back to be a slave under those dirty dogs, and give my life sooner or later, so that they can preserve their gentry apart from the British gentry, instead of together with it. For that is all this matter comes down to.

How do you see that, Jamie? asked Maloney.

There are two thousand, six hundred and odd men here in this camp today, and they have followed after the Committee for only one reason, not for a bellyful of food and a swig of rum and a dollar in their pockets—but because they are proud and because they would be free. A different kind of pride from what the gentry has, and a better kind for my money.

And where shall we lead them, Jamie?

Into hell, if need be. Into hell and be damned! But not into polite "Our grievances are this and that, and if you satisfy them we will come back and beg you to lead us once more."

Danny Connell was watching me. I hold with Jamie, he said.

Oh, you would, said Jack Maloney. Oh, Christ, you would—my fine lads—for you are both good for a fight, where there is no more sense needed than to pull a trigger. But what shall we do? That is the heart and core of it— what *shall* we do? By now, without question, every body of soldiers under Congress is marching here toward the Line. Shall we fight them all?

No soldiers will ever fight the Line—unless you speak of British troops. I swear to that!

Shall we proclaim "the Republic of the Pennsylvania Line"? Shall we execute the three officers? Shall we march into Philadelphia and imprison the Congress? In the name of God, Jamie, what *are* we to do, now that the Line will follow us? Where? Where? Whatever kind of strange dreams you have, the world has not yet made them real. There is no other way than to come to terms with the gentry . . .

His voice rose now; pitched up and woeful, he cried: For withal it is a bloody Revolution, this is their war! A little crust of the bread is for us, but the slice is theirs, Jamie, and God help us, there is nothing we can do but come to an agreement with them.

I would rather die.

Maybe I would rather die, too, Jamie—but the men of the Line are extremely practical, and they have chosen us, and we will lead them. They have no intentions of dying. They, at least, have certain practical demands for pay and clothes and discharge, and every trust they put in leaders before was betrayed. Shall we betray them too, Jamie?

What else are you doing?

You thank God I love you, Jamie Stuart, and know you well too, or I'd cut your heart out. The devil with you!

And he went his way—and I went mine.

*   *   *

But that afternoon, after their hours of talk with Wayne and Butler and Stewart, the sergeants called me in, and this they said to me:

You take over Princeton, Jamie—every inch and corner of it, and make it secure so that a mouse couldn't creep in.

The taverns?

Yes, the taverns, Jamie, and all the rest; but be easy and gentle with the townsfolk.

Then Billy Bowzar motioned to a bearded, mud-stained man who stood close to the fire, warming himself.

This . . . he said . . . is Sergeant Dekkerholts of the 2nd Regiment of the Jersey Line. They have been ordered . . . he said, his voice becoming flat and toneless . . . to march against us. But they will not march against us, he said—Is that so, Sergeant?

They will not, said Dekkerholts. They will not shed your blood.

He turned around from the fire, a small, flaxen-haired, travel-stained and travel-weary man, his beard long and full, his overalls rent and patched, his feet bound in canvas instead of leather. He looked at me, and then he looked at the sergeants of the Committee, as if he had not seen them before, and then he looked at me again out of his large, bloodshot blue eyes, and he said:

Who in hell are you?

I am Jamie Stuart, and responsible for the safety of the encampment.

I told you they will not attack you, the Jersey men, he said, sullenly and somewhat sadly, for they are going to rise up and cast out the gentry, just as you did—just as you did. And now I want to go to sleep.

And with that, he sat down in front of the fire, his knees

drawn up, his arms around them and his head pillowed upon them. I stood there, looking from face to face—and sad, troubled faces they were—until Billy Bowzar reminded me:

You know what you must do, Jamie. I put little stock in what he says, since he has walked too much and slept too little. We also have information that the Light Horse Troop is riding up from Philadelphia to join the officers. So get on.

And if the Jersey Line rose, what is the Committee prepared to do?

We don't know that they rose, Jamie—only that they are intended to do so. We will see. . . .

We will see, I nodded—and I went out, happy at least that I had work of my own that I understood; I found Angus, and together we worked out our plans.

But before I go into that, I must say just a little of the encampment at Princeton, where we now spent a week of our lives. Not that it was a perfect achievement, or any sort of a dreamlike place. Men deserted; men ran away because they could not face the terror of what we had done; men got drunk and men whored: but these were the exception, and by and large, in those seven days, we established a working, cooperative means of living together. In the very first day, we cleaned out the upper floors of Nassau Hall, and established there both a hospital and a school. Two women and three men were found among the regiments who were equipped, some better, some worse, for teaching—and the children of the Line, almost a hundred in number, from the little babes to the twelve- and thirteen-year-old drummer lads, were put to letters; which was a great wonder in an army where not one in twenty could write his own name. More curious still, those classes for the children—short-lived as they were—were packed always with soldiers too, for we had a hunger for some sort of dignity and learning that was almost as great as our hunger for food. Having neither paper nor ink nor crayon, we made slates out of board and burned and shaped our own charcoal. We had no books, but, for the time we were there, the small knowledge in our heads was sufficient, just as what crude medical remedies we owned had to be sufficient for our hospital. There was a wonderful inventiveness and facility in the Line; every trade was among us, and there was nothing we could not make if given a little time and a minimum of tools and goods—candles, rope, cloth, furniture, shoes; yes, and we would have made paper and a press to print books and a newspaper, if it had not all finished so soon.

Maybe there was much more that we would have made—for word that the Jersey Line would rise stirred a brief vision in me of a new kind of republic that might come out of this long and sorrowful war; but, like other dreams I had then when I was young and strong and filled with my own power, this one is unfinished and befogged with all the years that have passed since then. I tell myself sometimes that now I know better what we could have done; yet when I listen to the same, half-formed dreams on the lips of the Abolitionists—of the young Yankee men who will sweep the whole world with their banner of freedom for all—I am none too certain. I see the thread that ties things together, but where it began and where it will end I do not know.

There was a Roman priest who came into our encampment at Princeton, a little, round-faced Irish man, who was bitterly poor and much despised, as the Romans were in our land then, and who had walked all the way up from Philadelphia when he heard that the foreign brigades had made a rising. Dusty, dirty and cold, his black clothes worn paper-thin, his wide-brimmed, flat-topped hat perched comically on the top of his head, he was brought into our lines and brought to me, and I asked him what he wanted of us and why he had come.

Sure, he answered, when I heard that the Irish men were in a rising with all sorts of low company, Jews and Naygers and Protestants too, I said to myself, I will go up and share their enterprise and perhaps soften it somewhat.

Because he seemed cheerful, and because our hopes were low and morbid then, I told him:

It will as likely be a hanging as anything else, and if the gentry make a start, I assure you they will hang the Roman priest first.

Then I will not be the first Roman priest was hanged by gentry, he grinned.

To which I answered that it was certainly an odd attitude for a man of God to have, since with the rising every pastor had cleared out except William Rogers, who was not properly a Christian but a Baptist or something of the sort. The rest held that resistance, revolution and such were not becoming to a low type of man unless he was led and instructed by a high type of man.

But among the Irish, said the priest, we have had a lot of resistance, yet surprisingly few of the latter type. Myself, I will stay if you don't mind and if you can trust me. It seems to me that, while I cannot predict where this business of yours will end, I have an inkling of where it began....

*   *   *

I tell this in the way of threads, but I wander from the main tale of how we took Princeton city and made it an armed camp. I pause only to tell you that we did many things in those few days of our new army that are forgotten, and they were things that were good, not only the schools, but discussions in the hutments on such documents as the Declaration of Independence and *Common Sense*, the fine book of Mr. Paine, and we also framed out certain propositions on the rights of all men to speak freely and to assemble and to petition—things that were fanciful then but which came about later, with much additional suffering, in the time of Tom Jefferson. We also made common teams for the sewing of cloth and even for the weaving of it, and for this latter we made looms, although they were never put to use. We put new roofs on the huts and we repaired the bitter damage that the enemy had done to Nassau Hall. So much for that, and more later, but now for how Angus and I turned over Princeton and put it in condition for defense.

There was the town, with the pike running into it across the brook and the gully, so that we were enabled to have the bridge at one end for a boundary and the crossroads at another. We threw a regiment—as we planned it—to the north and another to the south. A regiment could cover the brook, beyond the meadows, and two more regiments could ring the town and block off the two stem roads. This would be a matter of five regiments, leaving five in reserve and one for relief and mobility, and with a light breastworks and concentrations on lanes and footpaths, a cannon at each cross-lane and another at the brook and at the bridge—why, it seemed to me that the little place could be held until Doomsday.

It was a fine feeling for me, to have a plan of defense in my own hands, after five years of running, leaping, crawling and scurrying to the plans of the officers; and there was more of that satisfaction when Angus protested that *they* would have done it differently.

I looked up from the paper on which I was sketching and answered:

To me, that is a commendation, and nothing else.

But ye have but one man to twenty feet of ground, and no corrie for them to crawl into!

And I want none. And if I had ten men to twenty feet of ground, it would be a thin defense, but the one man is a cleg, and he stings a little while we throw the five regiments where we will. And if we know a little sooner, there is our one regiment of mobility to nibble a bit, while we come at the flanks. We are sick with warfare where one puts up a breastwork and cowers behind it.

... In any case, I added from my heart, there is only one body of Continentals in all this land that will come at us—from my heart I know that and surely—and I say that is the Light Horse.

Ye would fire on the Light Horse, Jamie?

On any man that crosses our lines without our will.

God help us if that should be, Jamie.

Something else will be if the Jersey troops come to join us—for something pecks in the Connecticuts and others too, and maybe for once the men who fight for their freedom will win it too.

* * *

So we called out the soldiers to dispose them. We sounded the trumpets and had the brigades parade, the ten infantry regiments and the artillery, and we formed them up four square to hear the orders. Jack Maloney and Jim Holt joined me, representing the Committee, and they stood with me in the center of the square and listened as I read the plan. When that was finished, before we disposed ourselves, the whole Committee came and we had an inspection parade. We made a fine, proud, handsome square, and if we were not uniform, we were clean-shaven and we carried well.

We dressed like British show troops, and our bayonets were gleaming and rustless, and every man was smooth of face and sharp of spine, and the forty drummer lads stood across the corners of the big square, ten at each point, beating to dress. Every regiment had repaired its faded and tattered banners, and many regiments—because this habit like so many others had fallen into disuse from neglect—set to work to sew the banners they had not carried since '77, so that now the 1st carried its segmented rattlesnake, the 2nd its clenched fist, the 3rd its wolf's head, the 4th its depiction of Romulus and Remus nursing at the wolf's udder, and so forth and so on—while at each side a color guard of the Citizen-soldier Guard bore the Stars and Stripes. Our cobblers had been busy with every scrap of leather we could turn up, and there was not a man in the Line that day who was not shod with a piece of leather on his soles, even if the uppers were sewn from tent canvas. Overalls were sewn and patched and made presentable, so if you had looked at us from the road, as the townspeople did, crowding there to see our display, you could well have said that this was the prettiest, neatest, trimmest body of fighting men that had ever marched among the Continentals.

The artillery had formed inside the square, where every man could look at the six cannons, four of bronze, two of iron, all shining; and by every gun, stiff and proudly self-conscious that they served cannon which had never been left on a routed field—cannon which had been fought since the first engagement outside of Boston in '75—stood two gunners, two layers, two caddies and two plungers, while behind them were sixty buckskin men from Fincastle, not standing to arms-parade as were the regiments, but leaning on their long, six-foot, snakelike Pennsylvania rifles, dressed in smock and shawl, with a powder horn and a bag of shot girding every hip—these the only riflemen in the entire Line, and snipers for the artillery.

The women and children stood outside the square, some clapping to the drums, some weeping to see what a proud and strong thing we were with every man standing to his place with only a whisper or a word from sergeant or corporal; and indeed I could have wept myself to look at them, and I would have given all the years of my young manhood to march them on York city where the Enemy was and show the British how men could fight when they fought for themselves, for their own soil and their own dreams.

But the evening was coming on now, with its snapping cold wind to chill the unseasonable warmth of the day. The sun dipped down to the trees, leaving a dazzling warp of pink and purple, and there was much to be done. I threw a look at the Committee, where they stood alongside the cannon, all grouped together, their faces filled with pride and sadness and wonder and joy and bereavement, all of it mixed and struggling with the past and the future, the knowable and the unknowable, the victory and the defeat; and then I shouted:

Brigades to station!

And the regiments marched away to take their places. I checked with one and another as they left, put the Gary brothers on horse and set them to checking over the perimeter and establishing the easy contact of all the regiments, sent Angus to the inn called Sign of the College, to empty it and close it down, and then took twenty of the Citizen-soldier Guard with me to Jacob Hyer's inn.

It would be a lie to say that I did not relish the job. What would you have of a lad who was twenty-two years old and had known nothing but camp and march and battle in all of his precious youth, so that all the softness within had to be compensated for by a hardening of the shell? Hard we were, and I was a little harder than most, as you will see, hard at the beginning and hard at the end too, God help me.

But now it was still a long time from the end, and I led my men over to the inn, kicked open the door, and had them file into the taproom with bayonets fixed and the winter wind sloshing behind them. Oh, there was good business in the tavern, all right, for the rising of the Line had provoked a great buying and selling, and the commission merchants and the dirty and indifferent traders—who owed allegiance to the hard dollar and the pound sterling and to nothing else—were scurrying over the road between York city and Philadelphia like rabbits, buying low and selling high, spreading every filthy rumor they could concoct, buying what they did not own and selling it before they ever had it, dealing in uniforms unworn, shoes we never saw, food we never ate, guns we never handled, munitions we never shot and bodies not yet dead. They were all there as I have told you, packed in with the warmth and the smell of roasting meat and smoking rum, and I relished what I did, believe me.

What now, Jamie, what now? Jacob Hyer squealed, spreading his arms against me and pressing his great paunch to me as my men crowded into the room. Haven't I been a good friend to the Line? Haven't I sent, noon and night, a gallon of hot flip to the Committee? Didn't I roast up in my kitchen, special, a chicken pie and a hasty pudding? What now, Jamie? Is an honest man not to do his business undisturbed? Is that a way to have folk think of the Line, that you torment an honest citizen?

You're as honest as Judas Iscariot, I said, and if the truth were known, what a dirty spy's nest you operate here!

Not so, Jamie! You got no right to blacken my character. I'm a legal-commissioned colonel of militia, and as ready to serve—

To hell with all that! I interrupted him. I will not touch a penny you own or a stinking cut of beef from your racks, but the whole town is now within the perimeter of the Line and under the government of the Line, and I want every transient person out of here in ten minutes and out of Princeton too.

You mean my custom?

Precisely what I mean.

His face turned white, and then as the blood returned, suffused with an angry blush. I had spoken up and loud, and every person in that packed and silent room heard my words. Then a babel of sound commenced, led by the land-lord himself.

You got no right ... no justice, no right, no warrant! ... I will not submit to this! ... Here I stand, and my house is my castle! ... I will lay down my life first ... Here I stand, and you go no further into this, Jamie Stuart! You fat, foisonless man, I said, you shut your mouth, or I will drive a bayonet up your butt and pin yer tongue with it. What a cackle you make! And look at this room here, you damned bugger—look at this collection of scavenging crows! Look at them and you would never know that this is a country at war and that one or another has taken sides and that there's no inch of Jersey soil without a drop of American blood on it! What are they doing, traveling the roads between York city and Philadelphia? Honest work?

At this moment, Wayne with Butler and Stewart behind him appeared at the foot of the staircase. Wayne didn't come forward into the room, but remained there on the stairs for the moment, listening to me and watching, his long, thin cold face composed and emotionless. But some of the guests had risen while I spoke, and now one of them, a lean, middle-aged man with side-whiskers and a mustache and dark, calculating eyes, came over to us and interposed:

Son, how old are you?

Twenty-two winters if it is any of your damned business.

That's a harsh way of speech, my lad, and harsher for your elders. Don't you think it's a little foolish to drive us out of here this winter night? Will that bring you friends? There are many men in this room who would make good friends to you, for they are men of influence and instruction, and it would be better for you to befriend them. Now suppose you sit down at our table and have a glass of grog on this. Hot words and hot heads never accomplished anything constructive.

What do you do? I said. What do you do that you grace this world so?

I buy and I sell, he answered, which is as honest a way as I know.

What do you buy and sell? I roared at him, grasping his cravat and pulling him up to me. Do you traffic in men's lives and men's souls? What is north of here for an honest man to buy and sell? Do you sell a little information to the British enemy? Do you buy the dollars the people have, to make them more worthless than they are? Och, I could spit on all your sweet-tongued kind. Get out of my sight! And I hurled him from me, so that he went down and rolled over, crashing against a table and then crawling on his hands and knees to be out of harm's way. But Jacob went wild, gabbling and gabbling, running first at me and then to the stairs where he began to plead with Wayne. But Wayne shook him off and pushed him away and brushed the sleeve of his uniform where Hyer had touched it.

All of you! I shouted. Get your goods and be out of this inn in ten minutes! Ten minutes, or a bayonet will prick a little haste into you!

Help them along, I told my men—while the landlord was pleading with Wayne:

Will you let this be? Is no law and order left? Is an honest man to be robbed of his custom?

Standing there at the foot of the steps, Wayne listened to the landlord without particular emotion or interest, and he might have been hearing a dog bark for all the effect it seemed to have on him. When the landlord moved to touch him, he shook him off—and then, as the press of the people mounted the stairs, he and the two colonels stepped into the taproom and to one side, from where Wayne watched me curiously.

And out of the village! I shouted after them. Every one of you out of the village. If you came by horse, saddle up and get out. If you came by stage, walk out.

Jacob Hyer stopped gibbering, stared at Wayne for a moment, and then walked weakly over to the bar and leaned against it. But then he recalled that customers were leaving without paying their score, and prudence overcame grief as he dashed past me and outside, calling them to pay up. Meanwhile, Wayne sauntered over to me, followed by Butler and Stewart.

What does all this mean, Sergeant? he asked.

It means that we are placing the whole village inside our lines, and that anyone who doesn't live here is to get out.

Why?

I don't know why. I am given orders and I carry them out.

I think you know why, Sergeant. You're making a hard score for yourself, and, as you may have heard, I have a long memory.

That's just as it may be, General Wayne, and if you want to know more I'll take you over to the Committee of Sergeants and you can ask them.

I can wait. I'm a patient man.

As I am also. . . . And then I started to turn away, but he caught my sleeve and said:

Does that order about nonresidents apply to myself and Colonels Stewart and Butler?

It does not apply to yourself and Mr. Stewart and Mr. Butler. Yourself and Mr. Stewart and Mr. Butler can stay here, General, if you wish, or you can go out of our lines or you can go over to Nassau Hall—or do anything you damn please except talk to the men. I will leave six of these men of mine here at the inn, but they are only to see that you can go where you want to go safely, and as for talking to the men—well, you can do whatever talking you have to do to me or to the Committee. That's the way it is.

So that's the way it is, Sergeant.

Yes, sir.

And the news I am expecting from Philadelphia?

Who is bringing it?

The Marquis de Lafayette or General St. Clair or both, with Colonel Laurens, said Wayne—holding onto his temper remarkably well, which was something for him, since he was as hot-tempered as he was arrogant.

When they arrive, I will let you know.

You will not conduct them here?

I will not take them or anyone else into our lines until I have orders to do so.

Said Wayne to that, looking me up and down: We have an old saying, Sergeant, that if you would skip a jig, you must pay off the fiddlers.

Or, among the Scots, I grinned, that he who dances must pay the piper. But the hell with that, with the dancing I've seen these five years, and many a lad who had no ground under his feet when he danced and no breath for song, either. But I must say, General, I added, that we are a sober folk with the gentry, for when you cracked the whip, you were never one half so gentle with us.

We cracked it lawfully, whispered Wayne, and not for a God-damned cursed mutiny.

Ye have always had the making of the law, haven't you, General?

And will have it again, Jamie Stuart.

Then if you know my name, I said, and I didn't think you knew the name of any of the dirt you led, call me when you want something.

Then I turned away and told off the men for the inn. I put Aaron Gonzales over them, who was a lad with a level head, and I told him that if one dram of spirits was touched, I'd see that a court-martial took place. I was burning with anger—for no matter what I said, there was that cold, thin, assured face of Wayne to tell me who would have the last lick—and he knew that I meant what I said. Then I took the rest of my men and went out of the damned place, with Hyer plucking at my coattails and pleading his cause.

Let go, you scut! I threw at him, and marched off past the raging ousted guests up the road to the bridge. The men had done their work well, but such was my mood that I found grounds for complaint wherever I went. The cannon at the bridge was at the further instead of the nearer end; the barrier of logs and branches across the road was not filled in with dirt; the opening was too wide. At the side roads I swore because the men had crowded the roads instead of picketing the fields, and at the Philadelphia direction, there was a little knot of town girls, joshing the men as they made bastions and built match fires.

What are ye? I cried. Is this some damned militia picnic?

And when Button Lash, the sergeant in charge and the first man ever to enlist in the 1st Regiment of the Pennsylvania Line, blinded in one eye with grape at White Plains, without toes from the freezing winters, and sometimes addled in his head with all the woe he had seen, but gentle and dearly loved by all of us, said to me, Ah, Jamie—Jamie, my lad, ye have no call to wallop these boys for taking a word with a maid. They are good lads and working truly . . . I was sick and sore and speechless and did the rest of my rounds in silence.

Then I went past Nassau Hall where the Committee still burned light, found my hutment, pulled off my boots and crawled into bed, overalls and all. I was sick at heart and knotted in the belly and bruised inside with loneliness and frustration and hopelessness—and for that I slept poorly, tossing and turning and dreaming dreadful dreams of my childhood, dreams in which I stood naked in the midst of a circle of bearded, kilted gillies such as my father had told me of, and while an unseen arm whipped me they chanted, *Caper, Jamie, caper, for this is your lot and it will not be otherwise.*

Sweating and grateful, I awoke to someone's whisper and a hand on my shoulder, and there was Willie Hunt, unseen in the darkness but his voice specific enough telling me:

Jamie—Jamie, wake up, for we got some passing strange fish in our net and we don't know what in hell to do with them.

What time is it?

Onto morning, Jamie, but this is a dirty catch and the men will not wait.

Coughing, my stomach all sour and heaving, I crawled from the straw bolster and pulled on my boots and struggled into my coat, and then felt my way out after Willie Hunt. Onto morning it might have been, but there was no sign of that in the starless sky, which was as black as pitch. Benny Clapper from the 2nd was waiting for us with a lit brand, and in the light it cast we followed him over to the bridge. As we walked over there, I asked Willie Hunt:

How did you get into this?

I could not sleep, Jamie, so I stretched my legs over to the bridge, where I thought maybe I could pry a little tobacco out of the lads. And there I am, warming by the fire and gossiping with them to pass the time, when out of the night come these two very strange birds.

What are they?

Wait and you'll see, Jamie. You'll see.

We were at the bridge now, and there, behind the barricade in a circle of men, were two well-dressed but nervous gentlemen, one long, one short, both cloaked in black and wearing fine felted hats. Outside the circle and to one side, another of our lads held their horses, and in spite of the cold of that early winter morning, the two of them were sweating.

Here is Jamie Stuart, someone said, and the circle opened up to let me in; but the two strangers said nothing, only eyeing me nervously and speculatively.

Who are you and what do you want? I demanded.

We want to speak to the authority of the mutiny.

What mutiny?

The mutiny of the Pennsylvania Line.

Who in hell said there was a mutiny?

That is the intelligence we have.

And who in hell is *we?*

Who are you, sir? demanded the taller one suddenly. Who are these men? What security have we that these are Pennsylvania men?

That's the kind of dirty culls they are, Jamie, said Benny Clapper, and they got the white mark of Tory on them, I swear. They been standing here and talking in circles these twenty minutes now. And you know what I say they are? I say they're dirty damned spies, and we ought to string them up on a handy branch and have done with it.

Now that's a hasty opinion to come to, said the smaller man, licking his lips, his eyes darting from face to face. A hasty way of dealing with honest men. Are you the Pennsylvanians?

We are, I nodded.

We must see your commander. We must speak with him.

Now look at them, Jamie, said Michael Omalley. Me eyes have not seen two more honest men.

What do you want with our commander? I asked.

We have a message for him, a most confidential message, an exceedingly confidential message.

Message from where?

That is our intelligence, said the taller man hoarsely. We are honor bound to reveal that only to your commander. To no one else. I am sorry, sir.

All right, I said. All right—

And when they all began to talk, I cried, Shut up—the lot of you. I'll take them to the Committee. Benny and Willie, come along with me. The rest of you mind that road and stop the damned gabble. A fine lot of talkative soldiers you are!

But our horses, sir . . . the tall one began.

Leave your horses where they are. Do you expect to ride through the village at this hour of darkness like a bloody Paul Revere? If you're as honest as you testify, you'll have your horses soon enough.

And with that, we marched these two uneasy gentry down the road to Nassau Hall. By now, the night was breaking, the pitch-black giving way to murky gray, the houses emerging like ghosts from the darkness. The little town had that ultimate quiet that a place has in those very early hours, and the sentries in front of Nassau Hall were haggard and weary, their eyes full of the mysterious weight of the nighttime.

What's up, Jamie? they asked. What's up?

I must wake the Committee.

They bedded down late, Jamie, right there on the floor by the table, and it's only God's mercy to leave them alone.

I haven't much mercy lately, and here are two queer birds who can't wait. I'm thinking this is important enough.

All right, Jamie, go on in.

So we went in, with our two strangers and our torches, and woke up the Committee where they lay, stretched out on their blankets on the floor. It was a shame, a burning shame to wake men who slept so tiredly, such a sleep that it was like the sleep of the dead; but there was something about those two black-cloaked messengers that made my skin crawl, and I wanted none of them on my own. We lighted the candles on the table, and once again that queer, singular, almost worshipful feeling about the Committee of Sergeants came over me; for waked as they were now, at this unholy hour, with the splutter of torches in their faces,

they were nevertheless patient with a patience beyond belief and listened gravely to my tale.

Very well, said Billy Bowzar when I had finished, we
are the Committee which is entrusted with supreme command over the Pennsylvania Line, but we will have no
dealings with you, sirs, unless we know who you are and
from whence you come. And when you say this, you say
it with no restrictions—otherwise go now. This is a military
encampment of a Continental Army, and within our own
lines, this Committee is the court of law with all powers of
martial enforcement. Also, our law is not the law you
might be accustomed to, for we make our law to enforce
what we believe to be right and just. I say this to offer you
due warning.

I think we can do business, sir, said the taller man, so
I am ready to accept your conditions. You have been waked
out of your sleep and we have gone without ours, so I will
get to the point quickly and without further ado. My name
is Mason and this is James Ogden, and we come as emis-
saries from Sir Henry Clinton in His Majesty's loyal city of
New York. From the Commander in Chief of His Majesty's
forces, we bring greetings and good cheer—and it is our
good fortune to be the first to do so. We also bring a message of historic importance, which I will deliver into your
own hand.

Roughly and as well as I can remember, the foregoing
is what Mason said. He was not an imaginative man, and
he appeared unaware as he spoke of how stony and set the
faces of the sergeants became. Almost cheerfully now, he
took off his shoe, raised the inner sole, and extracted a
piece of lead foil. Then, with the same precise motion, he
put on the shoe again, unfolded the foil, and took out a

small piece of thin paper, laying the foil on the table and handing the paper to Bowzar, and still no one spoke.

Billy Bowzar read it. The writing was exceedingly small and cramped, and Bowzar had to hold it to a candle to read it, and then he passed it to another. Softly, Levy read it aloud for those who had not the learning, and it was short, direct, and to the effect that when the Pennsylvania men entered into accord with His Majesty's government, each soldier would receive a bonus of twenty British pounds, while each corporal would receive thirty and each sergeant fifty. All former deserters from the British Army would receive full and unconditional pardon. All men who desired to enlist would be welcomed. Those who did not could claim transportation to the West Indies, where they would be given land.

Finished, Bowzar looked from face to face. Jack Maloney said, I was once George's man, even more recently than Scottsboro, so let me say this. I say we should hang them now, before the sun rises.

They are dirty spies and dirty traitors, said Scottsboro. I say hang them.

I know what you feel, said Bowzar slowly and thoughtfully. They have robbed us of something. Just in coming here, they have robbed us and dirtied us . . .

We came in good faith, Mason began.

Be quiet, be quiet—Bowzar said quietly, but so coldly!— Be quiet. You did an awful thing when you came into our line. These are the Pennsylvania brigades—the foreign brigades. Do you know what that means? Do you know what kind of a trust we carry? I know you are just a little dog for a big dog, but how did you dare to come to us—who have lived and died these five years for man's freedom—with a tyrant's offer?

While he spoke, Bowzar had folded the message, and now he was wrapping it in the lead foil again.

That was a terrible thing to do, said Bowzar. We will give you to General Wayne, and that way maybe wipe some of the dirt off. There is no other way but that, he said, turning to the Committee. Do you agree?

One by one, they nodded.

Ogden began to plead. He fell down on his knees in front of the table, crying as he pleaded. That he was a family man, he said. He had been paid for this. A man does a job that he is paid for. He emptied his pockets and the coins rolled this way and that way across the floor. Do you kill a man who comes to you in good faith? Turn him over to the officers . . . Hadn't they revolted against the officers? What kind of insanity was that? At least forget it—forget it and let them go. Let the whole thing be forgotten, as if it had never happened . . .

But Mason said never a word, for finally he realized what this Committee was, and the knowledge of the foreign brigades came to him, even if it came too late.

Take them to Wayne, Jamie, said Billy Bowzar.

We prodded them out of the room, Ogden stumbling so that he could hardly walk. Outside, I picked up the sentries for a guard, and we went across the road to the inn. It was dawn now, a cold and cloudy winter morning, and when I rapped on the tavern door, Gonzales opened it to me.

We herded Ogden and Mason in, and I told Gonzales: Wake up Wayne and tell him I must see him here immediately.

He won't like that, said Gonzales uneasily.

The hell with what he likes!

So Gonzales went upstairs, and we stood in that cold and sour-smelling taproom and waited. Jacob Hyer came in while we stood there, but when he saw my face, he said nothing but went about building up the fire in the hearth. One of his women came in rubbing her eyes, a big woolen wrapper coiled around her. Morning, Sergeant Jamie, she said, to which I answered surlily, Go to the devil and begone. Then Gonzales came back with the officers.

They had pulled on their boots and thrown their greatcoats over their nightshirts. With the sleep still in their eyes, without their big white wigs, they were less formidable and less proud, closer to life and closer to death. Death was around. That big, cold, sour room smelled of death that morning.

What does this mean, Sergeant? said Wayne.

Absorbed in himself, he was, but the other two saw Mason and Ogden, and they knew what it meant. I gave Wayne the piece of lead foil, and he opened it and read what was written on the paper. He passed it to Butler and Stewart.

When did it arrive? he asked finally.

A few hours ago.

With these two swine?

With them, I nodded.

White and quiet, they stood there, quiet and dreadful and hopeless—and it ran through my mind what an awful, monstrous thing war is, but more awful than anything the war where men strike for freedom—for there is no forgiveness, not by the masters and not by the slaves; and I knew more than that: I knew with deep finality that my dreams—wherein this kind of hatred and cruel practice would be no more—were not for accomplishment in my time or my children's time, and I knew what it was to be of a Committee of Sergeants which led men into a future that wasn't. Hate went out of me, and I was only tired and forlorn and young, thinking that there are always strange men like myself—and a little of the strangeness in Wayne too—who must chew the bitter cud of freedom and find some nourishment in it. The fruit was not ripe, but it was our sustenance, our only sustenance.

What are you going to do with them? Wayne asked.

What are you going to do with them is more to the point, I said. They are a gift from the Committee to you. Take them and be damned.

And I turned around and walked out.

PART EIGHT

Wherein I tell of the fate of the two spies, and certain
details concerning the Philadelphia Light Horse Troop
and the New Jersey Line.

WHAT WAYNE THOUGHT, I did not care, for I had no desire to be an honest or loyal man according to his lights. Later that morning, he wrote a note to the Committee, in which he used a good deal of fulsome language and said that his heart had been warmed and reassured by this deed of honor, and he also pledged, in the name of the Congress, an award of fifty gold guineas to each of the sergeants involved in the capture of Ogden and Mason. There was a price on the blood of two miserable wretches, and fifty gold guineas, which made more thousands of Continental dollars than you could count, was the kind of money that no soldier of the Line ever hoped to have, even in his wildest dreams. There I was, a rich man, and Benny Clapper too—but we talked it over and threw the offer back in Wayne's face; and there's the answer for those scholarly historians who have been so hard-pressed to comprehend how two such dirty and mean articles as ourselves could turn away a fortune in terms of gentlemen's honor. Well, we were not gentlemen and it was not gentlemen's honor, and nothing is paid for but something is bought. We didn't like that kind of deal, and when Benny Clapper and I had talked about it for fifteen minutes, we agreed that Bowzar should tell Wayne and the rest of them to take their dirty blood money and use it elsewhere. For myself, Jamie Stuart, this was not so hard, because I had neither kith nor kin and no lien on tomorrow, but was a wild and headstrong lad; but Benny Clapper had three kids and a wife in Bristol, and when the gentry boasted to Congress over the hundred guineas they had saved, they were by no means able to comprehend what it meant to a family man to give away security and free land and beasts and tools. But the devil with that, for Benny Clapper was subsequently slain at Yorktown, and no one except myself, an old and feeble man, knows his name today or remembers anything about him; and let the dead sleep, for they will not be awakened or honored in this time.

Mason and Ogden were hanged, but that was later, and I tell it now only so as not to dwell on it. We come to the end of things, and I must get on with my story. . . .

It was Friday, around noon, that the Philadelphia Light Horse arrived, with Lafayette and St. Clair. With them was Laurens, one of the brigade officers of the Line; and altogether there were forty cavalry prancing up the road from Philadelphia. There were building up by now a thousand rumors, the two main ones being firstly that Sir Henry Clinton had moved six thousand British troops across the Bay into Staten Island, and was marching from there to confront us—either to join him or be wiped out by him; and secondly to the effect of George Washington gathering together every Continental regiment to march with against us. As to the first, I think there was no man in the Line who would not have welcomed the release from tension that would follow a British attack, and I myself wanted it, for I sensed somehow that there was no other resolution of our fate than in battle. And as for the second, I knew now, even as Wayne knew, even as every man in our encampment knew, that there was no American soldier north of the Virginia border—except for the Light Horse Troop—who would raise a musket against us; and as for the Light Horse . . .

Let them come, the men said. Let them come, by all that *is* holy, bring them to us!

And at about two o'clock in the afternoon, as I was standing in front of Nassau Hall with the Jew Levy and Danny Connell, there was a burst of gunfire from the Philadelphia pike. The three of us set off at a run, and as we passed through the village, I saw Andy Swain talking to one of the girls, his long trumpet slung over his shoulder, and I shouted to him to get to hell off his behind and sound To Arms. But even then, the drums at the encampment were beating To Stations, and everywhere men not on duty were racing back to the parade to join their regiments and stand to arms, a remarkable point of discipline when you consider what an urge there was for them to go to the perimeter. As we passed Hyer's house, I saw that Wayne and Butler and Stewart were standing outside, Gonzales and his men around them, and Wayne called to me:

Can we come, Stuart?

The devil you can! Hold them there, Gonzales!

We ran on. There were two more shots, and then silence except for the shouting of men. We turned the bend of the road and came to the barricade, and there was our guard, raging, the cannon shotted up with grape and a lighted match over it. Powder smoke drifted on the wind, and a man of ours lay in the shelter of a tree, stretched out and made as comfortable as possible by his comrades, but spitting blood and retching clots, and dying, as anyone could see. He was a Polish man, Piotr Lusky by name, a broad-shouldered, quiet blond man, flat-faced and slow of speech, having little English for all his years with the Line, and one to be filled with hunger for his own faraway land. Well, he was going there or somewhere now, for he died in the next few minutes; and I saw that and also the cluster of the Light Horse down the road out of musket shot, and also in between one of them whose own horse had been shot under him and who had broken a leg coming down and now crawled on his belly along the road, pleading for one of his gallant gentleman comrades to come to his aid and bear him from our anger.

Next to me, big Andrew Yost, who was corporal over the guard, was sighting a musket on the crawling man; and I watched him, fascinated, waiting, gauging the pace of his finger on the trigger—until some spark of sense made me strike up his gun.

Ah, let him shoot the bastard, Jamie, a man pleaded, and Connell told them:

Och, shut yer mouths, the lot of ye! What in the name of hell made ye fire on them?

They called us names, answered Yost.

Names they called ye!

They fired first . . . someone else put in.

And what did ye call them?

The poor Polish man breathed out his life then, the Jew

Levy holding his head and wiping his mouth and whispering to him in his own heathen tongue. Angus MacGrath and Billy Bowzar came running up now with the whole of our own 11th on the double behind them, and it did my heart good to see how those sweet and terrible men of the 11th, whom Angus and I had given our hearts to so long ago, fanned out among the trees without a word of instructions needed, and took up their places in cover. Now all the cavalry on the continent could come up the pike, and all they'd have for their pleasure would be a bloody ruin in the dirt.

A few words told us what had happened. The Light Horse, led by General St. Clair, the Marquis de Lafayette and Colonel Laurens, had come up the road and demanded that they be let through into Princeton. One word led to another, and when one of the troopers would have forced his horse over the barricade, Piotr Lusky seized its bit and turned it back. The horseman drew his pistol and shot Lusky through the chest. A dozen men fired at him but the horse reared and received the lead and went down on the horseman, and the rest had clattered away out of musket range. That was when I came, when Andrew Yost was evening the score; and now Yost said:

It is a long shot, but you let me try, Jamie—just let me try.

No! cried Bowzar. We'll have no murder!

And was it not murder when they shot down that poor Polish man?

Let him be—let him crawl—let him crawl to them.

And Bowzar, making a trumpet from his hands, cried out, You can come back now, and safely! Pick up your man! We'll not shoot!

Stow that damn match, Connell said to the man hanging over the cannon. Ye make me nerves crawl.

And back on the wind came the thin reply:

How do we know you will keep your word?

Ye don't know! Bowzar shouted. Ye can go to hell or Philadelphia and be damned!

Children from the village were pressing up now, staring goggle-eyed at the dead man, and we shooed them away, nipped them over their behinds and sent them running. I did not know what would be, but it was no place for children; and I wonder now how many of the children who were there recall that cold, clear winter afternoon as the Light Horse troop came back, urged on by St. Clair and Colonel Laurens and the little Frenchman, who was mopping the sweat from his face, for all of the weather.

They were a pretty lot, that Philadelphia Light Horse, and in all the Continental Army there was nothing else like them. In those times, all around Philadelphia were the great manors of the squires. What they were in blood, I don't know and care less, for I have little taste for this business of blood and birth; but in every detail they aped the English squires; and their one passion was to tear up the fields of honest farmers, hunting fox. If a farmer protested, they could prove that they had the right to ride roughshod over him by law, decree and immortal grant. When the war came, because they were too close to Philadelphia to be comfortably Tory and because they stood to be rich in the way of land grants from a free Pennsylvania, they made sounds for our side and they organized themselves into what they were pleased to call "the Loyal Philadelphia Light Horse." They were rich enough to do it properly.

Every one among them turned out a fine chestnut mare. While we wore our canvas overalls into shreds for which there were no replacements, they kept Philadelphia tailors working on what they were pleased to describe as the sweetest suit in all America: brown shortcoat which was faced and lined with white twill, white doeskin breeches, white satin vest. Their black boots were knee-high and cuffed with white, and their gloves were of the best white chamois. White lace at throat and cuff, a little black hat with a stiff brim, all bound around with silver cord, the same silver cord that swept from one shoulder. Their harness was white leather, intricately worked, and the saddle on the horse we had shot down could not have been bought for five thousand paper dollars, so heavy was it with silver inlay and fine relief. They were great ones for parties and balls and dances of state, and whenever some foreign visitor came to Philadelphia, they were turned out to show what a handsome military force Continentals were, and whenever we of the Line marched into Philadelphia, they were to welcome us with their sedentary gallantry and maybe to reassure the Congress, who were never too easy about the black-hearted men of the foreign brigades; but whenever we marched out of Philadelphia, they remained behind, so that the ladies would not grieve for them. Each of them carried two pistols and a carbine that was a marvel of beauty and workmanship, each imported from the finest Italian house of gunsmiths, and each carried a saber of Toledo steel priced—to quote Jackson Lunt a swordmaker in my regiment—at sixty guineas; but I know of no occasion when their swords drew blood unless it was against the poor crippled, unwanted outcasts of the Line, who in '80 came to Philadelphia where they shook their stumps of arms and legs before Carpenters' Hall, claiming that it was not right for those who lost limbs in the service of the state to die of hunger and be forced to beg in the streets, and who were properly cut up and courageously dispersed by the Light Horse—who received a special regimental insignia for that deed; and I know of few occasions when one of their pistols or carbines had been lifted against a man until they slew this poor Polish fellow.

Now they returned, and they picked up their lad with the broken leg on the way. They sat their horses a good thirty yards from us and would come no nearer, those bold and gallant men of the saddle, and the three officers came on alone, St. Clair to the fore and Lafayette and Laurens behind him. St. Clair was superior to Wayne in Pennsylvania, and the one attitude of Anthony Wayne which we held in common with him was a lusty hatred for General St. Clair of the land of Pennsylvania. But you had to give St. Clair credit for the way he came on up to the barricade and the muzzles of our muskets and the hungry mouth of the shotted cannon, where he said:

A mighty strange welcome for the general of the common-wealth.

Bowzar had been to look at the dead man, and he walked now to the barricade, where he stood with his hands on his hips, staring at the haughty, flushed face of St. Clair.

You come with blood on your hands, General, he remarked quietly. Is this a curse on you? What a history you have of blood and suffering! We are good soldiers. We are disciplined soldiers. If we were not, you would not be alive this minute, you and those dirty Philadelphia barons behind you. How long is our patience to last?

St. Clair did not answer, not because he had no will to, but because his anger clotted the words; his face turned the color of a beet, and his lips trembled and coiled as he sought for proper speech. Meanwhile, Lafayette had advanced his horse up alongside the general's, and the French boy, throwing back his white cloak—heavy wool lined with silk of powder-blue—burst into excited speech:

Clods—what is this! How do you dare! This is Gen'ral the whole Pennzl'vania! How dare you!

But even that is only an indication of how he spoke; I can do no more than to suggest his accent, to give an indication of the babble of indignant sound, high-pitched, his body trembling, the saliva spattering out; until Danny Connell, who was observing him thoughtfully, his head cocked as he contemplatively rubbed his nose, said several things unprintable and told Lafayette specifically where he could go, concluding:

. . . Sure, for me nose cannot tolerate the scent of you!

I will see you all in hell! roared St. Clair, but Bowzar said nothing to this, only standing there in silence with his hands on his hips.

Now Laurens had pushed up his horse, and was speaking earnestly and quietly to the general, plucking his sleeve, and when the general shook him off Laurens said bitterly:

But I must insist, sir!

How dare you insist! You and Wayne! Damn it all to hell, why isn't Wayne here?

Please, said Laurens, softly but murderously, I will not hold this kind of talk here. I will not be responsible.

St. Clair swung his horse around and rode back to the Light Horse troop, Lafayette and Laurens following. There, they conferred again, Laurens arguing determinedly. Then Laurens dismounted, handed his reins to one of the horsemen, and walked up to the barricade.

I'm sorry, he said to Bowzar simply. I'm sorry as the devil, believe me.

It was a bad day's work, Mr. Laurens, said Billy Bowzar. It was murder, and that's all that it was.

Where is General Wayne?

He is at Jacob Hyer's house and comfortable enough, as are Stewart and Butler.

Are you holding him prisoner, Sergeant?

He's no prisoner. He can leave when he wishes to leave. Of his own free will he came, and of his own free will he may go.

Will you take the general and the marquis and myself to him?

Bowzar thought that over for a while, before he made any reply. Levy had come over to stand next to him, and he looked at the sad, bitter, hollow-cheeked face of the Jew before he spoke, saying:

No—No, we will not. We will not have any dealings or words with that man St. Clair or with that Frenchman. You must understand, sir, that when we cast out our officers, we were in deep earnest. So long as we are in command of the Pennsylvania Line by the edict of the men of the Line, we talk on our terms. You can take that or leave that, Mr. Laurens.

Standing there on the other side of the barricade, his cocked hat tilted back, his hands in the pockets of his great-coat, Laurens studied us shrewdly and not without respect. He was a very young man, was Johnny Laurens, only twenty-seven years old or so, and a very brave man too, and not long for this earth; for only a year later he was slain in the fighting in the South. He was one of the very few of our regimental officers who had some respect for the men who served under him; and when he fought a duel against Charlie Lee and near killed the wretch, it was not only because Lee plotted and connived and talked against Washington, but because Lee treated us like dirt and dogs, and because that sat poorly with Laurens.

Why do you call me Mister? he asked now, not angrily but curiously.

Because your rank came from us, and now we have taken it away.

I see, he nodded. And you are absolutely adamant about the general and the marquis?

We are that.

Will you take *me* to Wayne, along with one of the Troop?

Connell and Levy nodded.

If you wish, Bowzar said.

Laurens looked back at the Light Horse and the two officers; he sighed, shrugged his shoulders and walked back along the road to where they were. It was at least ten minutes he stood there talking with them, and then we heard him addressing the Light Horse. A word here and there told us he was asking for a volunteer, but there were no volunteers. He stood apart and raised his voice, and still there was no response. Then he returned to us alone.

I have no love for what you've done, he told Bowzar ruefully, but so help me God, I prefer the foreign brigade to those. Take me to Wayne, will you?

Take him along, Jamie, said Bowzar, and then come to us at the Hall where the Committee meets.

*   *   *

So Laurens and I walked back to Jacob Hyer's inn. For
a while, we walked in silence; then he said to me:

Well, Sergeant, you have sure as hell stood the world
upside down, haven't you?

A little bit of it, perhaps.

Well, he shrugged, I think you will take us back, Sergeant, though God knows maybe we don't deserve it.
There's nothing else to it, as I see it. Someday, perhaps,
your kind will get angry with the gentry and do us in
proper—and when I think of those damned Philadelphia
fops, I'm not all regrets. Only there are harder men than
those, Sergeant; and that's something to remember.

It is indeed, Mr. Laurens, I answered.

Sweet taste to that *Mister*, eh? But you will call me
Colonel, Sergeant, and when the time comes, I'll enjoy the
taste as much as you are enjoying your lark today. How is
it in the Book? *Ye are the salt of the earth: but if the salt
have lost his savour, wherewith shall it be salted?*—or
something like that. You need a new seasoning, Sergeant,
and you have not found it.

And you're damned arrogant for a man who walks on
this road by grace of the Committee.

Let us say confident, not arrogant, Sergeant. . . . And
there are my good comrades.

For we were now at the inn, where Wayne and Stewart
and Butler stood shivering in the cold, looking down the
road and waiting. Laurens laughed and waved at them, and
Stewart ran over and embraced him. I left them there talking and walked down to the parade, where five regiments
were drawn up to arms with knapsacks and whole equipment, and where the drummer lads stood cold and blue

waiting for the signal that would send them into battle—in the strange inhumanity of armies of the time, which chose children to lead grown men to slaughter. Jack Maloney and Jim Holt and Sean O'Toole were in command here, and I told them what had transpired on the Philadelphia pike and of Bowzar's call for a meeting. We dismissed the regiments, and then together we walked over to Nassau Hall, where the rest of the Committee already awaited us. In the other big room, to the right as you entered the Hall, the body of the Polish man was laid out on a bench, awaiting the building of a coffin and burial, and it was covered with the wolf standard of the 10th Regiment. Good-by, I said to myself, good-by and farewell, lonely Polish man. But no one said anything aloud, and we went into our headquarters to hold our meeting. We lit the candles, for night was falling now, and we listened to Chester Rosenbank, who was there by invitation and with no good words.

The Committee, he said—his solemn, German face owlish and regretful, his little blue eyes watering behind his spectacles—the Committee has asked me to report on the state of our supplies; I humbly submit the report.

Speak up, Chester! said Dwight Carpenter, and the schoolmaster looked at him reproachfully as he removed his glasses and wiped them with a rag of cloth. He had for his report some scraps of paper, and now he assembled these in front of him, squinted through his spectacles, cleared his throat and began to speak. He was not quite like anyone else in the brigades, but then, I may ask myself who was? From one or another of the states, they might have been cut from a whole cloth, but we were a union of difference, of distances, of extremes; and this German schoolmaster, who could sit for hours, dreaming over his flute and Johann Sebastian Bach, and would spend hours more teaching our fifers counterpoints and harmonies, was a very good soldier indeed and one of those who had enlisted in the first Pennsylvania regiment organized in Philadelphia in March of 1775. But soldiering had not made him other than he was before, and he spoke to us as he would to a classroom, explaining a painful and unhappy problem.

Considering first the question of ammunition, he said, I can be most explicit. We have at present in the whole encampment two thousand, seven hundred and twenty-two men—that is today. Our previous counts—well, they have not been wholly accurate. In this, I include the drummer boys and the riflemen, but not the forty-three men who are in the hospital; because when I discussed that with Andrew MacPherson, he insists they must be left here if we move. Now we have, all told, fourteen thousand and thirty musket balls, less than five rounds to a man even if you exclude the riflemen and the gunners. With rifle shot, we are better off, with almost seventy pellets to each rifle, and we have gunpowder to the amount of twenty-one hundred pounds. This does not include the contents of the individual powder boxes, since I have no way of determining that. But that is not good either, for until New Year's Day, no regular inspection was made of the powder boxes, and a good deal was used for flinting and for purging sick stomachs too. This, however, we have put a stop to. It is my estimation, nevertheless, that we have not enough powder in the boxes for the balls, unless they are undershot. We have, for the six guns, forty iron balls and twelve stone balls. We also have fifty-two rounds of grapeshot, which makes exactly one hundred and four cannon rounds, and

for that, you see, there is plenty of powder for undershot-
ting but not for dueling. But since we have so few balls,
we cannot go dueling anyway. The grape can be recast for
musketry, but that would leave us open, and the men
would not like it. We have neither bar shot nor chain shot.
That is the way it is with the ammunition.

This finished the first part of his report. We should have
known, but we didn't know, and I saw many a face go pale
as we listened.

But I myself, said Levy, counted eight hundred bars of
lead. In the hospital alone, there were three hundred bars.

We never finished rendering those—and the rest we left.
Just as we left the four dismounted cannon at the redoubt
at Mt. Kemble, and two hundred cannon balls and fifty
bags of grape with them.

If they are still at Morristown—began O'Toole.

No, no, said Jack Maloney. The Yankee soldiers are already there. If we should raid the place . . .

His voice trailed away, and no one else spoke. Once
again, Rosenbank cleared his throat.

As for food—he said—we are no better. We have meat
and flour for two days and corn meal for a third day. That's
all—and what we have is only because the farmers brought
it to us and gave it to us. We have no money to buy, and
the farming men here in the neighborhood—no matter what
they feel, they cannot support three thousand men. If they
give us all their food, what will they do then with no
money in exchange? We have eleven tents that are any
use; the rest we had to cut up for shoes and overalls, but
they were no good anyway. All the men are shod, but not
for marching. For perimeter duty all right, but not for
marching. We have some cows, but if we eat them we can't

milk them. But we have no fodder, so I thought I would trade with the farm folk for corn meal. That will give us enough meal for two days more, but then we will have a lot of sickness if we eat only corn meal. We have twenty-three oxen and forty-seven horses, and if we leave the wounded here, we can begin to kill the oxen; then we can burn the carts for firewood, but that is like eating our fingers to feed our bellies, like eating the horses, which would be like eating our feet to feed our bellies ... Our feet, our fingers ... I've thought all I can about it, I don't know what to do. There is food on the farms, I guess, but if we should take one grain of it, well, that would be the end—yes? It would be the end?

It would be the end, Levy answered. One chicken, one ear of corn—it would be the end.

Anyway, it's the same, someone said.

All right, Bowzar nodded, smiling. Thank you, Mr. Rosenbank—giving him that term because he was a scholarly man and deserving it—we are very grateful. Will you stretch the food as far as you can? Don't let the men go hungry, but don't waste food.

Food I would not waste, Sergeant Bowzar.

No. That's true. Well, we thank you. We are grateful to you. Maybe someday, if we ever have medals, we will be able to give you a medal.

A medal would be nice, said the schoolmaster thoughtfully as he rose to leave. When I go back to school teaching, it will be nice to wear a medal. Good night, he said. Good night.

He walked out, breathing on his spectacles and polishing them and rubbing his eyes. He will be weeping when he is outside, I thought.

Medals, said old Scottsboro.

Well, gentlemen? Bowzar smiled.

Medals, old Scottsboro mumbled.

If the British—said Levy, almost to himself—are marching on us from the east, and the Yankees from the north and the gentry from the south, all our problems will be solved, no? I won't mind a finish the way a soldier should finish, the way the Polish man finished.

Time for that, said Bowzar. There is the Jersey Line still, and nobody knows what they will do . . .

But before the night was over, we knew that too. All things came to us that day. Johnny Laurens came to us in Nassau Hall, knocking on the door and then smiling as he walked in, his greatcoat open, his youthful, handsome face flushed and healthy. He stood strong and tall and confident, looking at the twelve of us as we sat around the table, never bothering to remove his cocked hat, for we were twelve small, shrunken men who had prodded our dreams too much—whereas he stood there as one who had never overmuch had the need of dreaming.

Forgive the Jew Gonzales, he said, for I talked him into bringing me here, after he had intimated that you might meet all night long. What I have to say will not wait all night long.

What have you to say, now that you are here? Billy Bowzar asked him coldly and bitterly.

Only this: that Joseph Reed, the President himself of Pennsylvania Country, will come here and talk with you and treat with you on the terms General Wayne laid out. I am empowered to say that—your terms and General Wayne's terms. You must take this or leave this.

And what be them terms? asked old Scottsboro.

Three main points—the rest can be settled if you talk with the President. The points are these. *One:* No reprisals to be taken against any member of the Line. *Two:* All soldiers whose enlistment has expired to be discharged. *Three:* All proven bounties to be paid.... On your part, you must pledge the discipline and will of the men who remain.

That is very little you give us, said Bowzar slowly.

Or a great deal, depending how you look at it.

We will let you know tomorrow, Bowzar said.

Laurens smiled, nodded, and then, as by a sudden impulse, saluted. He turned on his heel then and left....

The salute lasts in my mind. We were finishing, but a brigade officer of the Line saluted us; and I sometimes wonder whether if Johnny Laurens had not laid down his life so soon, we might not have been remembered a little better—and then I wonder why we should want a better memory. What is the memory for all such things as we did? Johnny Laurens had a smile and a gentle manner and the juice of life ran strong in him, but there was never a moment's doubt where he stood. They stood in one place and we stood in another, and so it was until the end, and I must get on with the end, for I have told much and yet there is much more to tell.

Leaving the Committee to talk, I went out into the night and on my rounds. Filled with a great restlessness, I could not remain there with them and listen to them debating what could not be resolved; for when all is said and done, they were good, brave and strange men, not proud but filled with the sense of freedom, and thereby their debating came to nothing at all. If they had been adventurers, they could have embarked on some wild and terrible adventure; but though they came from all parts of the world to fight in the foreign brigades, they had come to have a deep love for the land on which they fought, for over many a year they had sealed a pact on it in blood. So they who led an army had no place to lead it—and they talked on and on, and at the back of their minds was the thought that surely they were not singular, and if the Jersey Line rose to join them, and then the Connecticut Line, could not the Revolution go on, in terms of the simple folk who did the fighting?

In a sense, they were not wrong; the bird that pecked in us pecked in others—even though we did not know it; even among the Yankees, for the Massachusetts troops had put their names to a petition, laying out the same demands that we had. And their officers responded more cleverly than ours: they marched; men who march have less time for brooding than those who sit still, and though their feet bled and though their limbs froze, the Yankee troops marched on and on through the forests of the North. Southward they marched until word came that the Midland armies had done strange and frightening things. But this we did not know, and we had no way of knowing it until that night, when, in my restlessness and loneliness, I walked from point to point on the perimeter of our Princeton defenses.

What a cold night that was—when a twenty-two-year-old lad walked among the defenses of an army he and a few others led! The curious Midland midwinter thaw had vanished, and the mud had turned into steel, with a thousand knifelike edges. As the cold increased, I heard that snapping, brittle winter sound, the small agony of the land's surface, and I drew closer the blanket I had thrown over my coat. I was out of my thoughts now; I went from fire to fire, exchanging a few words here and there in the easy way of men who have known each other a long time. At each place, it was *All's well*—but well only because no enemy was fool enough to come through those frozen woods and fields at night. And then I came to the bridge, where the two Jersey men were, half-frozen, crouching so close to the flames that they singed the edges of their clothes. Oh, like great, beaten dogs they were, with their dirt and their beards and the misery in their eyes.

As I came into the firelight, they looked up at me, their mouths full of toasted corn bread that crumbed over their beards; it is not pleasant, when your belly is full, to watch starving men eat.

Have ye no rum, Sergeant? one of them said.

These are Jersey men, Jamie, said Prukish, who was in command of the post.

Jersey men—said someone else—and the look of them! But they have had it bitter, coming all the way down from Pompton, where the Jersey Line rose up against its officers.

The Jersey Line rose! I cried.

Aye—one of them mumbled—aye, Sergeant, that is the truth of it. The Jersey Line rose, God help us. . . . A little rum would be a pleasant thing—he said, looking from face to face, stuffing his mouth again with the corn bread—ye have none? No. Well, that's the way it goes . . .

I shook his shoulder. What's this about the Line? I demanded. You hear me?

He nodded, and the tears from his bloodshot eyes ran down over his dirty cheeks.

He's a sick man, Sergeant, said the other.

That's right. I be a sick man now.

Talk up! I shouted at the other.

You got no business shouting at me, Sergeant. I came a long way, a powerful lot of walking with the cold weather on. I seen some bad things too. So I say to myself, with them Pennsylvania lads, I'll just rest easy and sweet.

Did the Jersey Line rise up? I asked softly.

Sure, Sergeant. They rose up and they was put down. They brought down the Yankee men, and the Yankee men shot us. They just stood there, them Yankee men, with the tears rolling down their faces, and when the order was given, they shot our lads. So that was that with the Jersey Line, Sergeant, and we two of us, we think, We'll off and tell the Pennsylvania lads, which is necessary anyway. You wouldn't never shoot us and we wouldn't never shoot you, but who would have thought the Yankee men would have done it? Not the Yankee men themselves, if you ask me, because they stood and cried like children when our leaders was brought out to be shot down. But they done it anyhow.

His partner, meanwhile, had rolled over close to the fire and gone to sleep. So close he lay that I could see the hairs of his beard begin to curl and crackle, so I kicked him awake and pushed him away.

Come both of you with me to the Committee, I said.

We done enough walking tonight, Sergeant.

Come now, come now, I answered gently, and there you'll find a warm place, and maybe a glass of hot toddy too. A blazing fire ye will find, and tallow candles stuck in sticks, while here in the open you can never be warm. So come along now, lads.

Thus they came with me, forcing each step that took them to Nassau Hall, and while they walked they told me. There was not much to tell, for it was essentially our own tale with all gone wrong with them that had gone right with us. There were many differences, of which I will tell you; for the Jersey Line, while it was a Midland body with many foreign folk in it, was not like our Pennsylvania army, just as no force on all the continent was like ours. There were only two regiments in the Jersey Line, the 1st New Jersey, with two hundred and thirty-nine on its rolls, and the 2nd New Jersey, with just a little less than that— but it was not only in numbers they differed. They had nothing like our Committee and they could not make theirs into something like it, for there were not in the Jersey regiments men who had fought through every engagement from Boston to today, like the grim and knowing veterans of the 1st Pennsylvania, who had been made into sergeants and corporals for our whole Line. Also, while the men of the Jersey Line had dwindled, they were overburdened with officers—one for every four men—and their condition of sickness and starvation was even worse than ours. For all of that, they had driven the gentry from their ranks and were on their own under their sergeants when the Yankee men came down, and that broke their hearts. The leading folk of their Committee were taken out and the Yankee men formed firing squads and shot them down—with the tears streaming, they shot them down; and these two had come on to tell us.

So I took them to Nassau Hall to talk with Bowzar and

Maloney and Williams and the rest. There I took them, but I did not go in myself.

I knew what the outcome would be. Regardless of how they talked or how much, we of Pennsylvania were alone—alone we were, at the end of the road. Now we would talk to Reed and make terms with him, and the dreams we had dreamed would be no more than fanciful desires.

It might take days or weeks from now on; but to all real purposes, the rising was finished.

PART NINE

Being an account of the leave-taking of the foreign brigades, how each went his separate way, and of what befell Jack Maloney and myself.

THUS IT CAME ABOUT that in time we made our peace with the officers, through Joseph Reed, the President of the Commonwealth; for we were alone now, and no place to go and no future of our making that we could comprehend. But it was no such peace as the Jersey Line made; even at the end, they took no liberties with the foreign brigades, but kept their word—all men who had served more than three years were free to leave if they chose to leave. The terms were our terms, but they were terms for departure not for remaining. Our terms for remaining were that we should choose our own officers, and that we should be clothed like human beings and fed and paid; this they would not or could not accept, but our Committee had an obligation to the men and the men were sick to their hearts with service under the gentry for the gentry's way of fighting a war.

So, still holding the Line intact and under arms, we paraded once again and formed up foursquare on the meadow at Princeton, on a cold winter afternoon with the snow clouds building up in the east. In a way, that was the end, although there is more to tell that must be told; for there at Princeton was the last time the regiments, the riflemen and the artillery company of the Pennsylvania Line stood together at dress formation to listen to the drums beating and see the old regimental flags flying and hear the order of the day read out. There were tears in many an eye before that afternoon was over, for the foreign brigades were something and they had made something, and now they would be no more. And many a lad was there like myself who knew little else but the camp and the march, and had no home to go to and neither kith nor kin. With the cold east wind blowing, we stood to attention, and then at our ease with our captured muskets grounded, listening to Billy Bowzar. He had climbed up on top of a caisson, and there he stood, legs spread, hands on hips in that manner we knew so well, his curly red hair blowing in the wind, his square face reassuring and becalming; for you listened to Bowzar and heeded him, in battle or out of battle; he was a calm man and a knowledgeable one.

My comrades, he said, when you chose myself and the others to be the Committee of Sergeants, you had the power to keep us or replace us, as you saw fit. You kept us every one, and for this we are glad. On our part, we tried to serve you in what ways we knew, and we served you as best we could. There were adventurous things we might have done, and if we had done them you might have followed us, but we reasoned that a man's life is not something to adventure with unless the cause is worth while. Therefore, we sought for a way in which the Line could serve your cause and the cause of our country and its folk—and yet remain as we were, with discipline but without the officer gentry.

How many hours we sat together seeking such a way, I need not tell you, for that you know. We found no way. When we heard that the Jersey Line would rise up, we thought perhaps the whole of the land would join us; but that is over, and there is no way left without shedding the blood of our own people. That would be sorry business, to turn brother against brother, and that we rejected. We were right in rejecting it—but we did not do so out of our weakness, but out of our strength!

Then there was a roar, and we stamped our muskets on the frozen ground, so that the *thud, thud, thud* of two and a half thousand guns echoed through the village and across the valley. Jack Maloney stood beside me, and he put his arm about me, tight as a steel vise, and he bent his head to hide the tears as they flowed, and he whispered to me:

Ah, Jesus Christ, Jamie, we have been given a moment of opportunity and a sight of glory, and we failed them.

I saw the Jew Levy weeping, the strange little man of his own council and his own peace whom I had hated two years for his being a heathen Jew, and then loved for three years for his being a patient man who never raised his voice or lost his temper or had anything but a gentle word for a man in pain—but knew him not ever, not in two or five years; and the big black man Holt wept, and old Lawrence Scottsboro wept, since his moment was past and finished. So I knew then that what Jack Maloney said was right and true, that we had been given a moment of opportunity and a glimpse of glory, and we had failed because we knew no better way of things than the gentry could offer.

We still have our strength, said Billy Bowzar, when the stamping of the muskets had finished, and we must use it well and wisely. We cannot remain as an army and have our own officers out of our own ranks, and we will not remain under the officers we cast out. Therefore, they have agreed to discharge every man with more than three years' service, which means the greater part of the Line. The rest will be formed into new regiments, perhaps in this Line, perhaps in another—and this they must do. I would to God that there was a way to hold the Line together, but there is no way. A thousand men have sworn that they will never serve their officers again, and we know of no way they can serve this Committee other than to peacefully go their ways. So that is it; yet we have proved something. We have proved that we, by ourselves, can make ourselves into a better army than whips and canes ever made of us. Someday, other men will remember that. For my own, I will stay with what is left of the Line, for that is the way I feel. I don't put this as a matter for anyone else's conscience, only for mine. Therefore, we will break camp in the morning and we will march to Trenton, where we will disband.

That was it, or something like that; for I cannot recall all of this exactly, and it was a long time ago, and I have no journals but only the pictures that were engraved on my mind. I have many pictures, but the clearest are of winter afternoons when the foreign brigades stood to square parade with the sere, cold sky overhead, with the old banners blowing in the wind, and with the drummer boys beating a roll, their little hands wrapped in pieces of wool, their fingers blue with the cold. And rather than the important it is the unimportant that lingers; so that in the moment when Billy Bowzar finished talking, I saw one of the drummer lads whose name was Harold McClintock

bawling like a child—which he was, for he was only thirteen years old and no larger than a boy of ten would be
these days—with his blue lips and his blue fingers and his
skinny, sunken chest; and I wondered what would become
of him and all of those lads who had been picked up here
and there along the way in the miles we marched, and
taught to beat a drum or blow a fife. Those things I wondered about—and what would become of the blowzy or
worn women who had followed us here and there and
everywhere; and where would the big Bantu black men go,
who spoke hardly any English at all but were runaway
slaves from the tobacco fields in the Southland; and what
of old Lawrence Scottsboro who knew nothing but soldiering? What of the Poles whom we picked up in York
city in '76 when the Polish brigade was shot to shreds, and
what of all of us, of all of us?

But it may be that those are partly thoughts of the years
afterwards and not of the moment. At the moment, I was
one of them—the only difference being that I had some
place to go to—and I made up my mind that I would go
back to York village in Pennsylvania and to the manse of
Jacob Bracken.

So after some time it was sounded to break ranks, and
the sergeants blew their whistles, and the men crowded
around Billy Bowzar whom they loved. But I got out of it,
and walked away by myself; I was not in a mood for fare-
wells and I did not know, then, that we would come together again soon enough.

We marched to Trenton, where we were mustered out.
I could tell of that, yet it was without particular incident,
and we were not what we were once, the Pennsylvania Line

of old. We were nothing at all now, except men of many tongues and ways of speech, ragged and aimless. We stood by the riverbank and watched our cannon loaded onto barges which carried them away to Philadelphia. We saw the Line dissolve like sand washed away, and it was done. Each went his own way, and to some of them we said good-by and farewell forever; and there was many a man there I never laid eyes on again. But there were others I saw soon enough, for it was not easy to break the bond and the habit of what we had been for so long; and of that I will tell in due time.

But now we said our good-bys, and Jack Maloney and myself together walked off down the road to Philadelphia. He had no place in particular to go; and for my part, the road to York ran through Philadelphia. We turned once to look at Trenton and the shrunken encampment that remained there, and then we went on. We were no more soldiers; we were discharged; we were free; but the taste wasn't sweet. We had no money and no future in any particular, and what we owned in the world we carried on our backs—our old knapsacks, our knives, our flint boxes. We had a piece of bacon, a pound of corn meal and a pinch of salt. These were the rations we had drawn, with an oath to go with them, from the plump, healthy commissary sent up by the Congress. We each of us had been given a threadbare blanket, and we had odds and ends of rags that we had held onto; in my knapsack was the banner of the 11th Regiment, which I had folded up and taken for myself, partly for sentimental reasons and partly because I considered its usefulness as a scarf in the cold weather. So we were off on our own, I myself a tall, skinny, rawboned lad,

Maloney a foot shorter—Handsome Jack Maloney, as we had called him once.

Two days we were on foot to Philadelphia, and it was a blessing that this was a mild winter, and not the terror of cold and ice we had known three years before at Valley Forge. Always the snow clouds hung in the east and the north, but the snow did not fall until the church towers of Philadelphia were already in sight, and the night in between we spent on the roadside with a good fire to warm us. Altogether, it was not bad. The road was fairly empty, except for occasional groups like ourselves, out of the Line and drifting toward the city without any certain purpose or intent. The only incident worth recalling happened when a patrol of the Light Horse came trotting along. We stood our ground—perhaps foolishly—and when they saw that we were out of the Line and without guns, they gave us a taste of their whips as they cantered past. Well, we had taken the whips of such men often enough, and we rubbed our faces and went on.

So we reached Philadelphia with a wet snow falling, tired, chilled and dispirited, and walked through the streets and saw the cheerful, bright-lit windows, the citizens hurrying to be home to the warmth of their firesides; and we smelled the food cooking and saw, through the windows, the children laughing as they went to dinner, the families gathering together with great certainty that all was right in the world. We saw the shape and heard the sound of something we had never known, and the misery of that winter night made it all the more poignant. And it was no pleasure to have citizens cross a street rather than pass two men of the Line—the same Line which had again and again made a barrier of its bayonets between this city and the enemy. Right or wrong, we had given five years of our lives to the war, and those five years the Philadelphian citizens had spent secure and comfortable.

So you see, said Jack Maloney, what it is to be discharged and a soldier of the Continentals.

Which is why, I nodded, feeling the icy water in my thin boots, so many come back to the whip and the cane. There are worse things than a whip and a cane.

Far worse, Jamie, for here I am just like a dog without a master. Here I am in the cold, wet snow with houses all around me, but to them in the houses I am a fearful thing. Have you any money, Jamie, forgive me for asking you again?

None.

Not even a copper penny?

Not even a copper penny, I said.

Well, said Maloney, kicking the slush out of his path, here we are at the great Carpenters' Hall, where fine words were said and fine documents were signed; and I have two hundred dollars of Continental paper in my sack, so let's get them out, Jamie, and eat and drink, and then we'll render in payment what was paid to us—if you are game.

Game I am, I answered him.

So we stopped in the square, rooted in his knapsack, got out the paper, stuffed our pockets with it, and went straightaway to Josef Hegel's Coffee House, where there was light and warmth and merriment, and all the other things cold, hungry men desire. Hegel's inn, called the Red Cock, two squares from Carpenters' Hall, was not the best place in the town but by no means the worst, which meant that while you didn't encounter the great merchants, neither did you encounter the great thieves; and Hegel closed his doors to street doxies, peddlers, cripples, beggars, if not to footpads, pimps and purse-lifters. It was one of those in-between places where a soldier could go if he had some hard money in his pants, and as we remembered it, there was a good piece of roast meat and good beer and good rum. We had gone there first after the occupation in '78, when we came into Philadelphia as liberators of a town which to a large degree, recognizing the difference between the golden pound and the paper dollar, did not particularly desire to be liberated; and we had come in hard and bitter, and the town was wide open for us in an unvirtuous display of virtue, whereby the women proved their loyalty and there was free beer in every tavern. The welcome had cooled since then, but we had not expected something so chilly as what met us when we turned back the door of the Red Cock, which invited all comers so merrily with its diamond-shaped panes of colored glass.

Well, there was merriment within all right, and the proper smells and the proper sounds, but as we stood in the little hallway, eyes were averted from us, and Josef himself came over, frowning and thinking of the neatest way to turn us out into the bleak wet of a night that had already changed to rain.

Innkeepers, said Jack Maloney, are cut of a mold, by God.

To which I answered that among the few pieces of wisdom I had inherited from my poor father was something to the effect of the selling of food and the other sustenance of man's soul and belly putting the seller apart from the race.

An evil practice, which gives rise to fat, dirty men.

The fat man was upon us, head to foot in his apron;

and I thought, this is my own true punishment, for the ghost of Jacob Hyer has arisen against me! This man had a pear-shaped face, little pig eyes of pale china-blue, and an enormous chin which swept, layer by layer, down onto his chest, for all the world like a majestic beard.

No soldiers, he said, short and sweet and to the point.

You buggerin' randy reaver!

What's that?

Scots, I said smoothly. And what in hell is wrong with you, Josef Hegel? Is this true German hospitality, that I hear so much of?

No soldiers, he said again. That's that.

Like hell it is, I answered—holding back little Jack Maloney, for I felt the little man begin to shake with anger—Just look at us again. I am Jamie Stuart and this is Jack Maloney, and in our time we spent a pretty penny on your lousy rum. Do you think you're going to turn two soldiers of the Line, two sergeants, mind you, out into that miserable cold rain? Guess again ... dropping my voice ... for we'll dance a pretty jig around your place. Now let us sit down quiet, and that will be that.

You got any money? he wanted to know.

I did quick arithmetic and answered him, To the face value of five guineas.

Show it, he said.

Now I will like hell. Sit us down, or—I swear to God—we will take this place apart and break it into little pieces.

Don't shout, he said. Now, all right. Just come with me.

And he took us to a corner through the hard and unfeeling eyes of his guests, who shrank away from two dirty and soaking men in overalls, swearing all the while under his breath at the various curses that plagued him—dirty, worthless soldiers being the first and foremost among them.

What will you have? he asked ungraciously, as we slipped off our knapsacks and sat down.

For each, a noggin of rum and a cut of that lovely meat on your flame.

The meat comes dear.

Well, we are great ones for dear things, so fetch it!

And when he left, Jack Maloney leaned back, sighed, grinned happily and observed that we would probably spend the night in jail, but that it would be worth it. He brought the rum and we took the first hot gulp of it down on our empty stomachs. The second drink went smoother, but already I could feel my nerves tingling. It was a long time since I had tasted rum, especially this thick, brown, syrupy stuff that was better than the best wine of Europe, to my way of thinking . . . especially since I was something of a connoisseur of rum and totally ignorant of the best wine of Europe.

So you see, Jamie, said Jack Maloney, when we had finished the meat on our plates and wiped up the gravy with good white bread—the kind of bread I had not tasted in at least twelve months, good white flour bread instead of the miserable corn pan we ate in the Line—So you see, Jamie, said Jack Maloney, what a queer thing this matter of life is. We have in our pockets two hundred dollars of paper, stamped with the name of the Congress and issued out to us as pay at one time, but since it is not worth the paper it was printed upon, we are thieves and sit here eating stolen meat and drink with a stolen roof over our heads. But you and me—who were a part of the Committee of Sergeants just a while ago—now we are despised, because we wear overalls and carry sacks. But on the other hand, Jamie, those men who remained by the fireside, blessings fall upon them, like little snowflakes from the heavens. Why are we accursed, Jamie Stuart? Is freedom a sickness?

A rare sickness, I answered slyly, my head light and airy. Nor catching at all, like the pox.

Nor catching, agreed Jack Maloney, and added: Except at times. Except at times, Jamie. . . . Except at times, he told the barmaid who had come beside us, putting his arm around her and smiling into her face.

Now what is? she wanted to know.

A sickness like the pox. Now bring us some rum, darling, a little rum. Ye do not hate soldiers?

Not when they look like you, little man, she smiled; and he pinched her behind and she slapped his face and went off with the noggins.

Jamie, Jamie, said Jack Maloney, Jamie, my lad, I am filled with sorrow at myself, for I am just a lonely man with no knowledge of anything but killing, and even that trade is gone. Pride is for the gentry, Jamie—we should not touch it. Pride brings us down. A man falleth with pride. I envy my good comrade, Billy Bowzar, who remained a soldier, which is all that any of us are good for. Will I find me a good, sweet woman someday, Jamie, will I now? And peace? Will I find me contentment, Jamie?

And he stared at me earnestly and drunkenly, his eyes wet with tears for his own sorry fate, his thin-featured, handsome face bemused and inquiring. And as the barmaid returned with our rum, he sang:

In London Town, in London Town,
The lassies are so fair,
That I who wandered off so far
Am sooth in deep despair.

His voice was high and sweet, but it carried; and eyes turned toward us, and a party of men at a table nearby regarded us with little love and much disgust. Their conversation turned on us, and they spoke, among other things, of the dirty, drunken mutineers of the Pennsylvania Line. Jack Maloney heard them, stopped singing, eyed them for a moment, and then rose up, mug in hand, and walked over to them.

I beg your pardon, he said politely.

They looked him up and down. They were well-dressed, well-fleshed, sober men, sitting over their supper and beer; they were shopkeepers or small traders of some sort.

I drink to the foreign brigades, blessed be their memory for ever and ever, said Jack Maloney.

Ha!

What does that mean, sir? asked Jack Maloney.

Gentility had overcome him, which he had absorbed from the years he served his British masters, and there he stood by the table like the very soul of politeness, delicate and small and very handsome indeed, as only he could be in his broken canvas-topped boots, his big, wet, stained overalls, his coat thrown open, his ragged mockery of a vest, and the old rag he wore around his neck with all the elegance of a ruff. He had raised his brows with solicitude, wrinkling his small, well-shaped nose—and one would take him for the least dangerous little man in the world, which he was not. So I reached out and wrapped my hand around the heavy pewter candlestick that stood on our table, and lay there against the table that way, watching and listening, too drunk to mind what happened now, too unhappy to raise a finger to prevent it.

Ha! It came again.

Shall I take that as an insult, an observation upon the brigades?

Get out of here, you damned, dirty deserter, said one of the men.

Deserter—deserter? asked Jack Maloney. Why? he said gently. Why are we dirty too . . . he inquired . . . unless because we tended to the war while you tended to other things? Five years I have been in the old Pennsylvania Line, gentlemen, and it ill becomes you, I think, to speak so poorly of me. Yes, even if I was a deserter right now— added Jack Maloney—for a man gets a bellyful of fighting and dying and hungering and the cold and the misery and the wet winter nights, and of all those things which you know so little. . . . So apologize, if you will.

I'll see you in hell first, said the man.

I'll see you there, said Jack Maloney cheerfully and emptied his rum in the man's face. Now Hegel was thundering across the room and people were rising everywhere, but the man who had gotten the rum was rising to fight, spluttering and swearing, and so were his companions, and he was with his hand in his waistcoat, looking for a weapon of a kind, so I considered it time for me to stop dreaming and do something. They were to crush little Jack Maloney like a cockroach, but they underestimated their man, as the large man usually will the small one, and he tipped the table upon them and crowned one of them with his mug. Another who would have flanked him, I touched gently with the candlestick—not enough to hurt him but only to deflect him, and then I put the heel of my hand in the face of roaring Josef Hegel, tipping him upon the man who had gone down from the stick.

It's time for the door, Jackie! I shouted, and we fought our way across that room in a fine fashion, sowing devastation around us, until at last, and more sober, we were out in the cold wet night and running down the street with a great outcry behind us.

Now come with me, you crazy damned fool, I told Jack Maloney, grasping his arm and pulling him into a dark little alley, the kind with which Philadelphia abounds; and I dragged him along to an old woodshed, where we crawled in among the shavings and listened to the hue and cry pass.

What a brave thing you've done, I said, for here we are without even our knapsacks.

Yet better than in jail, Jamie, you will admit, he insisted.

I will not admit that, you crazy, drunken Lobster, for there is enough dishonor to be made of the Line without you adding to it.

Did I add to it, Jamie?

That you did.

Ah, Jamie, he moaned, putting his arm around me and weeping on my wet sleeve, there you are, a little bit of a lad of twenty-two summers, and I am thirty-six years old and witless, and you will go off and leave me with proper disgust, and here I will be in this strange, wild land of America, a deserter from the King's army and a renegade to freedom. A renegade, Jamie, do you hear me, for what was our great rising in the end? What was it, Jamie? Naked we came into the world, and naked we lie here, two hunted men. What a kettle of stew the world is for our kind, Jamie—Jamie, my lad, look upon ourselves as those respectable men at the tavern looked upon us, two dirty, wretched soldiers who have turned their backs upon the struggle. I tell you, there was a great and immense rightness in their attitude.

Shut your mouth, I said angrily. You are drunk, Jack Maloney, and to listen to you turns my stomach.

Drunk, I am, Jamie, royal drunk, drunk as quality, but there is nevertheless a deep truth in my drunkenness. I see things clearly. I see Handsome Jack Maloney clearly, and it frightens my immortal soul to see him so. I am a little man walking with a heavy burden upon me, and the burden is freedom. What right had I to make a great blather over those citizens in the tavern?

Every right, I threw at him, for there they sat and swilled while we fought and died.

Yes, yes, Jamie, he answered me very softly. We fought and died. That was the essential of it. The cross we bear is like the cross of our Lord Jesus Christ, when his poor weary feet took him up the hill to Calvary. Did he turn and say, Lessen my burden . . . ? No—no indeed, Jamie, nothing of that he said to the citizens who watched him go past.

And you are not Jesus Christ, Jack Maloney.

As you say, Jamie, but did it never occur to you that we share something?

You talk like a damned parson!

No, Jamie—God forgive me that I should talk like a parson! Drunk I am, but not that drunk. Not with religion, Jamie, but with a little bit of the truth. A little bit. Did it ever occur to you, Jamie Stuart, to contemplate the truth, the immense awful truth of today and yesterday, of the present and the past and the future too, the way a man lies upon the ground and contemplates the stars in the sky in their vastness? Jamie, you are a young lad, so a lot that I say you will thread into one ear and out the other, but some years ago I was stationed at a place called Gibraltar where there is a single rock as high as a mountain and the little monkeys clamber all over it, and we in the garrison there made a mutiny and struck for our freedom, and afterwards forty good lads were hanged up by their necks, and then I climbed me the rock and lay on top of it upon my back, looking up at the soft summer sky which is so lovely in those far parts and asking myself, What is the meaning of a man who dies unknown and unsung and unremembered, with a curse upon his soul from all of the gentry and all of the quality, and all of the kings and their grand commanders, and even his own true comrades are questioning themselves to know whether what he did was right or wrong or good or bad—and who keeps a score, Jamie Stuart, of the whiplashes and the canes and the multitude of other sorrows since time began? Who keeps that score, and what is the meaning of all the ranks of men who stand up for freedom and are then struck down? Always, they are like you and me, miserable and lowly men, with no quality to them and no grand manners and not even a decent shirt on their backs; but it is the essence of this thing called freedom that we should have some understanding of it, while those who sit and swill in the taverns look down upon us. Do you know where the score is kept, Jamie Stuart?

Where? I asked, caught up, in spite of myself, in his drunken outpouring.

In your own heart, Jamie Stuart, and in mine too; and with that he rose up to his feet.

Where are you going? I asked him.

Back to the Line, Jamie, where I will enlist me. And I hope to God that you will go with me.

The devil I will! I cried. I will not return and serve under that cursed crew—never! I will lay me down and die first!

Then I'm sorry, Jamie, because it's a lonesome thing to travel singly. But I am going.

But not tonight, I said, grasping his arm. Not tonight, you drunken idiot. Wait until morning.

He shook off my hand and answered with immense dignity, I will not wait until morning, Jamie, and you can do as you damn please. I will go now while the pride is upon me.

And with that he went out of the shed and into the rain.

So Jack Maloney left me, and I did not follow him—and yet I saw him again. I let him go out into the rain and the dark cold night—and for all I knew, out of my life and away from me forever; and there was the last of my good and splendid comrades whom I had lived with and eaten with and by whose side I had fought ever since I was a little lad of seventeen years.

All alone in the world, you are, Jamie Stuart, I said to myself, as I lay there in that woodshed, all alone with nothing to show for the years you carried a musket and bayonet. Alone and alone.

And like a child, I put my face in my hands and wept tears of bitterness and self-pity. Then I heard a noise and a scratching, and drew back in fear, but it was only a bedraggled cat seeking the same shelter I had. I purred to him and he came to me, and I gathered him close in my arms, and that way, sleeping sometimes, awake and shivering sometimes, I passed that unhappy night.

If the commonwealth of Pennsylvania and the Confederation gave me nothing else, I could thank them for a body that was hard as nails and more or less inured to every variety of cold and sickness, and I could thank them that I was able to walk out of Philadelphia the next morning on the turnpike to York village. The clouds had blown away, and it was a clear, cold sunny day, with blue sky and a clean wind from westward. So I said good-by to Philadelphia, which was no town to my liking, and I turned my steps to the only place that had some aspects of home to me. There were my memories and there was sweet Molly Bracken, and there were the old houses, the old church and the old mill—and all the childhood matters that one dreams about.

So there I went; and because I was young and healthy, my spirits soon picked up, and I strode along the pike with long steps, whistling as I walked.

PART TEN

Wherein I tell of my homecoming to York village in
Pennsylvania, and of what took place until that day
when I heard the beating of the drums again.

IT IS HARD TO imagine today how far away one place was from another in those old times, for as you know there were no railroads then anywhere in the whole land, and no river steam vessels, and no smooth surfaces on the highways for fast stages to dash along, but only the lumpy pikes and post roads, which were for the most part two tracks grooved deep in the mud, soft and slimy in the springtime, dusty in the summertime, but murderously hard with knife edges in the frozen wintertime. The gentry went by horse, but poor folk walked; and I was just about as poor as a lad could be. So it took me four long days to walk the distance to York village, and when I came there, the soles of my boots were worn to nothing; and if I was thin before, I was thinner now, my cheeks sunken, my belly rubbing lovingly against my spine.

I ate well on the first day and a little on the third day, and otherwise I ate nothing at all on that trip. The first day, after seven or eight miles of the cold winter morning had made me ravenously hungry, I stopped at a farmhouse gate, with the dogs yapping against it and longing for a chance to try their teeth on me, and with the wonderful smell of frying scrapple coming from within. That was a food I had not smelled or tasted a long, long while now, and I stood against the gate looking longingly at the little house, with its strange yellow and blue decoration—which told me that Bavarians lived within—and its plume of smoke in the chimney. In all the world, there is nothing like smoke out of a chimney to make a homeless man feel his condition. There I stood, until the door opened, and a small, neat, motherly woman appeared, with a veritable horde of children somehow managing to find shelter behind her skirts.

Her corn-colored hair was bound tightly back, and her tiny blue eyes regarded me shrewdly, as she said, *Was willst du, knabe?*

I had little enough German then; I wanted to say something else, something about myself and my homelessness, but I came out with, *Kleine Mutter...* and then added, *Hunger ich.*

The children giggled at this very bad speech, but something touched the lady deep to her heart, and she slapped them into silence, called off the dogs and invited me in. How I did eat that morning! An immense platter of scrapple was put before me, and with it I had three bowls of wheat porridge, good and salty, with lumps of fresh-churned butter melting in it. There was fresh cottage cheese and little yeast rolls that were taken out of the oven as I entered and a big wooden dish of boiled potatoes, with cream for a sauce. And for a side dish, for a nibble as we call it, there was smoked duck, cold and sliced thin with sliced hard-boiled eggs. And up and down the table were earthenware pots of jam, peach and apple and crabapple and the marvelous carrot jam that one finds only in this part of Pennsylvania. And to wash it all down, there were big clay jugs of milk, fresh taken from the cows only a few hours before and hot and sweet-smelling and delicious. It was such a breakfast as I had not eaten for years and years, such a breakfast as one could only find in the South Country of Pennsylvania, and I could have wept for the look and the taste and the smell of that food.

I sat at the table with the family, a weather-beaten, work-hardened man of fifty or so, his wife, and five children, the oldest about twelve, the youngest just a babe; and since they had no English at all, I tried my best to talk to them in my bad German, and to answer the many questions they threw at me. First, they let me eat, seeing how hungry I was, and enjoying, the way simple people do, the quantity of my appetite. Seeing that they did not hold against me the fact that I wore a soldier's overalls, I told them what I could about myself in their language, who I was and from where. They listened to every word respectfully and attentively.

Continental, the children said. They knew that word, and they said, Yankee?

No, no, I told them. *Fremden Brigada—brigada.* I spoke with my hands and with English, and the farmer man laid a hand on his wife's arm.

Wir haben einen sohn—he said very slowly, so I would be certain to understand. A tall son, a strong son who had worked with him, but then he went off. And the woman asked me to eat, please eat more, eat until all the hunger was gone. But there were hungers that never go, and suddenly I was sorry that I had come in here. But in German words I shaped the question, Who was their son and where was he?

In dem fremden brigada, said the man.

Du . . . ? the wife asked, and the same question was in the children's eyes. And the man repeated slowly, *In dem fremden brigada.*

I was there, I said; but I did not tell them that the foreign brigades were no more, no longer, but dissolved and gone forever. Was the war gone too and dissolved forever? I didn't know, but I asked them the name of their son.

Hans Stuttman.

And I knew. Was there anyone in the brigades I did not know? But it was three whole months since he had run with the bloody dysentery and laid down and died. What was I to tell them?

Das Kann man nicht wissen?

No, I answered, so many men in so great an army. I knew him not at all. I thought and thought; what was he like and what had he suffered and what had he dreamed? But he would never come back to this little brightly painted house, never at all. No, I knew him not, I said. I rose to go and, with questions still an ache in their eyes, they filled my pockets with bread and potatoes, so I had supper that night and an empty belly the next day. The second day I had nothing, and two farm doors were closed to me until my pride forbade me to go near any others or to beg at the kitchen of an inn; for while I had been many things, I was never a beggar and would not turn one now. On the third day, I saw a gypsy wagon camped in a little clearing among the trees, and there I went and ate of a rabbit stew the Romany folk were cooking. Though I was welcomed among them, there was precious little of the stew, and I ate only enough to take the edge off my hunger. But I lay by their fire that night, having no flint of my own to make one with, and I listened to their sad Romany music and looked at their fine-featured maidens—but not with wanting now, because I was on my way to see a maid of my own. The yearning to move was more than I could withstand, and though they invited me to wait and ride with them, I was up and afoot before the dawn, and when the sun rose, it shed its cold light on the lovely foothills of my own land. And that evening I arrived at the village of York.

Ours was a quiet, out-of-the-way little village, with nothing in particular to distinguish it until the Congress was driven out of Philadelphia in 1777 and came there to sit; but long before I returned now, the Congress had gone away and back to Philadelphia, and the one simple straight street of York village and the two simple cross streets that divided it were very much as I had known them in 1775, when first I marched away. I came walking along the pike as the sun was setting, onto what we had called the Deeley Street when I was a boy, but which even then had lost that early name, and there was the house of the master cobbler where I had been apprenticed, and as I passed by I glanced in and saw Fritz Tumbrill, seemingly not one whit changed, even though I had lived lifetimes since I saw him last; and here across the street was the feed store, the chemist's shop, and the Halfway Inn, called that, I think, because it was roughly halfway between Philadelphia and the Virginias. So I moved down the street in the twilight, seeing this and that which was the same and seeing this one and that one, whom I knew very well indeed; but I lacked the courage to speak even one hello, and no one at all knew me, who had gone away a stripling boy with a downy face and came back a tall man with a week's growth of beard upon him.

Not that they didn't look at me, for a soldier of the Line was no common sight in York village, and if nothing else, my big, dirty, canvas overalls marked me surely for what I was; but there were other things too: the beard on my face, the slow aimlessness of my steps—for who else is so adrift as a soldier discharged?—the cut of one shoulder above the other from the weight of twenty pounds of musket I had grown to manhood with, and that wary walk of the man who has learned to use the bayonet. Every face was turned toward me, but none saw in me Jamie Stuart who had gone away once, and none addressed me as I moved down the street to the old church and the ivy-covered manse. For where else would I go but there, and what other friends in the world had I but Jacob Bracken and his daughter Molly? You would think, wouldn't you, that there would be a lot from York village in the foreign brigades? But though once there had been nine from this place, there was only myself, Jamie Stuart, left from them. One of them, Frank Califf, had come home; two others in the 1st Regiment had died at Monmouth, and a fourth at York city a long time back. Three had been taken by sickness, and the last had disappeared, as soldiers do, gone away and no one knew to where. But here I was back, and I could imagine these quiet and home-kept citizens whispering:

Look how he goes to the church, and is it not a sorrowful thing what comes of a soldier!

There walked by me Brenton, the tanner, who had once hided me well for stealing his apples, and though he looked me full in my face, he knew me not, nor did Mrs. Swinson, nor Grandmother Sturtz, who did my mother's wifery, as I have heard said, when I came into the world. So I walked on, my heart filled with wonder and terror that I would see Molly Bracken as I saw them, and that she, as they, would see nothing of the lad she loved; but I did not see her, and presently I came to the manse and knocked at the door.

Himself, Jacob Bracken answered the door in the color-run twilight of that evening when I came home, with the sun setting in the winter west, with one paintbrush of violet across the sky and with the red glow of eventide lighting that wise and gentle man who opened the door to me. But even his eyes were not discerning enough, and he looked upon me gravely, standing there tall and unafraid, his long, narrow face seriously inquisitive of a travel-worn soldier who knocked upon his door, his side-whiskers grayer than I remembered them, but otherwise no different—and all of that was immensely reassuring, for one who is marked and branded with revolution is apt to consider that all the world turns over with his own adventures; and here was this little village and the folk in it fairly much the same as when I had left them. His broad mouth held that slight, ready smile, which told you that here was a man of God not wholly unconcerned with the brown dirt and the folk who stood upon it, and he said to me quietly:

My good friend, what can I do for you?

And he told me afterwards that in this skinny, ragged soldier who stood upon his doorstep there came to him, all at once and like an accusation, the voice of a handful who like men accursed went on without end; but there was no accusation in my thoughts or my voice, and I must have sounded like a little lad when I said to him:

Pastor Bracken, this is Jamie Stuart, come back again.

Dreadful to me was the long, lasting moment of silence, while he stared and stared—and fear came; for how did I know that here was where I belonged, and how did I presume on those I knew so little? To older folk, five years is very little indeed, but the five years from seventeen to twenty-two are a whole lifetime.

Jamie Stuart, he said slowly and thoughtfully and wonderingly. In all the mercy of God, is this him? Come up here, my son.

He held the door open and I passed in and followed him to his study, where a lamp burned. The wick of this he turned up; and then, putting a hand on either arm, he faced me and examined me searchingly all over, but warmly and fondly.

Jamie Stuart . . . he repeated . . . Indeed it is he. A boy goes away and a man comes back, and I am glad to see you home, my son.

Not being able to talk, I just stood there and faced him and let the warmth of the room, the golden light of the lamp and the curling flames of the fire sink into me.

Then sit down, he said. Sit down and rest, and in a while, you will be yourself.

He led me to a chair close to the fire, and I sat down there and I began to cry, ashamed of myself and hiding my face in the wing of the chair. But I had walked thirty miles that day, and never a bite of food had I eaten, and this was unreal and uncertain; and I wept because it would vanish as dreams always vanish, leaving behind them only the aching memory which in turn grows dim and unrecognizable.

I am ashamed, for a man should not weep, I told him.

And how else will you rid yourself of your sorrows, he answered, and make yourself clean again? How else, Jamie Stuart?

He poured a glass of wine from a bottle on his table and handed it to me. I drank it and felt better and wiped my eyes and sighed, for the generous heat of that place was all over me and through me.

Now I will tell Molly, he said, who is in the kitchen this minute, and what will she think to know that Jamie Stuart is back here, safe and sound and whole!

He would ask me no questions, I realized, but I stood up and begged him, She should not see me this way—and do I know her even? I am afraid.

You know her and she knows you.

Is she married?

No, he said. Why should she marry, when she considered so much of you?

But she should not look at me the way I am! What a sight I am! . . . Yet I could not explain to him how in Philadelphia a citizen would cross the street rather than pass by a soldier of the Line. I stared down at the ragged ends of my overalls, at the broken shoes that showed below them, at the frayed cuffs of my threadbare coat. Months had passed since I had bathed, and after the Line dissolved, I never shaved, but let the corroding ruin of it show all over my body.

And I have nothing, I said. To show for it all, I have nothing, not even a copper penny to buy a clean shirt, nothing, and I am here like a beggar . . .

Make your heart easy, Jamie Stuart, he said, and come with me. You are right, and she will not see you the way you are.

Then he took me upstairs to his own room, and laid out his own razor and a clean shirt and an old but clean pair of brown britches and good woolen stockings, and then left me there by myself for a little. But while I was still shaving, he came up with a wooden tub and then with a great kettle of boiling water, and a washcloth and soapstone and a dish of oil—for in those days we had no soap such as there is now—and he added to the wardrobe underclothes and a handkerchief, which I had to touch and handle, so unused had I become to the sight of such things.

Does she know that I am here? I asked him.

Now wouldn't she know, Jamie Stuart? Who is this for and who is that for? she asked me, so I told her, and she stood looking at me the way you looked at me before. Is the war over? she asked me, but I did not know the answer to that, and after you have eaten, you may tell us what you desire to, and if you want to speak of nothing at all, well that is all right too.

I nodded, and then he closed the door behind him and left me alone. I finished shaving, and then I stripped off all my clothes, so that I stood naked for the first time since the winter began, and there was a great strangeness concerning the sight of my body, the white skin which turned black at the line of my boots, so that I wore stockings of ancient filth, the knobs of my joints, the long, stringy muscles, and the long lack of intimacy that made me ashamed, as if I were peeping surreptitiously at another. Standing in the tub, I poured the hot water over myself, and then scrubbed and scrubbed, oiling myself where the dirt was heaviest and working it out, scrubbing my hair too, every bit of me, until for the first time in so long I stood clean and fresh and sweet-smelling. Then I dressed myself in Jacob Bracken's clothes, with only my old boots to remind me of what I was once. From my own clothes, I took the few papers and documents which I had saved, my warrant from the Committee of Sergeants and the one or two other things I valued, and then folded the ragged bits of uniform together and placed them in one corner, thinking that the next day I would wash them, since they were all that I had.

Then I went downstairs into the low-ceilinged parlor of the manse. There Jacob Bracken waited for me, and he said:

This way, I would have recognized you, Jamie. You are not so different.

But inside—I thought to myself—there is a deep and profound difference, and how shall I explain that to anyone? And less and less able would I be, now that the events of Morristown and Princeton were so far away....

It will snow tonight, Jamie, said the Pastor Bracken, and it is good that you are here under our roof.

But where, I wondered, would Jack Maloney be when the snow fell, and where Billy Bowzar and Danny Connell and the Jew Levy and all the rest? Where would they be?

Taking my arm, Jacob Bracken led me into the little dining room, where the round table was set for three people, and where Molly Bracken waited.

Here is a man to see a woman, said the Pastor, and I said:

Good evening to you, Molly Bracken.

Good evening, Jamie Stuart, said she.

And then she gave me her hand, which I held for a moment, but more than that I could not do, and what I would say, I did not know. This and that out of the past is unclear and indistinct, but I see Molly Bracken plainly

279

enough as she was on that evening when I came home, with her black, black hair so shining and lovely, and with her eyes so blue, the fullness of her womanhood lessened only a little by the size I had gained in growth; and this was the dream I had over and over for five long years. Well, my throat was big and my voice was hapless, and overgrown and awkward I stood, like a large and hapless lad, until she asked me, simply enough:

And are you hungry, Jamie Stuart?

Never a bite of food did I taste today.

Then sit down and I will bring you my cooking, and you can see what a fine cook I am.

So the three of us sat down at the round pine table, with its pretty painted top and its four pewter sticks, which I remembered so well, and the pewter mugs and the yellow dishes that were made by the Dutch folk in Philadelphia, and the two-pronged forks that had come over from the old country; and the Pastor bent his head and said:

Lord God of Hosts, Who is merciful in His strange ways, we give Thee thanks this night not alone for bread which we eat, but for bringing home to us this lad who, without kith or kin, is dear to us and close to our hearts.

Then Jacob Bracken looked up and smiled and said, Bring in the food, Molly lass, and we'll see if the lad has improved his appetite along with his ways.

But I sat there with my head bent and the tears coming again, hating myself for my weakness, for I had been a strong man and a hard one, hearkened and respected by the soldiers of the Line. Not until Molly had gone for the food did I raise my head again.

In those times, the South Country of Pennsylvania was fruitful, and even a poor Lutheran Pastor set a good table, and if as a boy I ate poorly in my apprenticeship, it was less for the lack of food than for the contempt of men, child or otherwise, that the whole system of master and servant bred. Tonight, there was fresh baking, suet pudding and boiled beef with turnips, with pickled apples on the side and small beer. It was good and filling food and I ate well, but mostly with my eyes on the table, and almost as little as I spoke, Molly spoke; but the Pastor kept up a running history of the five years in the town, who was born and who died, and what had taken place when the Congress fled Philadelphia and came here to sit. In this very manse had sat Peytons from the Virginias and Schuylers from York colony and such other men as Stewart and Adams and Reed and great gentry of like kind, and what would Molly Bracken think of me sitting here now, the orphan child of Scottish bondslaves who did not even know his own grandfather and was owner not even of the clothes that he wore? But Jacob Bracken had no mind for that, and on and on he went; a sawmill had been set up, and with the new loan from France, it was turning out wood for muskets day and night, and it was done on shares, so that Tumbrill was no longer merely a cobbler, but held a per-centage of stock in the mill, as did Jackson Soakes, who had set up a banking establishment here when Congress came—which bank still flourished; and there was talk of iron molding, since if campaigns were to be fought in the South, why should not ball ammunition be dropped here? Many were the changes that I had never noticed, and he said:

These are new ways, Jamie, but I can't say that I like them. It troubles me that the war, which we never see or feel, brings us wealth so strangely...

Father, said Molly Bracken, never a word can Jamie get in when you go on like that.

I am merely filling in the years.

Yes, Father, said Molly Bracken patiently, that you are, and he comes straightaway from where there are things doing and battles fought and grand encampments and cities—but never a word of this will you give him a chance to tell.

When he wants to tell it, he will tell it, said Pastor Bracken. When my son comes home, I do not ask him why he comes. It is enough for me that he is here. When I opened the door, Molly, and saw a soldier of God's own angry army standing there in the cold winter night, with the ragged overalls that Christ's soldiers wear, I did not think to catechize him on where he was from or where he was bound for, or whether he was coming from the battle or going to it; for who am I here in the comfort of mine own house to question those who freeze in the open wintertime and march all footsore and weary? I think, sometimes, that we are too proud, too proud, and such as we would not hasten to lighten Christ's burden if he came by with the great weight upon his back, but would rather point out that his clothes were ragged and his face unshaven. So if I would give shelter and comfort and confidence to a stranger—which no man is in all truth—should I do less for my son here?

I didn't ask for a sermon, Father, said Molly patiently, but simply for a moment for someone else to get a word in.

Jamie, he said, these are new times, with less respect from a child than my father got from his. Is the war over, Jamie?

No, I answered, and then I told them what had happened. Wholly and completely, I told it, keeping nothing back, and there we sat at the table while the candles burned down, with no interruption except when Jacob Bracken rose to throw a stick of wood on the fire, and all of it came out of me, even to the last betrayal of my comrades. So I finished and said:

This is what I did, and I came home to the only place I knew as home, and as to whether what I did was right or wrong, you can judge.

I cannot judge, said Jacob Bracken, and that is something that only the Lord God can do, so I will not judge, Jamie. Meanwhile, go into my study and pull up a chair to the fire, and while Molly finishes the women's work, I will burn some rum and we will drink a glass with butter and talk as friends, which is what we are, Jamie Stuart. So go on in there, Jamie, and build up the fire and draw the chairs close, and soon we will join you.

This I did. And then with the dry wood spluttering in the hearth, with the little room just as warm and cuddly as a squirrel's nest, I went to the window and watched the first real winter's snow begin to fall. You know when it is the real snow, the deep snow, the abiding snow that comes to blanket the ground and remain. Each flake is large and firm and turns and twists with great assurance as it comes to the ground, and then for a man indoors there is the mighty security of roof and fire, but for a man out in the field it is an awful thing to see the whole world turn white and cold and silent. So for all that I was here, with the fire blazing and the books lining the walls and the stuffed wild goose sitting popeyed and proud on the mantel, I was neither restful nor at ease; for the best of me was elsewhere, and what was I doing by the fireside with all of my good comrades gone away from me?

I was glad when Jacob Bracken came in, for I feared my own thoughts and had no desire to be alone with them. He gave me a mug of hot flip, and we sat down before the fire, and he said:

Well, Jamie, here we are, myself and you too, snug and safe in front of the fire—which in a way is God's judgment for whatever small good we did in our lives. Do you believe in God, Jamie?

It took a while for me to answer that, for in the flames and come to life, as pictures do when you sit and ponder a burning log, were all the troubles I had known in my own young life, and all the little bites of glory, and all the faint heart and fears, and all the marches and counter-marches since that long ago time when the 1st Regiment of the Pennsylvania Line had paraded through the streets of Philadelphia and then set out to join the Yankee farmers outside of Boston town, each of us with a sprig of May finery in our hats, each of us with something or other in our hearts. Thus moved the possessed and the dispossessed and we were one together, but I was not one with them any longer; and here was a man of God asking me if I believed in his Master.

I think not, I said finally and unhappily, for I never saw any judgment between the good and the bad which was not either the whim of chance or the working of the gentry. There was a little drummer lad in the beginning of this revolt, and his name was Tommy Mahoney, and while some drummer boys become mean and sly and bad in every way—which is not so strange, when you consider the terrible life they live—this one was good and pure, and he died without cause or reason, as did so many of my comrades in all the years of this bitter war.

And was the Revolution no reason, Jamie? asked Jacob Bracken.

Sure—reason enough, if you say that what we went away to strive for might have been. But soon enough we discovered that the grudge and gripe of the officer gentry was not our grudge and gripe, and it was only to serve their purpose that we existed. There was one class in the Line of the foreign brigades, and there was another class who led us, and never was there a meeting between the two or any kind of understanding. They turned us into dogs; it was the whip and the cane, week in and week out, with no pay and no food and no clothes—and soon that became no hope, which could not be otherwise, it seems to me. We in the Line were Jew and Roman and Protestant and black and white, and we learned to fight and live and work together; so when you ask me if I believe in God, what should I think about the big Bantu Nayger, a slave and unbaptized without grace or salvation, and he came into the Line with blood on his hands and a heathen name, Bora Kabanka, a great black man who had slain his master? What should I think about him, when at Monmouth he picked me up in his arms and bore me from the field under fire, like I was a little babe—and if I had a guinea for every lash he took from the officers because he was a proud black man, then I would be rich indeed? There is dying for a cause, which is one thing, and there is dying for the proud folk who do not give two damns for us. I leave that. I will not go back and serve under them again, and I will not believe in a God who stands firm behind the man with property but has only a curse and a blow for men like me.

Well, Jamie, Jacob Bracken said thoughtfully, there's a way of looking at things, and belief in God is not an easy matter to argue, is it? I don't hold with those who say *Don't discuss religion*—for what is better meat for chewing than the food of one's own soul? Now I believe in God and in the Lord Jesus Christ the way I believe in my own right hand, and I attempt to serve Him, you know; but consider that I who talk of God with such certainty have never ventured in His behalf any more than a little speech and now and then a bout with a sinner, whereas you who deny Him, Jamie, have given five years of your life in His holiest service.

Have I? I said.

Indeed you have, Jamie, and on that point I am completely clear.

Well, I wondered, what of the King's soldiers, who are blessed with the blessing of God when they put on that lobster suit of theirs?

Now, for the first time, Jacob Bracken lost his calm manner; a flush came over his long, narrow face, and the broad mouth roared out:

Who said?

The Archbishop of Canterbury, for one.

The servant of the Devil! he cried. On his lips, the word God is an abomination! Ye hear me, Jamie? An abomination! Every sacred martyr of Protestantism is proof of that! Cursed is the Church of England as the Church of Rome is cursed—

But, I interrupted, a great many of the lads in the brigades were Romans.

Jamie, he roared, have you become a damned theological pettifogger? Do my words mean nothing to you?

He was half serious, half humorous. Jamie, he said, there is not that much obscurity concerning the works of God.

Molly joined us now. Across the village, they could hear you, said she.

And with reason.

That I doubt, she answered him, drawing a chair up to the fire, so that the three of us sat in front of it now, and in this all my dreams were realized. Yet the rum I held was without taste, and Molly Bracken was a stranger to me.

Jamie, said the Pastor, surrender not grace that easily.

But I had surrendered, and staring at the flames, I held my rum untasted and tasteless.

Outside, said Molly Bracken, a great storm is making. And it will snow and snow.

Said the Pastor, Jamie, when you made the uprising, you and your comrades, what was in your minds?

Not God, I said sourly, not anything like that—but only that it was unbearable.

Yet there must have been a thought of what would be afterwards.

How do I know what the others were thinking?

I will not lose my temper with you, Jamie Stuart, said Jacob Bracken. You are under my roof, and under my roof you shall stay.

Molly said, Leave him be. Leave him be. Look how tired he is.

This I was thinking, I said suddenly. I was thinking that we would strike a flame that would ignite everywhere, and everywhere plain folk like myself would join us. And that we would sweep the British into the sea and make a place here of justice and decency.

That's a grand thought, Jamie, said Jacob Bracken.

And look what it came to. Where are the foreign brigades now . . . ?

Consider, Jamie, said Jacob Bracken, that you have given five years, and how many have given nothing!

I have given nothing! I cried. How can I tell you?

But there was no way in which I could tell them, and they were more gentle and good to me than I deserved; and presently Jacob Bracken led me up to the little attic room where my bed was, and I crawled in between the clean sheets and lay there, looking out at the big flakes of snow that drifted past the window. . . .

So it was that I came back to York village and to my friends and to what life had been before I went away, and I picked up this thread and that thread, and presently the numbness in my heart, which had been there ever since Jack Maloney left me that cold and rainy night in Philadelphia, eased out, and I began to forget the whole violent wash of war that had surged up and down and through the Jerseys for so long. Here, we were a long way from Jersey; life went on here, and in the wintertime, when the roads were closed with snow, this was a world to itself.

The town made no fuss over me; Jamie Stuart had gone, and now Jamie Stuart was back, and it mattered very little indeed. The war was something they had long since become used to; and like most Pennsylvania people in good circumstances, they were only nominally in favor of it. Perhaps a little more in this town than in others, since the war had brought business and money, but the fact that the Pennsylvania Line was no more—a piece of news that came to the village from this direction and that—gave them no great concern. This was a war that had gone on too long. If Jamie Stuart washed his hands of it, that was sound sense from where it was least expected; for what real good could come from a miserable Scottish lad born from parents who had been bondslaves?

I stayed with Jacob Bracken because I had no other place to stay; but often enough I thought to myself that it was time for me to be moving on, and I decided that when the snows began to melt, I would take the road for Philadelphia, perhaps to sign onto one of the sailing vessels, or to get a job in the ropeworks, or even to find a place there as a cobbler. York village was not for me, and Molly Bracken was a stranger, as if she had never kissed me upon the lips, as if we had never exchanged words of love; but she was a grown woman now with the need to think seriously of the future, and what was the future of a soldier out of the army? In no way did I hold this against her, but I tried as much as I could to avoid her; and when they took me on as a hand at the sawmill at half a guinea a week, I saw her almost not at all—for it was up at the dawn and back with the night, and only at the table did we exchange a word or two.

Once or twice I said to Pastor Bracken, I have no right to stay on here like this, and suppose I found a room and board elsewhere?

But his response was always something to the effect of my wanting to drive home a disagreement; and indeed I did not take too much persuasion, for there was nothing in York for me now but the sight of Molly Bracken, if even for a little and without hope. And when, here and there, one of the long-tongued gossips in the village let it drop that they did not approve of the wild and wicked Jamie

Stuart living under the same roof as the poor, motherless Bracken girl, Jacob Bracken's spine stiffened like a ramrod.

Now you stay here, Jamie, he said firmly, and from his pulpit he thundered at those who carry false witness.... Aye, we have a militia, he told his congregation, but a militia waits for the war to come to it, and the good Lord has seen fit to keep the war far distant—for His own purposes—although one gunshot in freedom's name might be a better sermon than all my words. But who else is there except one orphan lad among you who has ventured his life in what we discuss so glibly? ...

And I squirmed and avoided the eyes of those around me; but Molly Bracken sat with her head up and smiling, and that made me wonder.

But themselves, the townsfolk were a little afraid of me; I was not only different from them now, but the distorted tales they had of the rising made them think of me as a wild and lawless person, and when finally I came face to face with Fritz Tumbrill, he was a meek and a chastened man.

It was when I had my first half-guinea in my pocket that I went to his shop to order a pair of boots, which was my greatest need at the moment. Believe me, it was a strange thing to be back there now, to see how small the shop had become in its insignificant frame building, all covered with snow, so insignificant a reality in comparison with my memories—and I often think now that there is the best sign of maturity, the reality of things instead of the unreal threat of them. My world had been a world of spirits and demons and witches and ogres, but I had faced real fears and found them not so awful as they might be, and death itself is not the worst thing in the world if you can face it with your eyes open. And here was this man I had feared so, all shrunken and old and small, and now he was afraid of me.

But let me tell you how I came in, how I pulled at the latch and how the little bell tinkled, and how a child's voice told me to come in, even as I had once told people to enter. Inside, nothing at all was different; a boy at one bench and Fritz Tumbrill at the other, but when he looked up and saw me, his face became pale; his big jowls shook; and he said to me, almost pleadingly:

Why, welcome home, Jamie Stuart.

Good evening to you, Fritz, I nodded. I have come to have a pair of boots made.

And glad I am to see you, Jamie. I tell you now, they will be the best boots I ever turned out of my shop, and not a penny will they cost you. All the time when you were off to the war I said to myself, There is Jamie Stuart gone with never time to give him a little gift. So this will be a gift in a way of speaking, Jamie.

I want no gifts from you, Fritz Tumbrill, I said. I will pay you what the shoes are worth.

Are you holding old scores agin me, Jamie? he asked, cocking his head and looking up at me.

Well, I had been, I had been; but looking at him now and from him to the thin, pale-faced boy who sat on the other bench, his head down, his skinny little hand frozen in midair, clenching the hammer, his mouth full of tacks— looking from one to the other, my hatred for this fat, gross man who was now part owner of a mill went away, and I asked myself, What are you doing here, Jamie Stuart? What are you doing here with this fat shopkeeper, in this fat and contented town, living with a pastor who will patiently convert you to God again? What are you doing here, Jamie Stuart? I asked myself, remembering the worst of times I had known—and the worst of them were not like this, not like this in this place, where the Roman was hated and the Jew maligned and the black man considered an ape from dark Africa. Yes, standing there in the cobbler's house, I felt that my soul was shriveling up within me, and all the goodness and greatness that had been mine once when I marched in the companionship of Revolution was plain to me now and made plain too late; and as my heart had never hungered for anything, so did it hunger for the ugly little men of the brigades who were my comrades.

Old scores? I questioned. No, cobbler—no; there are no old scores left. Make me my shoes and be done with it. . . .

So I had new boots and work at the mill and a home with Jacob Bracken, who spoke to me gently of God and of humility and of my future. The month passed and March came, and with March the warm sunshine to shrink the snow—so that by the middle of the month it already appeared that spring was at hand. There was one fair Sunday when I took Molly to church to hear her father preach, and I sat as I always did in the church, stiffly and uncomfortably, counting the minutes until it was over, filled with a turmoil of doubt and unsatisfied longing and hesitation and the brooding wonder that attempted to extract some meaning from my life and from my deeds. When the service was finished, I rose to leave, and Molly Bracken said:

Look at the day, Jamie, with the sun shining like in summertime. Will you walk with me a little?

If you wish, and if you are not ashamed to walk down the street alongside of Jamie Stuart.

What a thing to say! Now I am not ashamed but proud.

And after we had walked a little way, she said to me, Why should I be ashamed, Jamie Stuart?

Because I am not like the others in this place.

Maybe you are more like them than you think, Jamie Stuart.

No, less like them than you would think, Molly.

We passed out of the village and along the road, walking slowly, side by side, and saying nothing until we had gone quite a way. And then it was Molly Bracken who asked what gnawed inside of me, the way I was.

What way?

Like a stranger, Jamie Stuart, like I had never known you before and there was nothing at all between us of any worth or meaning or reason for remembering. Sometimes, you frighten me.

As I frighten other people, Molly?

Yes . . .

Tell me why, I said, as gently as I could, for now I realized clearly enough that it was not the difference in herself but in me; and here was a beautiful and womanly person who wanted myself who was nothing and less than nothing, an orphan and a penniless soldier out of the Line; and the bitter sorrow of it was that he did not want her.

I can only tell you part of it, she answered, but you never made to kiss me or to touch me or even to look at me full in the eyes. When you came home that evening, and my father came down and put a kettle onto the fire, and I said to him *Why?* and he told me that Jamie Stuart was upstairs and would wash off the dirt of marching and fighting before he would come before me—and when I heard that, I thought I would faint from gladness, and there was a song in my bosom that said over and over and over again, *Jamie Stuart is back—he is back to stay, and he will never go away again.* See how shameless I am to tell you all of this—

Not shameless at all, Molly Bracken, but tell it to me only if you desire to.

Why am I telling it to you then, and you ask me how are you strange? The winter is gone, Jamie Stuart, but the cold clings to you—do you know that?

I didn't know that, I said unhappily, and if it is true, then God help me.

How can He help you when you don't believe in Him, Jamie Stuart?

You hold that against me?

Oh, I don't hold that against you, Jamie Stuart, but you hold it against yourself, and you have no belief in the people here or in the war or in me either—but only a terrible hatred that makes me afraid when I look at you. What do you hate so?

Many things, I answered her, many things, walking step by step and so slowly, my eyes on the road, kicking stones out of the soft mud as I went along—and wondering what I could tell her, but wanting underneath not to tell her anything, for what was the use of cataloguing hatred when nothing I hated could withstand the scrutiny of my thoughts? It was less the gentry and the village and the pinch-souled cobbler, and the narrow self-concern of these people here and the hypocrisy of their lives, and the limit of their vision and the complacent relationship they had in each of their churches to their God, than the fact that I knew of nothing better than their way. When my comrades and myself took into our own hands the strength of the army, we marched into nowhere; and that was the way my hatred went—into nowhere.

So I said many things, but I could not tell her what the singular of it was. I hated in its wholeness a life that twisted the souls of men, but I knew of no living that did not; and thereby it had come about that I was a stranger wherever I went; but that I could not tell her, and I could not tell her that the only men who were my kind were those men who had marched with me in the brigades—and less could I tell her that I felt a closer bond and a purer sympathy to those poor damned women who had cast in their lot with us, whores though they were by any of her standards, than I did to herself, so young and fine and lovely. None of that could I tell her, but only that I hated many things.

Then God help you, Jamie Stuart, if you do not even know what you hate.

I have never known Him to help me or any other man.

Because you close your heart to Him.

About that I don't know, I said sadly. It may be.

Then we turned around to walk back, and walked on for a time in silence. We were almost back at the village, when she took my hand and held it tightly for a moment.

Jamie Stuart—

Yes?

Jamie Stuart, were you thinking of going away?

I was thinking of that, I answered.

Will you tarry a little while?

If you want me to, I will, I said, but I was afraid it would only make it painful for you and for me both. In some

ways now, I am only half a man—and I am no good for
myself or for you.

For me, Jamie Stuart, you are good.

But even though I answered her that way, the thought
of going never left my mind. As Danny Connell had said,
a bird pecked in me, and I tired of the work at the mill,
the sameness of it, the boys off the farms who worked
alongside of me, with their talk of this girl or that one
and never a thought of anything else in their heads—and
no curiosity either about the boundless world that
stretched away in every direction and only contempt for
me who was the child of bondslaves and was five years a
soldier with never a penny of hard money to show for it.
But when I began to think that they were truly like animals, I would remember that I had been very like them
before I went away; but I never ceased to wonder that, at
one and the same time, a great war could be going on in
the same land where these people lived from day to day,
with never a thought of the war in their heads or a care
for it either.

Sometimes, I went into Jacob Bracken's study and
looked at his books; but there were few among them that
could interest me. Most of them were heavy and dry theological tomes, written by serious and outstanding Protestant authorities, and there were various editions of the
Bible and commentaries upon them. There all of
Shakespeare, but little enough of it could I understand. And
in a book of seven poets, such men as Wilmot and Prior
and Pope, I found once these few lines by William Collins,
which I said to myself until they lodged in my memory and
remain there still:

How sleep the brave, who sink to rest
By all their country's wishes bless'd!
When Spring with dewy fingers cold
Returns to deck their hallowed
   mould,
She there shall dress a sweeter sod
Than Fancy's feet have ever trod.

It made me dream of what a fine, rich thing it would be to write some poetry of a sort about our own Pennsylvania men and what we had done, but not like this, but rather proud and angry; and this thought, I knew, struck only a cord of lament for my own bereftness. But once, I recall, I was looking through a book of sermons that had been published in Philadelphia, for the use and convenience of men of the cloth, as it said; and therein, written by a Yankee called Jonathan Mayhew, I found something that beat on my mind like a brief flash of light, so that my groping almost found something to hew onto out of these words:

Tyranny brings ignorance and brutality along with it. It degrades men from their just rank into the class of brutes. It damps their spirits. It suppresses arts. It extinguishes every spark of noble ardor and generosity in the breasts of those who are enslaved by it. It makes naturally strong and great minds feeble and little; and triumphs over the ruins of virtue and humanity. This is true of tyranny in every shape. There can be nothing great or good where its influence reaches. . . .

This above, I read with great excitement, like the key to a door that might open and admit me; and my excitement was such that later I interrupted Jacob Bracken in his work and begged him to listen while I read it aloud.

Yes, he said, that is part of a preachment of Mayhew, and I know it well. It is from a sermon he preached some twenty or thirty years ago. I should have liked to hear him preach. He is said to have been a man with a rich color of speech, but there is nothing new or particularly original in what he says, Jamie.

But there is, I protested. Tyranny *in every shape*, he says. Not one tyranny, not another or this one or that one, but in every shape. Then it means to destroy all tyranny— not only the tyranny of Britain and George III—

It is not to be taken literally, Jamie, he said patiently, for Mayhew himself distinguishes between what is a just and what an unjust tyranny.

How can there be a just tyranny? I demanded. If all men are created free and equal . . .

Created, Jamie; yes, indeed, created, Pastor Bracken said, his long, sober face expressing a mixture of concern and annoyance, but after the creation there is a natural order of things. One must be master and one must be servant. One must be rich and one must be poor. This is not matter of equality but of the order of life, which is another thing entirely, and man was conceived in sin not in perfection, and it is idle to dream that it could have been any other way or ever will be different. Here are you who have learned to read and to write, and as an educated man, Jamie, you can have a future in something better than running sticks through a watermill. And if you should find grace, Jamie, the ministry is open to you, and I will do all in my power to help you—and indeed I know of no better calling for a man who believes in justice and right. On the other hand, when this unhappy war is over, this will be a country of boundless opportunity, and many a lad like yourself has started in a Philadelphia counting-house with no more than the coat on his back and found himself a rich and respected merchant. Such men as these are a mighty bulwark in our struggle against the corrupt and insidious Church of England and the decadent and monstrous King who keeps it in power. And sooner or later—

Who taught me to read? I interrupted.

I know what you will say, Jamie, but I assure you, Jamie Stuart, that if I had not taught you, another would have, for the desire to learn and know was within you, and this desire to learn and know will never be within all men. Some are wastrels and others are thoughtless, dull people, and that is why even in so just a war as this one, we are forced to open the prisons and poorhouses to find men to serve—so that we come to understand that in the highest cause, the lowest of men will find a place, not because they love liberty more, but because they are fitted to take orders and thereby fitted into the eternal scheme of things. This is a wisdom beyond our understanding, my boy, but we must accept it. And when we accept it, we find that it is the best of ways.

I see, I said.

I hope, Jamie, that you do not think I meant any reflection upon your comrades in the foreign brigades.

What difference does it make, I said slowly and strangely, since I have left them and gone away, but they are dull and thoughtless and see nothing else but to go on serving without pay and without reward? What difference does it make?

I hope, Jamie, said Pastor Bracken, that you will come to think differently about many of these things ...

I came to think less, perhaps; and I did my work, and the days passed; and April came, with the sweet singing and budding springtime of the Pennsylvania hills. Then I would have been far less than human to remain in the same house as Molly Bracken and remain this cold, aloof and self-sufficient thing that I prided myself on having become; for there was a certain bitter perversity in what I did, as if I took some pleasure in my separation from all the natural things of life. And one evening, when her father sat in his study, writing, I entered the kitchen as Molly Bracken was coming out and went head on into her, and then we were in each other's arms and I was covering her face with kisses, while she said:

Jamie, Jamie—how long and how much you hate me!

I love you the way I've never loved anyone.

And she pulled away and smoothed her hair and said, How you've showed me your love, Jamie Stuart!

I could not.

And what now, Jamie Stuart? What is different? Is it the springtime that scents a bitch?

God damn you! I cried. God damn you to hell!

Why, Jamie? she demanded, standing cool and aloof and apparently undisturbed now. Because a parson's daughter talks that way? Do you talk to me like I was a whore because you want a whore?

Shut your mouth! I cried.

No, that I will not do, Jamie Stuart. For long enough I held my peace, while you lived here, hating us and eating our food and taking our shelter—

Because you kept me here! And I offered to pay, but you would not take my pay, so that I would be beholden to you!

And you would not be beholden to anyone, Jamie Stuart? Twenty-two years old you are, and the heart inside of you is like a flint rock that nothing can scrape, and what I said before is true, that wherever you go, the winter cold goes with you! But here I waited five years, dreaming of my fine lad that had gone off to the wars, because whatever you were—and even that first time when I saw you sitting on the cobbler's bench, your hammer in your hand and your mouth full of tacks—there was a purity and a goodness in you. But there's no purity and goodness in you now, Jamie Stuart, and the man I waited for died somewhere.

Then I'll go! I cried. By God, I'll go!

Go on, Jamie Stuart, and see if I keep you here. Go on out and see if you can find the heart and soul of Jamie Stuart wherever you have left it! You should not have come home for somewhere you betrayed yourself and destroyed yourself!

And wasn't five years enough?

She was weeping now as she said, More than enough, more than enough, God help me, if you could have kept your own soul. But this way, Jamie Stuart, you should have stayed where the rest of you is.

I left her, stormed out and paid no heed to her calling after me, and went straightaway down the street to the inn. It was the first time I had been there in my ten weeks in York village, and this night was the first time I was drunk in my ten weeks at York village. But I knew what I wanted, for once; and when Simon Decorman, who kept the place, began to welcome me with, *Well, Jamie, and is it not fine to see you down here with human faces?* I cut him short and told him: I have not come here for companionship or gabble, but for a mug and a pitcher of rum!

Now is that a way, Jamie—

Damn it to hell, do you serve rum or don't ye?

If it's a drink ye want, with no word of kindness or good cheer, why you can buy it and be damned!

As to that, I'll decide, and you can speak to me when you're asked for it!

So I got a table in a corner and the rum, and I proceeded to make myself drunk in a right royal fashion. Gradually, as the supper hour passed, the place filled up, with the lads from the farms and the mill coming in to have a pint of beer or something hot, and many of them were surprised to see me and came over to pass a word with me. What I said to them, I don't remember, but it was not gentle words, and if it had been anyone else but me, there would have been fighting in the inn that night. But there was something in me that made them afraid, and they left me alone.

Of that night, there is little I remember and less that I desire to recall. Even in so small a place as York, there were the necessary forms and places for a man who desired a little taste of hell, and I had my taste and found shelter, finally, on toward morning, in the barn of Caleb Henry, where I burrowed into the hayloft and slept until the sun was high in the sky. Then I awoke with an aching head and a burning throat and very little desire to live altogether—though the last was diluted somewhat when I got to Caleb Henry's brook unseen, and soaked my head and drank my fill. Then I quartered across the field away from the village and toward the Philadelphia pike. Thus I would go as I came, with the clothes on my back and nothing in my pockets—and nothing in particular in my heart.

Oh, it was a lovely day, all right, and I will not forget that, nor how the wind blew so warm and softly from the west and how the little white clouds sailed across the blue sky. For all my misery, a taste for life would not be denied, and I felt myself expand and yearn toward this mighty and beautiful and limitless land of mine, with its hills and its valleys and its triumphant and unmeasurable spaces; it sang a song for me as I walked along, unshaven and un-washed, my cotton shirt covered with the filth of the night before, and in that song were the echoes of my own unborn poetry of the good struggle I had fought, side by side with the good and brave companions I had known. I was leaving all that I had, but there was a merciless truth in what Molly Bracken had said to me, and all that I had was nothing and less than nothing. And if I was miserable now, it was that misery of youth that is never complete and never un-mixed with something else. So it was in that mood, as I neared the pike, that I heard the beating of the drums, that old, old sound that was as familiar as my own pulse and as native to me—but in the mood I was in, the drums were a part of my thoughts and seemed to come from the inner rather than the outer world.

That way it seemed to me at first; but then I stiffened; my skin prickled all over, as if a wave of icy air were flowing over me, and my heart beat faster and faster. *There were the drums*—still far off, but real, and nowhere in the whole world but in the foreign brigades were drums beaten that way, not as the Yankees beat their drums, not as the British beat their drums, but in a cross between the skirling of the pipes and the haunting Slavic rhythms of the Polish men, singing a song of defiant, wild and angry sorrow, telling people who hear to beware of men whose lot cannot be worsened but only bettered, men who go into battle with nothing to lose; and coming as it does from the skinny hands of little children, there is a pathos added that once heard is not forgotten.

And now I was hearing it, and I began to run. Across the fields I ran, my heart pounding, bursting through a hedge, leaping a brook, panting and sobbing—but then losing all of my courage as I neared the road, and finally crawling into a patch of blueberry bushes, where I could see without being seen.

And there I lay, while the drums beat louder and louder, until finally they came into sight; and then when I saw them, I wept. First came Laurens and Stewart, leading the file and mounted finely, but it was not for them I wept, but for the little column of less than four hundred men, which was all that remained of the brigades. First there were the drummer lads, eight of them, little Tommy Searles and Jonathan Harbecht and Peter O'Conner and the rest, just as small, just as shrunken, just as pinch-faced as ever; and behind them marched Chester Rosenbank with four fifers, and then came the regiments—the two regiments that remained. But there they were and I saw them: Billy Bowzar and Jack Maloney and the Jew Levy and the Great Nayger man, Bora Kabanka, and Danny Connell—alone he was, and I wondered what had become of his fair maid— and Lawrence Scottsboro, older than ever, his back bent as he trudged along, and Angus MacGrath, towering over the others—yes, there they were, but many others were gone, and I wept as the little company marched past toward York village.

A long time I lay there, part of the time thinking, part of the time with no thought but the sudden peace I knew. And then I rose and walked back to York village, with my purpose clear in my mind.

PART ELEVEN

Which is the last part of my narration, and which tells
how the foreign brigades gathered again at York village in Pennsylvania and what befell them there.

S O I COME TO the last part of my tale of the foreign brigades of Pennsylvania and of their rising against the officer gentry; yet a little more must be told before I can let my memories be and let the dead sleep as they should sleep. Since it is of myself that I write, I must take some time for my own thoughts and my own broodings, which is what I know—and little enough do I know of my comrades. That they were not mean and lowly, I do know, and this I will assert again and again; for they had a store of courage and nobility that was nowhere found in my own soul. This I assert, before I write what became of them and of me.

Myself, I went back to York village after I had thought about the matter sufficiently and knew what I was going to do; I did not know whether it was right or wrong nor did I greatly care at the time, but I knew that I had to do it, because a man is no good when he is broken into many fragments, a piece here and a piece there, but only when he is whole. And I knew that it would make me whole again in the only way of wholeness I cared for.

So I walked back to York village after a time, and I walked down the street to Lemuel Simpkins's cow pasture, where the Pennsylvania Line had encamped. By now, it was late afternoon, and already the tents were raised, the pickets posted, and the men were engaged in clearing the grounds, laying out the parade and gathering wood for their night fires. They had stacked their muskets in the European manner, by fours with one bayonet fixed—which is peculiar to our brigades—and from the look of it you would have thought that there had been an encampment there for many a day past. They had put out sentries, raised up a flagpole, and were beginning to build brushwood shelters, so it was evident that this was no quick bivouac but an encampment of some duration; and everything they did was carried out in the easy, competent manner of men who knew their work well enough.

Simpkins's cow pasture rolls down and away from the road and the encampment was set a good quarter of a mile back, with the command tent on a little knoll. Already, half of the townsfolk and just about all of the children had gathered along the road to watch, and already the children had begun their game of hide-and-seek with the sentries. Oh, it was a familiar enough picture: the children and the excited people, and the seemingly bored sentries in their torn and dirty overalls, and the little knot of officers importantly discussing the situation with the town clerk and the town council, and the girls preening themselves and the drummer boys standing back and hooting at them, and the horses clustered near the command tent and the soldiers off duty sprawling gratefully on the grass, and one wretched little captain showing his authority by giving parade drill to a platoon—all of it familiar and terrible and wonderful at the same time.

For a while, I stood off, looking to see whether Molly Bracken was in the crowd; but she was not there, so I went past them and circled around, to come into the camp from the farther side. I walked up to a sentry, and it was Arnold Gary, and he took a long look and said:

By all that is holy and critical, is that Jamie Stuart himself and in the flesh?

It is, I agreed.

Then he threw down his musket and put his arms around me and rocked me back and forth, and I hugged the smell of him, the sour, rancid smell of the dirty overalls on a man who has marched all day long, the feel of him, of a man of mine own kind who was a brother to me; and he said:

I knew it, and I told them, You mark me, when we come into York village, there will be Jamie Stuart, fat as a plucked chicken.

And what are you doing here with the brigades—or what is left of them, God help me—so far south and away from everything? Is the war over?

This stinking war, said Arnold Gary, is one that will never be over; for if it was, what in hell's name would our lousy officers do with themselves? And for the sins of my blessed mother—who never taught me the writing or the reading—here I am still, and will be forever most likely. And as for being here in York, well this is a rendezvous, the way they say, to see if we can make a Line out of ourselves, so that we can march off south for a campaign upon which they have set their hearts, there being damned little to squeeze out of the Jerseys any more, while this Pennsylvania country is as fat and tasty as a pig's ass. Ye can see that I envy you, Jamie Stuart, standing there in them fine shoes and fine breeches with never a care in the world, while my own reward from the damn uprising is special treatment with the cane.

How is it then?

It is lousy, Jamie Stuart, if you must know the whole truth.

How do you mean?

I mean that they are exacting payment in their own sweet way. For the exact letter of the rising, it is true that they have kept their word and exacted no punishment, but if you break step you get a cane on your back and twenty lashes for just whispering at parade, and for the Jew Gonzales, because he talked back to that dirty little rat Purdy, one hundred lashes, from which he died, just as Jim Holt, the Nayger, died when he talked back to Butler and they 'spontooned him in the belly. Oh, Jesus Christ, that was a thing to see, for he lay there on the ground, twisting and turning and begging us not to pull out the fat spear, but we had to, and then he rolled over and vomited out his lifeblood. And can you imagine that the fools of the Committee remained? Even Jack Maloney, coming back from Philadelphia, where he said he left you.

I know that, I said.

And you are free and clear, Jamie—what a blessing!

Depending on how you look at it, I said, for I have come here to enlist.

No!

It's true, so I'll thank you, Arnold, to let me go through to their damned command tent.

Are you crazy, Jamie? Are you clear and raving mad?

Possibly. What in hell—

He interrupted by tapping my chest and saying deliberately, Go away from here, Jamie Stuart.

And why don't you run away? I demanded. Off across the fields and away, and who would ever find you, Arnold Gary?

Where would I run to, Jamie? And what do I know except to heft a musket? But yourself—

Myself is my own conscience, so let me go past.

All right, he said. All right, Jamie Stuart.

And then he picked up his gun and went on his round, and I walked along into the encampment; and one after another the men saw me and recognized me, and many of them hugged me close, so I knew how it was to be back with them again.

Here I met Bowzar and Jack Maloney, who said, Have ye come to look down at us, Jamie Stuart?

Down or up, I answered; what in hell is the difference? And I walked past him over to the command post, where Butler and Laurens stood talking and then looked up and faced me in silence. But the men, my own old comrades, they kept their distance and stood together, watching quietly.

Well, here I am, I said, and I've come to enlist.

Laurens smiled in a way that might mean anything at all, and Butler put his hands in his pockets, spread his feet, and looked me all over and up and down.

Jamie Stuart, he said.

You have a long memory, I answered calmly enough.

Longer than you would ever imagine, Mr. Stuart, and

when you address me, why you will address me as Colonel Butler, if you please.

Yes, sir.

Yes, Colonel Butler!

Yes, Colonel Butler, I repeated.

Now in that there is the making of a good soldier, Jamie Stuart, so if you go over to the tent, the Jew will make your papers for you, and then you can draw a pair of overalls from Captain Kennedy at the supply depot over yonder and report back here.

I answered, Yes, Colonel Butler.

But he paid no more attention to me, going on with his conversation with Laurens, who now carefully avoided my eyes; and I walked to the big tent and entered. There Levy sat at a camp table, with the journal of the Line, that old, weather-beaten, leather-bound book which we had treasured so carefully through our rising, open in front of him— wherein he was composing the details of the day's march; and he looked up as I came in, his thin face a little more worn, a little more lined, his hair streaked with gray, but otherwise no different, and he squinted at me because my back was to the light.

Hello? he inquired.

I walked over and showed him my face, and a slow smile came and wrinkled him all over, and he stretched out both his hands for mine.

Jamie Stuart, and God be praised for keeping you sound and healthy.

And how goes it with the Line, Leon Levy?

This and that, Jamie Stuart. Some are dead and some are gone, and now there is a great campaign brewing in the Southland, but where will men be found to fight it? The people are tired of war.

You look tired, my friend.

We get tired. But what should I say about you, Jamie Stuart? You are different. Are you happy here in this pretty place, and are you with the beautiful lass whose name is Molly? Is it a good life here?

It's a good enough life, I answered him, but I am here to enlist in the Line again.

To that he made no reply, but looked at me searchingly for a long while; and then he nodded and got the papers and prepared them.

Sign your name here, lad, he said.

I signed my name, and once again I was a soldier of the commonwealth, and then I went and drew my overalls and put them on, and then I reported back to Butler and Laurens.

So you see, I have a long memory, said Butler.

I stood at attention and said nothing.

An astonishing long memory, and your overalls are torn, Stuart.

They were issued to me this way, sir, and I have not had time to mend them.

And dirty.

Nor to wash them, sir.

I said before, specifically, Stuart, that you were to address me as Colonel Butler.

I am sorry, Colonel Butler.

Sorrow, Stuart, is not an admirable quality in a soldier. Discipline is more becoming, and it seems to me that twenty-five lashes would wipe out your sorrow and instill a decent regard for soldierly qualities. Do you agree?

He wanted me to plead or protest, and I would have died before I did either. Laurens stood beside him, silent, but watching me narrowly; and I knew that he would not interfere, nor did I desire him to.

Do you agree, Stuart? Butler pressed.

You are my commanding officer, Colonel Butler, I answered him.

We will add five lashes for insolence. A round thirty. Have you anything to say to that, Stuart?

Nothing.

You are taciturn, Stuart. Never were there a more loud-mouthed, dirty-spoken lot of unhanged cutthroats than the men of the 11th Regiment, but they have all become admirably meek and silent. I am pleased to find you no exception, Mr. Stuart.

So there was my introduction to the Line, and they did it properly, that same evening, as the sun was setting, drawing up the men to parade and laying on the thirty lashes with the drums beating and with a fine concourse of townsfolk watching from the road. As an evidence of humor and understanding, a short man and a tall man were instructed to handle the whips, so that Kabanka and Levy were forced to administer my punishment; and then the same two, when I was finished and fainting with pain, carried me gently to the hospital tent, where Andrew Mac-Pherson rubbed bear fat into my back and Jack Maloney and Billy Bowzar tried to cheer me.

I am cheerful enough, I said evenly, and happy enough, so leave me alone.

And because they understood me and knew me, they left me alone there with my own thoughts and the strong, soothing fingers of the barber....

*   *   *

Why did they whip you? Molly Bracken asked me, when I returned to tell her what I had done and that I would live at the manse no longer.

Because they have long memories, and they have not forgotten what happened in January, I answered her, looking at the fine, ripe wholeness of her, looking at the sunlight which came through the window and lay upon her hair. She sat in her parlor facing me, her hands in her lap, her back straight, a strong, contained woman and like a rock to my eyes; and I, who would be twenty-three years old in a day or two, and old enough and proper enough to have a house somewhere and a wife to care for it and children to raise up, stood in the coarse canvas overalls that marked a man apart from the whole world.

And as I stood there, looking at her with fondness and wonder and a certain separateness too, a hint of the logic of my life came to me; for my youth had passed away, as it does at one moment or another for all men, and the cold consciousness of death faced me and I faced it and recognized it and greeted it equitably and fairly—there in that sweet and sunlit country parlor, with its soft olive-greens and pale blues that were so much a part of that era. Well and gently do I remember it, the country furniture that was already old with the satiny quality of our good white pine, shaped by German cabinetmakers already dead and moldering in their graves, the hand-hooked rugs, the small, high windows with their diamond-shaped panes of glass, not the glass you see today, but the glass of an earlier time that played with light and made an enchantment out of it, and the spring sunlight all over the place, on the pewter, on the broad, pegged boards of the floor, on my Molly's hair and on the Dutch maids who danced all over the wallpaper. In there, in that quiet place in the old manse, I began to understand the forces which drove me and the necessity which I recognized and obeyed. No man is anointed, but in many men the blood flows and the heart throbs only if they seek the freedom of their own kind; and then this freedom is not an abstraction but a liberation for themselves from their own chains. It is the salt with which they savor their food, and without it they would starve.

So when Molly Bracken said to me, Were you not ashamed that the whole town should stand there and see you whipped? I was able to answer, This was not something for me to be ashamed for.

Could they punish you for doing no wrong?

What is wrong for them is not wrong for me, I told her. Do you understand that?

How can I understand that, when I understand you so little? You love me and yet you hate me, and when you look at me a part of you is here and a part of you is elsewhere. What honor is there in a dirty pair of overalls—and why should it be you when the whole world is content to abide in its place?

Because I am not content.

And you will never be content, Jamie, never.

But I will, I answered her, I will, Molly, and you must pity me because I will.

Who ever pitied you, Jamie Stuart?

No one, I said, no one. But you must.

Why? Why?

Because I love you the way no one else will ever love you, and I can't have you.

It's a love that comes of talk and nothing else, Jamie

Stuart, and your heart is not involved—for when a man loves a woman, he marries her and takes her for himself.

I will not do that.

Because you cannot, she said bitterly.

Because this world is no damned good as it is, I cried, and the bread I eat is too salty for me to swallow! What cursed indifference there is in this place; and for five years I fought for the freedom of my country, and this is my country where my mother and my father died as bondslaves, chattels, flesh they were to buy and sell, and I will not be bought and I will not be sold, for there is something in me that is as proud as any man who ever lived and there is something in my comrades that is proud too, and in the gentry who lead us there is also a pride, so I will follow them and fight for them and take their lashes across my back—because now it is their turn and I move a step with them, but someday it will be my turn, even if I am dead and rotten in the earth, someday it will be my turn! But that you cannot understand, for in this cursed place there is no pride and only a crawling the way animals crawl—and that is the way I crawled into the kirk to plead with God to allow me to live forever!

To allow me to live forever, I said to her, and to hell with that! I will not crawl and abase myself and scrabble for myself and only myself and cheat my neighbor and find an apprentice whose hands I can live from while I starve him and cut muskets to sell a government which never pays or thanks the men who die with those muskets in their hands or apprentice myself to a church and pray while other men fight and die for freedom—no, thank you, I want none of it! I want no such life forever! But every one of my comrades who laid down his life, every one of them lives a little bit in myself, and in that way myself will live and can never die, because my blood is here and mixed into the earth of this land. And this will not be like other lands because the foreigns came here and died here, and that can never be wiped out—never! It's a better immortality than the other kind!

And is that what you believe?

It is what I believe.

Then God help you, she said, because I cannot.

She was crying now, and I turned up her face and looked into her eyes.

I was wrong, I told her, in what I said before. Never pity me.

I never pitied you, Jamie Stuart, but you will pity me.

I will not.

Promise me, she said.

That I promise you: that I will not. It will mean such a lonely waiting—a year or five years or ten years—

It will mean such a lonely waiting, she whispered.

And will you wait?

If you want me to, she said. If you want me to, I will wait—or if you want me to, I will go with you and live by the camp the way the other women do.

Then never cry no more, and you I will never pity but only love. For once I could not love, and there was no love in the boy you walked the fields with and picked flowers with and lay in the grass with and taught to read the printed word and taught to speak gently and softly the way you speak so gently and softly, my beloved heart, my darling. I am learning to love. I am learning to be strong and whole, the way a man should be, and I will be that way when I return to you.

When you return . . .

When I return, I whispered, when I return, my dear.

And then I held her tightly in my arms, and on my back I felt her hands, pressing against the open welts that the whips had left.

And that was in May, ten days before we marched out of York village to the South, and of those last days I must now tell and then make the finish—for though we little knew it then, we marched from York village to the last great battles of the war.

I must tell of Jack Maloney, who was in many ways like a brother to me, and few enough men like him there were; if I paid a price for my part in the rising, he paid it tenfold, day in and day out. There was a particular hatred for Jack Maloney, because he was a soldier in a way that few enough of the Continentals were, and it was through him, and a couple of hundred like him who had deserted the British at the very beginning of the war and came into the foreign brigades, that we became singular among the armies of the states. In his lifetime, he had forgotten more of soldiering than most of our officers ever knew, and for this they could not forgive him. His discipline, his exactitude, his bayonet which always sparkled like it was made of silver, his overalls, clean and neat always, his face shaven in field or camp, his manner, his bearing like a king, his inner calm which was never shaken—all of these combined in a goal which they must conquer to prove themselves. But it was no easy thing to conquer Jack Maloney, and he took what they gave. I think only I knew what it took for him to stand up to the cane and the sword-flat; and he said to me once:

Jamie, we should not have taken them back. When this is over, they will cast us away like dogs.

That's done with, I told him. That's over and done with, just as the old Line is done with.

How much can a man stand?

What he has to, he can stand.

It was about then that our recruits began to come in, a handful of raw lads from the militia, some sailors from Philadelphia, some Naygers of the Virginias and some riflemen from the back country. One by one, the brigade officers returned, each with a handful of men, until the new recruits numbered a little better than three hundred, and they were formed into two regiments and kept carefully apart from the rest of us, of the old foreigns. Day after day they were drilled, in a hurried attempt to make some semblance of soldiers out of them, and the very haste of the officers made us think that the Southern campaign would be joined soon. Often it occurred to me that this forming them into separate regiments was the best proof of the absolute incompetency of our officers, since without question they would bolt at the first volley of ball or the first load of grape; but afterwards I learned that our gentry were by no means incompetent in their plans.

Soon after this, all leaves were canceled, and I saw no more of Molly Bracken. Pickets and sentries were drawn from the militia, and the camp was closely guarded as final preparations were made for a long march. And then, a few days before we left, Anthony Wayne arrived, bringing with him four cannon, an artillery company of some sixty men and a small baggage train, which held a few hundred pounds of corn meal and a great deal of coopered powder and shot bar. The artillery company were all of them strange men, and many of them had the voice and appearance of Yankees. They encamped about half a mile from us, on the edge of York Common, and we saw nothing of them before we marched.

The day after Wayne arrived, the two regiments of the foreign brigades were drawn up for parade inspection. Having no trumpeters, we were awakened before dawn by the drums beating us to arms, and we turned out in the smoky, wet morning with full equipment and knapsacks on. No one knew what this meant, whether we were about to march or whether there was some trouble in the area or whether this was an ordinary parade. If the last were so, it was exceedingly early in the morning, without even sufficient light to allow for any kind of proper inspection.

The only officers present at the beginning were four captains and seven lieutenants, and they ran back and forth as we turned out of our brushwood shelters and our tents, shouting at us to double our time and bend our legs and laying their canes across our shoulders with lusty abandon. Captain Gresham, a burly lad who had come to us two years ago from the Light Horse Troop, went at Jack Maloney who was crouched down lacing his overall leggings, and told him to stand up like a man and get to hell into ranks.

I'm still dressing, answered Maloney, standing up.

Dress before you turn out, damn you! cried Gresham, jabbing his cane into Jack Maloney's belly.

Mind the cane, protested Maloney, mildly enough. The ranks are still forming.

And mind your lip! roared Gresham. I will have none

of your damned insolence! he cried, lacing out with the cane and catching little Jack Maloney on the side of the head, so that he went down like a tenpin.

As Maloney struggled to rise, Angus MacGrath thundered like a bull and charged the captain, who turned to run. But MacGrath seized him, raised him in his hands and shook him like a puppy until he dropped his cane; and, still as with a puppy, Angus cast him away, picked up his cane, and broke it into pieces. Now the other officers came running, drawing their swords, and it well might have been murder and revolt then and there, had not Maloney himself called:

Stand to ranks! Stand to ranks!

The drummer boys took his hint and beat to parade as manfully as they could, until the roll of their drums echoed like morning thunder—while we ran on the double and fell in. In less time than it takes to tell it, our regimental lines were formed, and we were each of us standing to arms and looking straight ahead. Gresham had picked himself up and the other officers were grouped around him, talking excitedly in low tones. And still it was before sunrise, and only now was it light enough to see anything clearly. Now the drummers stopped their playing, and the officers came toward us in a group. Jack Maloney stood alongside of me, and I squeezed his arm and whispered to him:

Easy, lad, and easy does it. You're an old soldier.

God damn them, Jamie!

God damn them, I agreed. God damn them to hell and back again, but they are the officers and we are the men of the Line, and that's that. So easy does it.

Now the officers were standing in front of the ranks and about a dozen yards away, the eleven of them in a close group and still whispering to each other. The two regiments were side by side and four ranks deep, and making a right angle at the end of our parade were the drummers and fifers, with Chester Rosenbank standing in front of them, his face white and sick—for there was something terrible and brooding upon this wet field on this cold May morning, and there was something that all of us knew and yet none of us knew. And I said to myself, We are not the Line and the Line is dead and dissolved, and we are naked here. And I was afraid the way I had not been afraid in a long, long time. Then the first burst of morning sunlight—not the sun yet but just the light—cut into the gloom, and the night mists fell until we stood knee-deep in a sea white that slowly broke up and rolled away; and then all around us was the gracious Pennsylvania countryside, bathed in the pure morning light and cleansed with the pure morning air. The crows rose from the meadows and sadly bid the night farewell and a rooster somewhere sang the morning in. The mists fell away from the tents, and from the other end of the encampment we heard the drums beating to parade, beating up the militia and the recruits. All this we could see on that green and golden morning: the distant figures of the new recruits, the horses grazing in the pasture we had made, the morning birds in the air—the intolerable sweetness of a new day still unmarred.

The officers came toward us. Captain Purdy stepped forward from the group and called:

Stand to arms!

We stiffened and presented.

MacGrath!

Angus MacGrath stepped forward and waited.

Advance six paces, soldier MacGrath! snapped Purdy,

and in answer to his command Angus counted off the six paces and stood waiting. Watching him, I wondered again as I had wondered so often in the past what force commanded us and moved us; for here was this miserable little man, Purdy, hurling his orders at the great Scottish dignity of Angus MacGrath, Angus MacGrath who was like a mountain of endurance and courage and forbearance, tireless and simple and wise in a manner Purdy would never know and could never know. Yet because we were steeled in the years of discipline, we responded and obeyed.

Then why, I had to ask myself, had we revolted once? What had happened then, and what was lost now?

Kneel down! said Captain Purdy.

Like a man made of stone, Angus stood there, motionless.

Kneel down! cried Purdy.

Still Angus stood like stone, and like stone stood the ranks of the regiments.

Drawing his pistol, Purdy cocked it and presented at Angus, but I saw that his hand trembled and the big pistol wavered back and forth in front of the motionless man.

I gave you a command, he said, pitching up his voice. Either obey it or take the consequences!

And then Billy Bowzar spoke up, relaxing the awful tension of myself and of others. Billy Bowzar spoke up in that dry and even way of his, his voice cutting the situation into all of its separate parts, and . . .

May I speak a word, Captain Purdy, sir? he said.

I think Purdy welcomed the interruption and welcomed the opportunity of a way out. He had gotten himself into a bad position, and I do not think he would have had the courage to shoot Angus. It is a bitter thing to kill a man in cold blood, as well I know, even if you hate the man, as Purdy hated Angus.

So he said, This is no part of your affair, Bowzar.

Yes, sir, agreed Billy Bowzar quietly. But may I say a word, sir?

Well, speak up then, snapped Purdy, still covering MacGrath.

I only want to say, sir, that it cannot possibly help either yourselves or us to go on with this matter. We stand in our ranks, and we stand under discipline now. We are good soldiers, sir—and we are ready to march off to a campaign. We are going to fight and die, together, sir, and that is what is important. I saw the incident between Maloney and Captain Gresham. It was a mutual misunderstanding, sir, and it would be better if no blame was to be attached.

I'll thank you, Bowzar, not to instruct me in matters of discipline, said Purdy. You are being damned insolent!

I am trying not to be insolent, Captain Purdy, and I have no desire to instruct you in matters of discipline. That was not my intention at all, sir. I only felt that things will go hard if we continue in this. MacGrath lost his temper, but that is understandable.

You will not instruct me in what is understandable, said Purdy. That is God-damned insolent! MacGrath was ordered to kneel down and accept punishment. When he does, this matter will be over.

I will not kneel! said Angus suddenly. I will dee and damn you!

I could see Purdy working his courage, building his courage, jacking up his courage, and then Jack Maloney stepped forward and took his place beside Angus, presenting his musket, so that if Purdy fired, he would be in a position to fire back.

Then I'll go down with him! cried Jack Maloney. Damn the lot of you, you have no hearts and no souls, and a man is a dog to the lot of you! Now who will stand with me? he threw at us over his shoulder. Who will stand with me? Is there a man left in the brigades?

The officers closed in, but the Jew Levy and Danny Connell and Lawrence Scottsboro and Stanislaus Prukish and the black man Kabanka took their places alongside the two, some quickly, some with the damned resignation of men who realize that they have come to the end of something. An officer broke away—Lieutenant Collins, it was— and ran like the very devil was after him across the fields toward the camp of the recruits. Purdy fell back, the rest of them with him, so that now a group of seven faced a group of ten, and still the regiments stood in ranks unmoving. It was not enough; whenever I recall that morning moment, I realize how precariously the scales were balanced, and it would have needed only Bowzar and myself to tip them over—so that if we had moved forward, the ranks would have moved behind us. All of it was in my mind and through my mind, and already I could see where the lieutenant who ran off was approaching the militia; and faintly, I could hear his shouting, and now I knew why Wayne had kept the artillery so carefully apart. And all of it lived and acted in my mind, and in my mind I saw the ranks surge forward behind Billy Bowzar and myself, and in my mind I saw the ten officers go down before our bayonets and our clubbed muskets; and in my mind I saw our foreigns, better than whom were no soldiers in all the world, greeting the militia with spaced volleys until the green grass was like a slaughter pen; and in my mind I saw the artillery coming, the outriders whipping the horses, the guns bouncing over hill and hummock, and in my mind I saw us retreating into the woods with the stain of blood and death all over us—we who had slain our brothers and ignited the spark that made this war a fratricide—all of this I saw in my own mind's eye in those few minutes when the two groups stood at bay. And seeing it, I knew the hopelessness of it, the uselessness of it, the deep and woeful and pathetic uselessness of it; for it was only another road into nowhere, into a hope and a dream that had no existence, and we had traveled that road once and we knew it well. And if men died now—as I knew already they must die—they would be forgotten, and the foreigns would lick their wounds and we would march off to the Southern campaign, and we would finish what we had started together with the officer gentry. And it must be finished—this I knew.

So when Jack Maloney—Jack Maloney who was like a brother to me—called out, And are there no others? And will you not come, Jamie Stuart?

I answered him, No, I will not, Jack Maloney—I will not because there is no hope here, and once I did it!

Then be a man and do it twice! cried Danny Connell.

No—I cannot and I will not!

And then the time was past, for two men on horseback were spurring down on us, whipping their mounts, Wayne in the lead and Butler close behind him; and after them, at a headlong run, came the regiments of the militia and the new recruits. The officers reined up their horses, and the militia, panting and sobbing for breath, made a ragged line at right angles to our regimental parade, covering with their muskets Jack Maloney and Angus MacGrath and the five others. Purdy and Gresham were speaking to Wayne at the same time, and as he listened to them, his face became murderous with anger. And through all this, the sun rose and bathed the morning in its golden light.

Stand back! cried Wayne, and he reined his horse back, followed by Butler and the officers, until there was a clear space between the militia and the seven of our men. Then Wayne swung out of the saddle, strode over to the militia, and cried, Take aim at those men!

There was a sigh, like a woman in pain, out of the ranks as the muskets converged on the little group of soldiers. They drew closer; they pressed against one another—and frozen, paralyzed, I and the others in the ranks remained without thought or movement, only looking at these seven men who were our comrades, Jack Maloney, and big Angus MacGrath, and the Nayger Kabanka and the Polish man, Prukish and the Jew Levy, so small that he and old Lawrence Scottsboro looked like children, if you did not see their faces, and Danny Connell who had once sang sweet songs in another land—and they pressed shoulder to shoulder as Wayne cried:

Fire!

Forty muskets roared out, and a terrible groan went up from the ranks, a groan of awful and unforgettable anguish. Six of the seven men sank down in a horrible mass of broken flesh; one, Jack Maloney, his left arm shattered and almost torn from his body, remained standing—and facing him, the militia stood behind their smoking muskets and wept, even as we in the ranks wept.

But Wayne did not weep. I do not blame Wayne; I do not condemn him; he is dead and gone these many years, and I have no hatred for him. What he had to do, he did, and someday what we have to do, we will do.

But he did not weep; cold as ice, he was, and hard as stone, and with no more than a glance at the awful carnage of those six dead and the one living and standing, the one who was Jack Maloney who was like a brother to me—with no more than a glance there, he approached us and walked across our ranks, looking from face to face until at last his eyes fixed on me, and he said so softly and bitterly that almost only I heard:

Stuart.

Weeping, I stood there, and the smoke drifted away across the morning meadows and little moans of pain came from Jack Maloney, and we who had known every conceivable kind of horror were unable to look at this particular horror any longer.

Stuart, he said, fix bayonet!

Like a man in a dream, I obeyed and fixed my bayonet, and this dream went on, for he said:

I have a long, long memory, Stuart. Advance!

I moved forward toward that pile of horror and toward Jack Maloney, and Wayne moved with me. He drew his pistol and cocked it and held it a few inches from my head, and the hundreds of men around us stared in silent disbelief, and Jack Maloney was watching me now.

He is dying from that wound, Wayne said softly, and in bitter pain. Drive your bayonet through his chest.

For a time I stood as motionless as Jack Maloney, as Wayne, as the men in the ranks. . . .

You have one minute, and then I will blow your damned brains out, Wayne said.

Then kill me now! I suddenly shouted. Do it now, and God's curse on you!

One minute, said Wayne.

And then Jack Maloney said, Do it, Jamie, do it, Jamie! Do it for my sake! Do it and put an end to my terrible pain, Jamie Stuart. Do it because you were right and I was wrong—for the love of God, do it, Jamie! Do it!

His voice rose to a wild, vibrant note of command, and I lunged and drove the bayonet through his chest. And then I was down beside him, his head in my arms, weeping and weeping, and trying to tell Jack Maloney what I knew but what there were no words for. And then there were Billy Bowzar and Andrew MacPherson, and they lifted me up and took me away and talked to me. . . .

We broke camp the next day and set out on our march southward to Yorktown, where we fought the last great battle; and with my musket slung from my shoulder and my knapsack on my back, with bullets in my belt and a pound of powder and a pound of corn meal to keep me, I marched alongside of Billy Bowzar. Thus we marched, and in the course of it, he would say:

How is it, Jamie Stuart?

I'll never sleep again, and waking, I'll never forget.

You'll forget enough, he said, and too much you don't want to forget, Jamie Stuart. Because there will be a time for remembering.

And when will that time come?

Not too soon, God willing, Jamie Stuart. Not before the time is ripe, and then, God willing, we will know the road we take. We are like a seed that ripened too soon, too quick, for we were planted within the gentry's own revolt, and we grew a crop they fear mightily and neither they nor we knew how to harvest it. That will take knowing, Jamie Stuart, that will take learning. Be patient. The voices are quiet this moment, but they will rise again. Be patient.

PART TWELVE

Wherein a little is told of the last days of the Pennsylvania Line, and of those whose acquaintance you have made.

IF THIS TALE I have told here were something spun out of my own imagination, then this would be as good a place to leave it as any; but it would seem to me to be incomplete without a few words concerning the fate of the handful of us who remained from the old Pennsylvania Line. For me at least, in the course of this long narration, they have come to live again a little as they lived in those old, old times, and it is hard to part with them sooner than the point of firm parting, when the Line was dissolved forever.

From York village in Pennsylvania, we marched south to join in a general movement of troops toward Yorktown in Virginia, and toward the battle which to all effects and purposes ended the Revolution. Yet for us there was some special destination.

We found it on the 6th of July, on the James River, where, fronted by a morass, the core of Cornwallis's army lay waiting, better than four thousand men, well armed and well placed. It is said that Wayne's information was bad that day, that he had reliable word that less than a thousand British troops confronted us; it could also be said that he was looking for death, as he had searched for it before. In any case, he led the less than eight hundred men who composed the Line into a frontal bayonet attack upon the British—and the attack was led by the two regiments left of the old foreign brigades.

So there we perished and there was the end of the Pennsylvania Line. Only one hundred and twenty of us survived that attack, which was the wildest, maddest and most terrible bayonet charge of the entire war—and which incidently gave the British the blow which sent them reeling back to Yorktown. Of that fight on the James River, however, I have no heart to tell in detail. We cut our way into a British army more than five times our size, and then we cut our way out again, but of all the men in the 11th Regiment only I was left, and of the Line, only a handful of torn and bleeding men. Somewhere in that swamp Billy Bowzar lay, and MacPherson, and the Gary brothers, Arnold and Simpkins; there too died the German schoolteacher, Chester Rosenbank, and the drummer lads Searles and O'Conner—and how many more I have no heart to detail. Why I survived, I do not know, but it may be that I wanted to particularly and would not die even when all law and rule and precedent said that I should. For with two musket balls in my belly, I lay for five feverish weeks in a makeshift and horrible hospital outside of Yorktown. Yet somehow I lived and survived, and eventually I was able to walk.

In November, I received my discharge in Philadelphia, two hundred dollars in Confederation money, and a certificate attesting to six years of service in the Pennsylvania Line of the Continental Army. . . .

*   *   *

All this was a long time ago. I have had many things out of life and much that I never looked forward to, and I would be telling less than the truth if I did not admit that life was sweet to me, and rich and rewarding. I married Molly Bracken and we saw our children grown and married to others, and we saw their grandchildren. As it is said, there have been generations in this land, and the old times are best forgotten; and who am I, who gained so much from so little, to speak of injustice?

Yet it is not for the cause of justice or injustice that I have set down this narration. When I mastered the law and took my place at the bar, I gained some understanding of justice; and I do not come with any suit in the cause of the men of the foreign brigades. However it may seem in the course of my tale, I for one do not believe that they perished in vain or that they suffered in vain. They were never causes first, but results first and causes secondarily; and it is the peculiar nature of mankind that with his life so short—and often so miserable—he will nevertheless always find among his numbers those who are willing to spend themselves a little sooner than need be, a little harder, in the cause of human dignity and freedom.

Nor is it strange that, with all the monuments that have been erected, there have been none to the men whose tale I told. A monument, it seems to me, signifies a finish, a point of rest; and if these men rest, they rest too uneasily to have tributes raised to them. Their story is only half told. Another chapter is being written by those angry souls who call themselves Abolitionists, and I think there will be chapters after that as well. There would be no hope in such a tale as this if it were not unfinished.

BUNKER HILL:
THE PREQUEL TO *THE CROSSING*
ISBN: 0-7434-2384-4

Howard Fast has long been one of the most vivid and passionate chroniclers of American history. Through such works as *The Crossing* and *The Immigrants*, he has shown us the dreams and ambitions of the men and women who built a nation. Now, in *Bunker Hill*, he provides insight into both American and British points of view during the battle for control of Boston in June 1775—the outcome of which would dramatically influence the strategies of George Washington and Sir William Howe for the rest of the war.

A gripping story of betrayal and courage, cowardice and heroism, *Bunker Hill* is a masterful work by one of America's greatest historical writers, and inspires a feeling of pride in our origins as a nation.

THE CROSSING

ISBN: 0-671-03897-4

The riveting story of Gen. George Washington's greatest challenge: crossing the Delaware River

This definitive new edition of Fast's work reverberates with the dramatic events of Washington's re-crossing of the Delaware River—a pivotal moment in the American Revolution. It is an amazing testament to Washington's leadership of the young volunteer army fighting in summer clothes against the bitter cold, the snow, and the almost impassable Delaware.

Crisscrossing through Pennsylvania, Delaware, New Jersey, Connecticut, and New York, this is also the tale of Col. John Glover, the leader of a band of New England fishermen; of Tom Paine, the first American war correspondent; of the dreaded Hessians themselves.

Dispelling the myths of history, Howard Fast has written an unforgettable and true account of a key event in America's struggle for independence that all Americans should know and understand.